BETTING ON FOREVER

Battle Born MC- Reno

Book One

BY

Scarlett Black

DEDICATION

A great deal of time went into writing this book. Time that took away from my family. That is the most precious time of all. My man and lover, you really did support me while I obsessively worked hours to complete my very first book. It is amazing the feeling of accomplishment to have your support, even during the times you wanted to kill me the most, so thank you from your woman and mother to three very self-efficient kids.
#ForeverWild

BETTING ON FOREVER

Burned... like tires smoking on the street. That's how Alessia's last relationship left her. Vowing never again to trust a man with her heart, she moved to Reno in search of a fresh start.

Little did she know, everything would change with the rumble of an engine.

Into her bar sauntered a dark and sexy biker by the name of Blade, with club politics on his mind and the MC in his heart. Under pressure to deliver answers, retribution, and the money he's looking for, the last thing the new Prez had time for was the sizzling chemistry between him and Alessia. But it would take a stronger man than him to resist the desire for the alluringly fiery woman.

When sparks fly and desire burns hot, will Alessia take the biggest risk of her life with Blade and bet on forever?

PROLOGUE

Alessia DeRosa

two years ago

Standing on the sidewalk in the dark, I can hear the sound of cars driving by, people talking, friends laughing. The aroma of food and the crisp spring air hits my nose. Me? I'm hiding my feelings from the people who pass me by. Hiding from the reality I'm about to face.

The spring air chills me to my bones with a gust of reality so cold, the world stops. A slap of reality that brings me back to the present when my long, brunette hair whips me in the face.

Nothing. My heart is numb to the pain. The cold, dead part of me is shattering to the sidewalk when confronted with what my eyes are seeing.

Derrick, my husband, is walking out of a restaurant with a woman. An even younger version of the woman I am not. Carefree, beautiful, and so very soft.

Laughing with her, he guides her, hand in hand, to his bike. I notice a familiarity to their touch that only a lovers' intimacy can reveal.

Here I stand, alone, looking at what I thought my life was. Derrick, the person who used to be my best friend, is now someone I don't know at all.

Grabbing the helmet off his bike, he places it on her head and gives her a sweet peck and swat on her little ass. As soon as his leg swings over, our gazes collide.

Shock, maybe even regret, shines in the eyes of the man I once knew. We hold each other captive, neither one of us able to look away. So many words pass between us. But none are spoken at all.

The woman follows him, throwing her leg over the bike, cuddling her body close behind him. She whispers something close to his ear, but Derrick doesn't move or respond. Doesn't turn his bike on. Nothing.

What am I doing here? Taking one step back, then two, I run into a passerby when my shoulder hits him. My world fast forwards and I cannot hear what he yells at me. I turn and sprint back down the busy street. My heart is pounding erratically to an uncontrollable rage and pain. The roar of Derrick's bike coming to life enrages me further.

Embrace the anger, push the pain away. Breathe in, breathe out.

I keep those words streaming in a constant loop through my mind until I'm on my own bike, kicking the bitch on and peeling out, willing my tires to punish the road. I roll side to side as it makes the sharp turns, tempting fate to take me, hurt me further. Daring the heavens to open up and swallow me whole on this road to hell.

My mind swirls of possibilities. Will he go to our now shattered home, looking for me? Does he even care? None of those things matter, not even one.

The tires squeal when I slam on the breaks and park at my Papa's clubhouse garage. I cover the bike I love with a white, old, ratty oil stained sheet, then pull out my phone and call the one only man I have completely trusted my entire life. My Papa.

"Papa, I'm in the storage garage, putting up my bike. I'm getting out of town. You have an untraceable car you can loan me for a couple of weeks?" Cold determination laces my voice.

"*Sí, mija*, I was correct? What you found, was it as I expected?" Papa's voice is steady and quiet, so others can't hear, but the rage I hear in it is lethal.

"*Sí*," is all I say, all I want to say.

"*Mija*, tell no one, we never speak of this again. In the right bay of the garage use the car that is parked there. Leave your phone turned off in the desk drawer." He exhales his resignation before he lets me go.

"Go to Dana's house, park around the block. I'll have a new car and phone for you in the morning.

Answer to only me or your brother, *sí? Te amo.*" The line goes dead.

As soon as I'm off the phone I hit the road and I am at Dana's within minutes. My best friend pulls me inside and anxiously waits to hear from me what happened tonight. She sits across from me on the bed in the small bedroom of her apartment and we wait for the Jenn.

My father wanted me to keep this quiet, but the grief is eating me alive. He has his club to support him and I have my girls. His voice plays in my mind like he's sitting next to me, *"Words of defeat show weakness. Never show others your cards."* But I cannot be alone, not tonight.

Finally, my other friend, Jenn, walks into the room, shutting the door behind her. Only then, do I crumble, screaming the story off the top my lungs. Tearing my soul apart with each tear I shed over my husband, over the loss of my hopes and dreams.

After the weakness is purged from my heart, I fall into a heap of recovery. Jenn and Dana never leave my side.

What feels like days later, I will my swollen eyes to open. With them barely cracked open, I take in my surroundings and the crushing yet again reality of my life.

A moment is all I give myself before crawling out of the soft comforter and dragging my feet across the floor to the bathroom. The hot water of the shower washes over me as I start formulating my next plan. Staying here sure isn't an option.

Doubt that I can leave him crosses my mind for a second, because, leaving my family and friends? Feels damn near impossible. They are my whole life. But, Derrick is here, I can never escape him, us. My mind starts spiraling with all the *what if's*.

Goddamn it, I am stronger than this. Alessia DeRosa, will not fall to his lying feet. She will not bow to the mercy of pain. Fuck no. I will fight for myself. Does this hurt? Absolutely, but a coward I will not be.

After my shower, I quickly get dressed and make my way to the kitchen to find my girls. Dana sees my face, the puffy eyes and red cheeks, and tilts her head in curiosity. I think she suspected she'd see me damaged today and still crying. Nope, we are on to the next phase, damage control.

Fuego, my father, is sitting at the table with my mother and brother. Surprised to see my mom, I hold strong, for her, and for me too. If anyone could break me down now, it would be her. I give her a tight hug and sit next to her. My hand squeezes her tightly to show her my strength. Tears well up in her eyes and she looks away while I give her hand another squeeze.

"I have a plan," I break the silence. "I'm not asking any of you to uproot any of your lives, but I am mine."

Jenn looks at me with some kind of understanding.

"I'm cashing out every single asset I have. I'm leaving California as soon as I can."

Mom and Dana both gasp back a breath.

It's happening. There's no other option.

CHAPTER 1

Vegas

present day

Pumped for the night at the bar, I dress in my black high-heeled, peep toed pumps, my tight shredded camo pants and black loose tank.

Tonight is going be a great night, I smile back at myself in the mirror while tracing my lips with scarlet red lipstick.

I look forward to the second Friday of every month. Not only has my period passed, but it's girls' night at The Black Rose. That means no dicks allowed, meaning no human with a dick is allowed into the bar. Well, except for the dicks we call in from Las Vegas to dance for my girls. It costs me quite a bit, I don't make a whole lot on this night, but it keeps these girls happy here in Reno. Who am I to deny them of sexy and sweaty strangers?

Grabbing my worn out, black leather jacket, I pull it on and then my long hair out of the back on my way out of my room. Heading toward the kitchen, I grab the keys to my black Tahoe and I'm ready. Except that I forgot Tugger. Placing two fingers into my mouth, I whistle loudly, "Hey, Tugg, let's head out!"

Outside has that autumn chill in the air and I take a deep breath as I look around my yard at the yellowing leaves. A peace surrounds me in my soul that I haven't felt in a long time. A flicker of calm that is igniting fire back into every step I take. It's me finally snapping back into place, like a missing piece of a puzzle.

Tugger comes running up, excited, barking and wagging his tail. I open my door and let him jump in the passenger seat. Once we're both in, I rub his head. "How's my man? Ready to watch these girls have fun?" I scratch his ears. "Let's get to work."

Tugger is one of my three best friends and the only male, not related, who has stayed faithful to me. He is about two years old and I picked him up off the side of the road late one night. I figured he had to have gotten out from somewhere. He was so small and scared when I found him. That was when we first moved to Reno and I took it as a good sign. I never did find the rightful owner of this cute black lab mix, so I took that as him being meant to be mine.

We wind our way down the freeway and park around the back of the bar. Tugger always comes to work with me. He helps security by keeping the freaks out. If Tugg doesn't like you, you're gone.

Together, we hop out of the truck and head over to the back door. James, my head of security, is taking the last drag of his smoke, casually leaning with one leg kicked up on the wall next to the entrance. He puts it out in the ashtray that's sitting on the picnic table, with a shit eating grin on his face while he exhales.

"What's got that big ass grin on your face, dude?" I look up at him, bald and six feet tall, with a lot of man beef packed on him. He's a hottie, but I can't fraternize with my staff, we all know that shit never works out well.

James only smiles wider at my question. "Well, shit, hmmm, what has this smile on my face?" Rubbing his goatee with his thumb and pointer finger, he continues, "It isn't those pretty boys that dance around for you girls, that's for sure. I would say it's the pussy already crawling in there." Lifting his thumb over his shoulder, he points toward the bar area.

Sure enough, when James pulls the door open, the bass is jamming, and the girls are grinding to the beat. I walk in first and head toward my office with Tugg at my heels and James coming in right after me. Through my office door, I can see bitches are starting to pack in.

The music begins pumping a rhythmic beat, and the girls are grinding on each other. Damn, it's going to be a wild night. My house DJ, Jammin' Jenn, is rippin' up her tracks. She looks over at us and waves. I catch James smirk over at her, and I wonder when he will ever learn. She isn't going to go there with him, but whatever.

James heads back to his spot by Jenn, watching the floor. After placing my purse in my desk drawer and my jacket on the chair, I head out to the bar, shutting the office door behind me.

"Let's get set up, Tugg." He runs and sits down behind my usual spot at the bar.

Dana, my bar manager and one of my best friends, is here already. We take turns opening and closing, and she has been slammed early by the looks of it. She notices me walking in while passing a drink.

"Vegas, about time you got here, it's been crazy. I almost gave you a call to get you here earlier."

Reading the next ticket, I grab a vodka bottle and start on the next drink. Dana may look a little frazzled, but she's got this.

"No way, you can handle it, always do, but I agree, they started early tonight. We better keep their drinks light."

It's not that I want to cheat these ladies out of what they're paying for. I just want to keep them upright and safe. We give them a small discount on the mix drink special tonight, that's strawberry margaritas.

Feeling the vibe in the air, I shift into my bar persona and chat with customers. Left and right, drinks are moving, and cash is flowing. Smiling big at my next customer, "What are you having tonight?", I ask.

I freakin' love my bar.

It's hitting midnight. We are packed with customers and there's no sign of it slowing down. Between the two of us, we barely keep up with the flow. We have a bachelorette party, a birthday girl that just turned twenty-one, school teachers and college party girls in the bar tonight. It is one big mixed party of all kinds and different personalities.

Looking out over the squealing, laughing and hooting crowd, one of the very fine sexy strippers jumps up on our small stage. He's tall, tan, and has that very dark and dangerous vibe. Ugh, no thanks, been there and done that type. Girls are pawing at his jeans and stuffing bills into his pockets or belt, wherever they will fit.

Sexy stripper man grabs the hand of the bride to be and Jenn slams down the track to *Bailamos* by Enrique Iglesias. Damn, she's good, that girl can play for the crowd. The stripper guy grinds all over the red cheeked bride who appears about to faint in his arms.

Dana giggles next to me and I glance over before swiping a charge. "Vegas, he's going to give that girl second thoughts. That, or her brain is numbed from all those Raspberry Kamikaze shots those girls keep drinking. I eventually just made a pitcher of them."

I can't help but to smile at Dana, remembering when we worked that eight-to-five-day job. Just like most of these girls out here. It makes me happy to give them a place to let go.

Before leaving California, I cashed in my benefits, and here we are. Never regretted it, and it only gets better as time goes on. That's why she calls me Vegas. I went all in and bet my life savings on this place. Because of her, now most of the others have also caught on to it and call me Vegas.

"Nah," chuckling, I shake my head. "She's thinking if her man walks in at any moment, she's dead. I know her man, and she's getting her ass spanked if he sees or hears of this."

"Well, shit, some cocks got through", Dana tilts her head in the direction of the door, and, sure as shit, in walk a few very rough, but very sexy, men.

"Ah hell, Vegas", Dana says with a little stress in her tone. She's worried we could have problems with this rugged looking crew.

Walking back to my office, I grab my silver nine-millimeter and tuck it into the waistband of my pants. Then, with steal determination, I go back out to the floor. I head straight for these cocks that are uninvited. James is also making his way toward the trio, along with one other security guard.

Beating them both there, I greet the unexpected guest. "Well, boys, I'm sure security at the front door let you know it was a girls' night, right? I'm sure you also saw my *No Cock Allowed* sign lit up out front?"

Raising my eyebrows in question, I point with my hand toward the lit up, giant rooster with a red circle slashed through it. I love that cock, I had it specially made for this event.

Three men wearing Battle Born MC cuts turn around and look me up and down. That shit pisses me off, to be dismissed and then to be eye fucked. I am the boss here.

The cockier one in the middle speaks first as he steps into my space. I don't back down or step back. This is my place, and no one pushes me around.

Holding his hand out for me to shake, he introduces himself. "I'm Blade, and this must be your dad's bar? Is he here? I need to speak with the owner."

Taking his hand, I pull us deeper into each other's space. My tits barely graze his arm. Dominant move? You bet your ass it is.

Taking in a long pull of air so he can hear it, I breathe out slowly, right into his ear as I speak. "Well, if you really wanna know where the owner is, you're talking to her, thanks for asking." I hear him exhale his breath as I stand back.

Satisfaction hits me hard like a freight train to see that I affected him. Good. I smile, and his eyes are trained on my blood red lipstick. Fucker. Losing the smile, I purse my lips tight.

"My apologies then, beautiful," he raises my hand, placing a soft kiss on the back of it. Okay, so he's just as aggressive.

Pulling my hand back, I reassert, "As I mentioned, this is an all-girls party tonight. Why don't we move this to my office." It's a statement. I'm not asking.

Turning and heading that way with Blade at my back, James also joins us with the two other security guards. I can feel Blade's eyes all over my ass as I walk into my office. It's making my heart beat faster, adrenaline spiking up through my limbs with excitement.

I turn and lean on the front of my desk, opting not to sit down. You never know, and I really don't want to be sitting if something does go down. Also, I really don't think they're here to sit and chat.

As expected, the three of them walk in and start closing the door. "Don't think so, boys", James says and holds the door open as he and the other two security guards start patting all three down.

Tall and Broody, Blade, with his dark hair, the sides shaved tight and a small mohawk on top, is smirking at me. After they are cleared of no weapons, my three guards go to stand behind the desk.

Smirking back, I look into his eyes. "Let's start over with names and why you're here."

Mister Tall and Broody speaks up first. "I'm Blade, the President of the MC that recently moved into the area. This," he points to his right, "is Axl, and this," he points to the left, "is Tank. We thought old man Mac still owned this place. It's been a while since I've been back here. I have some business to offer. Don't suppose you're interested?" His eyes intensely focus in on mine, daring me, drawing me in.

Taking a few moments, I study their faces. *'Look them in the eye'*, Papa always taught me. *'Don't back down'*. Embracing Papa and his strength, I come back at Blade.

"You're right, Mac did own the place. I bought it from him right before he passed. His wife, Emilia, still works here. As for business, that totally depends on what you're offering. And let's be straight from the get-go. I won't be dealing in anything illegal."

My face is stone, but, surprisingly, Blade has his harder, making his brown eyes very dark. I don't know if I like this player yet. I squint my cat lined eyes his way.

"You always so pleasant and judgmental to people you just met?" Mister Growly barks out at me. Laughable. He thinks *I'm* rude?

"Well, let me say this. If I had a dick and said that, would it have offended you? Or, would you respect my bluntness? Because I have a vagina, it makes me judgmental? This is business, Mister.... Blade. Straight up is the name of my game. Don't like it?", I shrug, "go ahead and take the fuck off."

My hands square on my hips, *give me your crazy, asshole*. The anticipation, the rush of it, is a drug to me.

The guy to the right, Axl, snickers, bringing his hand to his mouth. I stare straight ahead at Blade as Axl says with a trace of humor, "Look, babe, Blade here, along with the rest of us, are looking to open a tattoo shop. No shady shit, just business. You also own the building next door?"

Blade moves his stare from me to Axl. So, he isn't happy about his MC brothers speaking up? Interesting. My right arm drops to my side, my spine relaxing just a bit.

"I own the building next to me, yes. If you're interested in opening a tattoo shop, we can sit down and arrange a meeting. I need to get back out there." I am worried that Dana and Jenn have the whole bar to look after by themselves.

Blade's focus is on my arms. He takes one step closer to me. One hand slides up my right forearm, while his fingers start tracing the roses that trail up my arm and around my collarbone.

"Who did your work...I didn't catch your name?" His voice drops to a soft, husky notch that has my eyes closing.

Taking in short, measured breaths, I feel myself overtaken with lust. An intense craving for the feel of his strong hands on me. I freeze with his fingers ghosting across my skin while my heart is racing like a junkie's. One hit of this man and I am hooked.

Shit, the thought of him pushing into me hard and unyielding leaves me wanting much, much more of Blade. His voice and hands yield my irrational thoughts.

He's bad for you, Vegas.

Catching his fingers when they reach my collarbone, I twist his arm behind his back and grab him by the back of his neck, pushing him forward until he's face down on my desk. Just as low and husky as his voice was before, I say into his ear, "My name is Alessia DeRosa, and the next time you touch me, I'll shoot your hand off." I let go and step back.

Blade's eyes are furious as he rises back to his full height, shrugging his cut back into place. His irises are dilated, but then he smiles and leans into me. "Pleasure to meet you, Alessia. Next time you put your hands on me, be prepared to finish what you started. Last and only warning, you get me?" Blade's eyes are tracking me, waiting for me to come back at him.

I'm about to argue, to tell him he started it, when James steps between us and backs Blade up a couple of steps. James glares at me over his shoulder for a second, for putting myself too close to a bad situation. I'm his boss, so he can save it.

He looks back at Blade, assessing. "You can give me your contact info and I'll pass it along to Alessia." There's frustration in his voice, any patience now long gone.

Blade chuckles and grabs an invoice off my desk, flips it over and jots his name and number down, then sticks my pen in his pocket. This cocky fucker pisses me off, anger replacing any lust I just felt. He turns to walk out, throwing over his shoulder while looking at me with laughter in his eyes, "Call me, so we can finish what we started."

The three of them stride together toward the bar area, then leave the building. James and I step out the back door of my office, listening to the loud thunder of their bikes starting up.

"You really fucked up, Vegas. Putting yourself too close to that guy. He was calling your tough girl bluff, and then wanting you to up the stakes. Don't play into that shit, next time let me do my fucking job."

I just sigh and shrug. What can I say?

I turn around and there sits my faithful dog, wagging his tail back and forth at the door. "Couldn't you bite him in the ass?!"

Deep inside of me, the rhythm of the bikes calls to me from my feet to my head, and I itch to take a long, hard ride.

CHAPTER 2

Blade

Riding off down the freeway with an uncomfortable hard-on pisses me the fuck off. The cool wind is doing nothing to calm me down. I can't stop the images of her blue eyes and plump lips with red lipstick that should be wrapped around my dick from popping into my head.

I've had enough of the club pussy to last me a lifetime. That fiery little bitch has me hard just from her smart, fucking perfect mouth.

My tongue was dying to trace where my fingers touched her skin. I wanted to bend her over her desk and spank that very fine ass hard.

Groaning, I close my eyes for a second. The release is calling to me, but only she can satisfy me. FUCK.

The club girls will bend over at a nod of my head. It's pathetic and unfulfilling. I'm getting older, and tired of that shit. Let alone, now when they see my Prez patch, their legs drop open, hoping I'll fuck 'em and love it enough to keep them around.

I want to own a woman who's mine and submits only to me. Strong enough to be her own woman. Who has enough grit for this hard life. Not these cunts you fuck and throw away. I need a wild cat to tame just enough to be mine, and only mine.

An Ol' Lady on the back of my bike suddenly became my fantasy. I've never, nor will I ever, let one of those club bitches on my ride. My bike is my number two behind my club, no one touches it.

My old man loves my mom with everything he has. He's always said that good Ol' Ladies are few and far between. My mom is loyal to my dad and to our club.

I don't know what is changing that's making me think this way. But it's hit me like a brick to the dick after only a few minutes of meeting Alessia.

Maybe it has to do with me turning thirty-seven, and I'm itching to slow down a bit? Wanting to have someone close to me, someone to watch my back, and not worry about all these club sluts. Yeah, most of them are fun, but my mind wonders off to that stubborn and ballsy as shit princess at that bar. She definitely doesn't need a man to tell her what to do or put cash in her bank.

No, that woman needs a tough man, with a strong hand, one who can control her in the bedroom. I can still smell her perfume, and I wonder what it was. Her hair felt soft on my cheek when she pushed me face down on her desk.

Yeah, she caught me off guard. I could have easily gotten myself back up, but I liked the little cat and mouse game we were playing. I groan at the thought of her perky ass and the handful of cleavage she gave me a peek of.

Axl, Tank and I pull into the garage and both of those fuckers have shit eating grins when they jump off. Tank starts in. "So, the Prez has a claim on the brunette back there? Or can I roll up tomorrow and see if she's a little less hostile with me? Or was that some foreplay you into, Prez?" His grin is taking up most of his face.

Axl jokes back to Tank, "Nah, bro, you seen that right. I think if I call her 'babe' a few more times, Prez may lay me out cold. Doesn't make a difference to me, that bar was full of fine ass. Tank, did you see that bartender next to Alessia? Bitch had some legs on her with those short shorts and long, blonde hair."

They keep bullshitting as we walk up to the door of the Battle Born MC clubhouse, the Reno Chapter.

I'm damn proud of it, and so is my old man, Stryker, the Prez of the Mother Chapter of the Battle Born MC, out of Las Vegas. He turned this clubhouse over to me this year, after he had enough of the shit that went down with the Nevada Knights MC.

Stryker threw out the old Prez and we patched over a couple of the men. The rest, we sent to the ground after we found out they were sex trafficking and going through the Battle Born territory. We could have let them keep their club name, but that ain't Stryker's style. He takes what's his and doesn't give a shit. They took something from him, so he took it all from them.

We turned this club into a Battle Born chapter and grew our business. Reno is also centrally located, so it was a no brainer to take it all.

Nickelback blasts through the speakers while laughs filter around beer bottles. Those club sluts I was just thinking about come running up. Shaking my head at them, I tell them to get the fuck away. Those tame little Barbies scamper off like the good little girls they are. Not in the mood for those dumb cunts.

I bet that fierce little Alessia wouldn't even acknowledge me, and that thought makes me smile to myself. So much fire out of her short, but curvy, little frame. Game on, princess, game most definitely on.

I take a seat at the bar next to Axl, my VP, and Tank, my Road Captain. We don't go anywhere unless the three of us can go together, especially on the important runs. We grew up together, and, without a doubt, they are my brothers.

One of our prospects, Solo, slides a few cold beers our way, and we chug the first half down. Axl questions first. "All joke aside, do you think Alessia will call? We need that location. The shop will work well in that area, and we need to get up and running and start making some flow, man."

He's nervous. This is important to all of us. After taking over the Reno area, we've had to make it on our own up here. Find our own cash flow and grow a business the club can survive on.

Sitting back against the bar, I take another drink before answering. "I think she'll call. That place has stayed closed with no tenants for the last year, it's just wasting space. Good thing too is we can use her customers as our client base and vice versa."

Axl relaxes a bit at hearing my thoughts. "I'm just glad we don't have to take those runs down south anymore. I respect the hell outta your old man, but that shit was getting down right murderous in that territory."

He lets out the breath he was holding. The war we had a year ago crippled all of our chapters financially. None of us knew if we would be the next one dead and cold in the dirt. Not a year any of us wants to relive.

Tank is distracted, not listening to our conversation. He's watching one of the girls jump up on the pool table, stripping to give the guys a seductive show of the pussy they've all seen and fucked plenty of times.

Turning back around to face the bar, I keep talking to Axl. "She'll call, and, if not, I can always check in and see about a meeting." I kind of hope she doesn't call so I have an excuse to go and drop in on her.

My phone vibrates in my pocket, I pull it out to read the message.

Stryker: Intel on Buck, call me.

Stepping out of the room to call Stryker back, the anger and regret are thrumming through my veins. My old man picks up on the first ring, reporting to me what he knows of what happened with Buck, one of the longest standing members of our club. Time to gather the brothers for Church. Fuck.

"Tank, get your head together, man," back at the bar, I slap him on the shoulder. Axl and Tank zone in at my words. "We need a meeting. Now. Stryker just got word on Buck. The shit ain't good, man."

I chug the rest of my beer before slamming it down, and I turn around to stand and face the room. My voice booms with frustration, "Church! Now! Sluts, get the fuck out!"

The brothers drop shrieking bitches from their laps and tell them to hit it as they walk past them with no care or concern for them. Prospects do their jobs by escorting the cunts out to their cars, making sure they're all gone, while the patched brothers and myself head into Church.

I feel the venom pumping fiercely in my veins. The intensity coming off me feels deafening. You can cut the tension with a fucking knife. They all want to know why they were brought in here. The MC brothers are directing looks toward both me and my VP as they try to find answers.

Anger is clear in my voice when I speak. "Battle Born MC patched you all over after we settled what your old Prez was dealing and trafficking without my old man's clearance. So, if any of you have a problem, and you wanna be a pussy? Back out now, throw your cut on the table." I pause and look at each one of them again with steel determination in my eyes.

They probably suspect that we are in here looking for a rat. Patching members over takes time to develop trust. We just don't have time for that now. Makes sense that they all want to protect each other. They've been through club wars and deaths just like all the other Battle Born chapters in Nevada. Hell, every MC has this past year. No one has been immune to the treachery and heartache of losing brothers, cash and connections.

I have one question for each of the Reno members. Will they ride and die for their brothers? One of them could be a dirty rat fucker, and, when I catch him, if he doesn't already know, he will find out why they call me Blade.

My fingers twitch thinking about the retribution in blood that will spill when I sink my blade into their skin. The sharp edge of it smoothly cutting into skin gets me high.

Pushing those thoughts aside, I continue talking to my men. "I've been contacted by the Mother Chapter in Vegas, and Stryker has called in a nomad named Cuervo. He's the best at tracking with situations that went off the grid. Why would Stryker call in Cuervo, you ask? Because a member went missing for a week, and the Vegas Prez found him dead a few miles past the Indian Springs truck stop. Out in the desert, Buck and his bike were halfway buried, or we may have never found him. They took his cut, cell and wallet. The Game Warden was out there opening the fences for the local hunters. He called Stryker because we never leave a body out in the open or dump without him knowing.

We need all the Chapters to help. I'm not putting this to a vote if we should wait and help the Las Vegas chapter find who killed him or not. Save whatever shit you were going to throw my way. That was *our* brother, you get me? It looks like whoever killed Buck, they did it in a hurry not to finish disposing of him. He had to have come across something important. Buck made his run south and was on his way back. So, from what we know, this wasn't random. He was found north of Las Vegas. We need to find out why."

I look over at my Sergeant-At-Arms. "Spider, dig up his cell and bank records, look for a timeline. Look at his contacts and start making calls."

I'm not done barking directions. "Tank, call the Elko chapter and give them a heads up and to be on the lookout. There will be a two-riders minimum till this is resolved."

They will regret the day they messed with Battle Born MC. I'll carve the club emblem into their flesh and seal it with fire. Their loved ones will know who returned them back home dead. Too many good men have died because of shady ass, greedy fucks.

I sit at the end of the table and slowly look around the room, careful to make eye contact with each man. Seeing straight through to their souls, I own each one of them.

One man steps up from the back, Bear. He walks forward and starts pulling his cut off. He reaches the table, and, before the cut can drop, Axl throws a knife into his neck. Bear chokes on his blood, struggling to breathe and stand. Hands clawing desperately at his throat, he falls forward onto the table, twitching.

Standing up, Axl grabs his knife, wipes the blood off with disgust onto the dead man's shirt and tucks it back into his boot. Blood flows in a beautiful, lazy, crimson river over the table, and pours over, dripping onto the glossed concrete floors.

"Anyone else? No? Let's get back to fuckin' business then." Axl is smirking like the crazy fucker he is. We all are.

"Tank, brief all these assholes on what happened last week on your run."

Relaxing back in my chair, I light up a smoke, grinning at my men, challenging them to question his authority. Tank stands so he can be at level with the crew. Hah, I laugh at his ass in my head. Stupid fucker.

Tank starts talking. "Me, Axl, Hitch and Spider were coming back from our drop. We saw a semi moving into our territory. The dude wore a cut I couldn't make out from my bike. We followed him north into Elko where he shouldn't be haulin'.

I put in a call to our contact in Texas. He confirmed a new crew was moving bitches and shit. We knew it was them by the logo on the trucks they use for transport. Contact said this crew started putting a black angel on their trucks. Dumb fucks just as good as advertised it by painting that logo on the side of their haulers.

The Cartel knows their border for drop off is Del Rio. Someone has a side business brewing and has paid a lot of money for these drop offs. Question is, who are we looking for, and are they new? They had to be set up through references. That's who we need to find."

Tank finishes and sits down next to me, throwing a smug look my way. Idiot thinks he's the only one with contacts. His information is just the tip of the iceberg. Dipshit.

The first thing I need to do is get the names of the members *not* on the drop and where they were while the brothers were gone on the run. See if I can tie any of them to any MC or gang ties, because I don't think it's the Cartel. We've kept the peace with them for years.

The Cartel's been around long enough to know that if you grease a few palms, work gets done and your men stay alive. Makes me think someone is getting greedy and saving enough to take over the Battle Born's territory. That will show us how big this threat is, when we can pin down exactly what's being moved and who is being the mule in the operation in those painted-up, whore cargo haulers.

I take a deep breath and close Church with one final warning to everyone in the room. "I'm suspecting these two incidents may be related. I need ears to the ground! I don't give a fuck how you do it. You call up every distributor you know. GET THE FUCKING INFORMATION!" My hand slaps down on the table, letting everyone in the room know this situation just went to top priority.

"Get on top of this shit before we lose more members. I'm sick of putting bodies that wear our cuts in the ground. These motherfuckers will pay in blood for taking what's ours. Church this Sunday at six. Get the fuck out of here and get to fucking work."

Hitting my gavel on the table, I storm out, followed by Axl and Tank. Axl is already up in Cowboy's ear, whispering like the bitch he is about something. Probably about me and that fine piece of ass, Alessia

Spider shouts toward the bar, "Solo, grab the rock crawler truck and pull it around back. Bring a tarp and two more prospects with you. No more solo trips for a while. Dump this piece of shit in the pit at the mine."

Solo walks in with another prospect and get to work. Together, they quickly wrap Bear up and drag him out.

Not in the mood to hangout or hear more bullshit, I grab another beer from behind the bar on my way to my room, thinking over everything I saw in Church.

Something really sticks out to me. Earlier, when I said *Vegas chapter* and *Stryker*, a couple of the brothers paled and swallowed hard. I make note of which ones those are, so I can have Spider look into their backgrounds and financials later.

Spider, the Sargent-in-Arms, gets his name because once he gets your life caught in his web, he'll devour you whole, just like the Black Spider tattooed on his neck. Ride or die, fuckers. Ride or die.

Except, if you die for being a rat, then me and my boys, Axl, Tank, Spider and Cowboy, will be the last faces you see. Lying back in my bed, I give up the fight on my thoughts of these problems, choosing to try and solve a more beautiful one.

CHAPTER 3

Vegas

I feel every little thing. Remember all those late nights Derrick and I spent together. We were so young, only twenty-years-old when we married. The memories seem like it all happened yesterday. Happiness when he would touch my skin, as if he could touch my heart with his whispers and kisses. He could inspire my dreams. At one time, I thought that man would be my universe, take me to heaven and bring me back to earth. Except, when he didn't anymore, the betrayal shattered my world and I fled California.

The man my papa loved as much as me had a mistress. I exhale the crushing pain at the memory of seeing him at that restaurant, then walking out to his bike with her. In the MC life, there's only one woman who rides on the back of your bike, and that's an Ol' Lady.

Before he left that last evening, he gave me a kiss on his way out to work. Only, the bastard wasn't working that night. Papa called to ask me how our dinner was, and that Derrick wasn't answering his calls. He worked for Papa, and he never made mistakes.

Because Papa was the Prez, he couldn't come out and say it, but he wanted me to know. Derrick ran with his crew, and he couldn't rat a brother out. Papa couldn't punish a brother for what the brother had done to me. It's not within the codes they live by for the others to care.

However, he gave me a clue as best as he could. Where I could go look for Derrick. It wasn't hard to get the GPS to his phone's location in seconds. Derrick got sloppy and forgot who my family was, or what I was capable of.

I couldn't believe it was true even when I stood on the sidewalk with the cold wind freezing my shattered heart. Refusing to move from my spot, standing there until he saw me. Stubborn to the end, I waited until every piece that made us, us, was wrecked and left on the concrete.

Humiliation, that's what truly made me pack up my shit of the life I had left and move far away to start over.

How I got back to my bike without killing him, I will never know. Maybe it was my pride? But as soon as my helmet was on, I peeled out of there.

After talking to Dana and Jenn, we were all on a mission. We needed a new town, with new people and faces to start over. After a few weeks of careful planning and dodging Derrick, we were ready.

Except, he eventually caught up with me. My car was packed and ready to hit the road and hide from the memories. I was about to get in after opening the door to the new black Tahoe, but my body went rigid at the sound of his voice.

"Alessia, come home to me."

With my back to him, I was unwilling to turn around.

"Please understand, she wasn't meant for me, not like you are. I was so stupid to do what I did," Derrick's soft voice pleaded with my cold heart. His strong hand landed on my shoulder, squeezing lightly.

Still facing the Tahoe, my head fell forward, hitting the car. The touch that used to bring me comfort was killing me now. Dropping my shoulder, I gave in and turned toward him, willing my eyes not to cry. Embracing the anger instead.

"For what, Derrick, so I can be like every other woman who takes her cheating man back? Tell me something, would you want my body after another man has had his hands all over me? After I shared my body with his? Let him fuck my body? Dominate mine with his? Tell me you could still worship my body after I betrayed you," I glared into Derrick's shinny eyes.

Grabbing both of my shoulders, he pulled me swiftly into his embrace, knowing that was the end of us. He was holding on to something that had died a sad and agonizing death.

"I will always love you, Alessia, always." Derrick's hands cupped my jaw, looking into my eyes, searching for the love that used to be there. Problem was, it still was there. I could see it in his eyes that he truly loved me, some part still did anyway.

The contact, so intimate, was so painful that I had to close my eyes, and damn it. My heart wanted to beat for him again, but my mind said no!

Trying to control my racing heart, I took deep breaths that only helped so much. A tear streaked down my cheek. Derrick bent over and kissed it away, catching it with his lips. He pulled me back into his chest and softly murmured, "I'm sorry. I did this to us, Alessia, and I am so sorry for it. Please believe me?" Squeezing him to me a little tighter, I did believe him, every word uttered to me.

I stepped out and away from his hold, and realized that was the last thing I knew to be true between us. "I know you're sorry, Derrick."

His eyes had a little hope, thinking this was turning around for him. "Thing is, I can't have you after you've shared yourself with someone else."

Growing up in the MC you would see the women forgive and go back to their men. I couldn't be one of them because I had too much pride and something else that stopped me that I didn't even understand, yet.

Derrick's head fell forward in defeat and I turned my back on him, and us. The first step away was the hardest. Then I closed the door to the car and started the engine when I heard his fist hitting the side of it. The last thing I saw on his face was the same agonized pain and anger reflected in my rearview mirror that I felt inside.

Derrick would know me well enough, that I would be stone. I guess he had to try that day, but I loved my pride more than him.

Shortly after, when some time had passed and I lived in Nevada, he tried to get a hold of me again, but I never gave in to any calls or texts. Two months later, he finally stopped calling.

I will never allow another man to break me again. I will never feel weak, because no man will have my heart like that again.

There are rules that the men and women in my family live by. We never rat out. To this day, they don't know who I saw Derrick with that day.

Exhaling a frustrated breath, I wonder, why the hell I am thinking of this for.

Tugger starts pacing at the door before the knocking comes, and he patiently waits for me. Checking the peephole, I see Jenn and Dana holding their cups cusps up.

"Open up," Jenn hollers.

Chuckling, I unlock and open the door and get Tug out of his misery.

Inviting them in, I say, "Well, I guess you guys want the details from last night, or you wouldn't be bribing me at ten in the morning with Starbucks."

I grab the blueberry scone and latte from Dana while she and Jenn stroll in. They both shrug, not caring that they are guilty, and find a seat with me on the couches in my living room.

"Busted," Jenn admits with a shameless grin. "We want all the details of those hot biker boys," she wistfully tells me.

I shake my head at her, "Jenn, you know you and James are MFEO." I laugh at her because when she finally decides to see that man is in love with her, God help her. And him.

Jenn's not having it though. "Whatever, he's always all over those girls at the bar and I'm not in the mood to be played by a player. And *stop* saying MFEO! We are not in high school anymore. So, answer our question and stop deflecting, we aren't leaving till you spill."

Ugh, these nosy bitches are going to bug the living hell out of me till I give, may as well get it over with.

"Fine," I huff out, feigning my frustration. "The Battle Born MC wants to move in next door to us and open up a tattoo shop. Not sure if they are looking to lease or buy that part of the building. I pretty much just said I will schedule some time to talk business, and then they left."

Dana's face is perked in interest, and the questions are coming. I can see them sprouting as she starts. "Do they all have to be licensed to work in a shop? Is our area even zoned to open a tattoo shop?" I love that she's getting the logistics worked out for me.

"That's why you're my manager, babe. I bring the fun, you bring your brains and beauty, and DJ Jammin'

Jenn brings the jams. That's why the three of us," I hold three fingers up, "are the perfect trio." I've been thinking for a while now to bring them in as partners. It would only be right.

"Dana!" Jenn's sudden outburst startles us. "That guy with a nice, tight build and as tall as the bossy one, he was hot. And, he was totally eyeing you for the short time they were there."

"Psh, I don't think so." Dana waves Jenn off. "Guys always flirt in a bar, and then some extra with the bartenders, thinking they will get something for free. This girl can handle her own O's and take care of herself. No B.S. required. Plus, I don't think there was any air left in the room. I was being suffocated by Vegas and the broody dude." She wiggles her eyebrows at me like I know what she's talking about.

"Seriously?" I question Dana and her sanity. "That guy, his name is Blade by the way, and the one Jenn is talking about is Axl, and there wasn't any air in the room left because he had his ego to inflate it with. The guy is a total douche, control freak, arrogant prick." I mock disinterest, because there's no way I'm telling them how hot our encounter really was and how much it got to me. Let alone my joy ride into ecstasy last night with my fingers with thoughts of his hands on me and his voice rasping demands from me.

"Hmm," Jenn's inquisitive eyes laser in, prying further, "You really are worked up over Blade. With most guys, you don't even care to take the time to cuss them out. He's special." Jenn is batting her eyelashes at us. Dana and I start laughing in sync over Jenn's tender thoughts.

"Well, I will call the pain in my ass, no additional comments necessary, Jenn," I hold up my hand at her while shaking my head. "And schedule a sit-down with all of us."

We spend the rest of our Saturday relaxing and chatting. Eventually, we get up and start getting ready for work.

The week flies by since we are all busy catching up on paying our bills, cleaning and inventory. I may or may not have forgotten to call Blade and made myself very busy on purpose. I don't know, it's been crazy.

Thankfully, at the moment, it's mellow enough in the bar where Dana and I take turns working on the invoices and helping customers.

Jenn usually comes in a few hours here and there to scratch out some new tracks. She always helps to clean or do whatever Dana and I don't have time for. I just love her being here while I work to listen to what she mixes together. She makes new playlists every single day.

Tonight, though, her music choices are sad, and I wonder what she's going through that she hasn't told us about. She drops the remix of *Last Kiss* by Pearl Jam on the bar speakers and confirms my suspicions that something is up with her.

Dana feels it too and turns to me with the same concern written clearly on her features. "Do we need to stage a suicide intervention? Bitch is sad, do we need to hook her up or something? Since she's been back from Cali, she hasn't been the same," she tries to whisper to me, but I think it's louder than she realizes.

"I don't know what went down in Sacramento, but when she's ready, she'll tell us," I confirm back to her confidently.

Jenn must have heard us because the song she was playing stops. All I can do is put the bottles that I'm holding down. Because Jenn starts playing Warrant's *Cherry Pie* with a very devious, pissed off look on her face.

Dana turns and glares at Jenn, "Really, Jenn, this song?" She steps out around from behind the bar to get a better look at Jenn. "The one time I forget to pack Spankies for cheerleading and that asshole on the football team told the whole school about my partially thong covered vagina he got a glimpse of during one of our kicks. That whole year, everyone played that song every time they saw me! Asshole!" Dana's face is red from her outburst and stands there, glaring daggers at Jenn.

Jenn is bending over, laughing hard at her too. "Yeah, I do remember, thanks for 'cheering' me up."

I'm shaking with laughter. It's been forbidden for a long time to play this song. It makes my heart and mind feel lighter as I remember the good times we had growing up.

Getting back to work, I pull the small stepstool over, stretching up to the top to grab the bottles I need to dust off. Not quite finding my footing on the step below on my way back down, I feel my center start tipping sideways, and I'm falling backward.

"Shiit," I yelp in surprise before masculine hands are on my ass, holding me up. What the …

CHAPTER 4

Blade

Opening the door to the bar, The Black Rose, I walk in and am gifted with the sight of Alessia's tight ass. It's the kind of ass you spank red, then bite the juicy, salty skin. My hand twitches about the same time my dick jerks to attention.

Alessia is on top of a stepstool that puts her fine ass at eye level. She can't find the step below, and she's tapping her foot around trying to reach it. She sways a bit, then gives out a startled squeal of, "Shit."

"What the fuck are you doing?" I shout, only to startle her more, which, makes her fall backward quicker. I run to catch her, and, before you know it, my hands are full of that fine ass. Fuck, it's nice and tight too. I bet she works out. A lot. Probably does those prissy ass yoga exercises. I absently wonder about it and my hands instinctively squeeze the globes to check.

"Uhh, you can let go of my ass now," I hear her low, cranky voice coming from above. She's pissed off that my hands are full of her ass. I give it one more tight squeeze and smirk up at her very annoyed, expectant eyes. That ass will be the star of my dirty as fuck fantasies from now on. What else would a man do?

She looks surprised by my grab, but I can't make myself to give a fuck. *Be mad, baby*, I tell her in my head. My hands roam up to her waist and easily pick her up and off the stool, then set her down in her cute white Converse sneakers.

Now I'm staring at her Guns N' Roses see-through t-shirt, and I can see the tops of her handful sized tits up this close. Would she be mad if I squeezed those, too? Definitely.

"Up here, asshole." She takes her dark red nails and trails a line from her tits to her eyes, pointing at them with two fingers. What the fuck? My dick is hard. I can't think past the pulsing heartbeat in my throat.

She pulls deep breaths in and out, but it only makes me notice her hardening nipples that graze my chest as she steps past me. On contact, her breath hitches again, and our eyes meet with a familiar spark of lust blazing through me.

We'll be neighbors soon, so why not enjoy myself? Unless... "You married?"

Startled by my abrupt question, she falters, "What?" Her face scrunches and appears just as confused as I am in this moment.

"A man. You got one?" I try explaining as I'm also checking for a ring. I can't really tell if she is wearing a wedding band or not. She has so many different rings on.

Still confused, she blinks up at me rapidly. Why haven't I moved? I *can't* move. Alessia captures all my attention when she's around, it seems.

"What are you doing in here anyway?" she huffs, annoyed and rolling her eyes at me. "And hell no! I don't have *or* need a full-time man."

"Good, babe." I release a breath I didn't realize I was holding. "It wouldn't matter anyway, because I would get rid of him." She glares at me and seems to be at a loss for words.

When she finally snaps out of it seconds later, she changes the subject. "Well, what are you here for anyway?" she demands impatiently.

That is such a loaded question. I need her naked, with that tight ass and pussy in my face. God, I need to get laid. Alessia may be too much trouble no matter how much I love the chase with her. I tell myself to reel this in and get back to business.

"I need to sit down with you, and hammer out the details of our deal," I reluctantly tell her, then move back a few steps, out of her space.

She stares at me some more with her hands on her hips, like she's ready for battle. The small t-shirt she's got on is stretched to the max by her tits that are being pushed forward. Fuck, I need to find a good lay.

I get my thoughts back together long enough to say, "I brought the paperwork for a business license, also came up with an offer to buy the property from you. When can we sit down and go over it?"

Vegas

In the corner of my eye, I see Dana stepping forward, wearing a very happy smile. I know that, since he came prepared, it impresses her. I go ahead and introduce them, getting this over with already.

"Blade, this is Dana Maraschino, my manager. Anything that needs to be said or discussed about this, she'll be there. You can give those to her, thank you."

Hearing a low chuckle at the end of the bar, I turn my head to see who it is. When did Axl and Tank get here? Axl has an infectious humorous tone to his next question.

"Dana Maraschino. As in the cherry? Maraschino Cherries?" He breaks out into a loud laugh. Dana is pissed, glaring at his face, but stays quiet.

Cherry Pie sounds through the speakers again, with Tank, Axl and Jenn full on laughing at Dana. Axl starts singing along, pointing at Dana and belting out the lyrics with the enthusiasm of a rockstar. He's now playing the air guitar and dancing, thrusting his hips as he moves closer to her.

Dana turns on her heel, snatches the papers from Blade's hand and storms off, elbowing Axl in the ribs on her way to the back room where she slams the door shut. HARD.

Out of breath, Axl heaves, "Oh, fuck, I'm in love." He grabs his heart with his hand, still trying to catch his breath. I can't help but throw my head back and laugh, and I really feel the laughter healing a tiny crack in my still cold and fractured heart.

I mention to Axl, "Any chance you had, my man, you just blew with that pelvis thrusting show. You have no idea what you just did. I will admit, though, completely entertaining, but good luck getting her to give you any of her cherry pie," I laugh out breathlessly.

He smiles back, "Nah, my charm is hard to resist. She'll come around and she won't be able to quit this." He zigs zags his finger up and down his body, thrusting his pelvis at us one more time.

"Down, playboy," Jenn says, cracking up while strolling toward us. "I'm Jenn, ya'll are looking to set up shop next door?"

Tank steps up to the group, suddenly more interested than before. Looking Jenn over, he adds, "You looking to get something done? I can hook you up," he winks at her.

Jesus, this is getting out of hand. Blade pulls us all back on point here, barking over in Tank and Axl's direction. "What I was talking with Alessia about was, when would it be a good time for us all to go over the contracts?"

Feeling more relaxed, I turn to look into his brown eyes. Jenn responds while still focused on Tank. "We close on Wednesday nights, except, we hang out here and pump some dirty songs. We relax and get pretty toasty, and BBQ. You can come hang with us tomorrow night, talk business, then we can all get to know each other better?"

I'm very pissed that Jenn just gave up our own girls' night to this meeting-and-get-to-know-each-other crap. I know what she's up to.

"Sure," I respond, trying not to give away that I'm too annoyed with her. "That will give us enough time to read the contracts, and Johnny to review them as well."

"Johnny?" Blade inquires.

"Oh, that's our lawyer," I tell him.

"And her ex, so he'll drop whatever he's doing to help Alessia," Jenn so freaking helpfully adds on. Blade has a pissed off look on his face. For what, I don't know, maybe he's hungry?

His voice is clipped, "We'll be here tomorrow at six, unless...?"

"No, six would be fine, perfect even," chipper Jenn responds. She is really not being my cool DJ Jenn right now.

Blade sticks his hand out and shakes mine very tenderly as he rubs his thumb over my knuckles. "I'll look forward to seeing you tomorrow, Alessia." His gaze travels over my eyes, down to my lips and back up. "Tomorrow," he promises and all three of them turn around and leave. Not fast enough, though, because me and Jenn are going to have our own meeting. Right now.

"Jenn, fucking seriously?" I'm frustrated and feeling exposed from seeing Blade, and I don't know why. So, I tell her angrier than I feel, "Why did you invite them to dinner and drinks? What if we all, and when I say all, I mean me and Dana, don't want to get to know these guys?" Dana emerges from the storage room to jump in on this conversation too now that Axl is gone.

Jenn stands a little straighter. "You know what?" she yells back at me, "Someone needs to get you out of your emotionless, romance-less world. Who gives two shits about what happened with Derrick? That prick-less wonder hasn't been bugging you and you've had two years to move on!" Jenn's voice gets a softer, sincerer tone. "By not living in these moments and chancing to trust another man, you are letting him win. Who really loses here, Vegas? You. Please, not you! Fight your fears and pride to trust again. Please."

Dana stands between us, her hand on each of our shoulders. She looks right in Jenn's face with a mocking tone, "Payback's a bitch, Jenn. When you're not expecting it, I will pay you back for all of that,"

We fall into a fit of laughter as James walks in for his shift. "What's so funny, ladies?" That only makes us laugh harder. "What? Seriously." He walks away more frustrated, mumbling, "Crazy ass chicks."

I look Jenn right in the eyes, and she blinks and nods in understanding. *I'll try if you do.*

CHAPTER 5

Blade

The boys and I step outside from our meeting with Alessia and her crazy as fuck crew. We light up a smoke before heading out, and I take a drag to calm my nerves. I don't know who this fucker Johnny is, but I'm going to find out. Why the hell does it piss me off that Alessia has a past?

Ignoring my thoughts, I flip my shades down and look toward Axl. "Axl, call Spider, have him..."

He cuts me off. "On it, already texting Spider about Johnny." He talks out loud while typing, "Get a last name, full background, including ALL relationships, especially with Alessia," Axl winks at me, the asshole, "bank accounts. Anything else, Prez?"

"Yeah, call Johnny's office and set up an appointment for us," I smile back as I'm thinking of showing that fucker my face.

Tank snickers, "You gonna cut off his dick, too?" I like the thought of using my knifes on that fucker since he probably put his hands on Alessia.

"No, not yet, Tank, but maybe we'll keep an eye on him, yeah?" The look on Tank's face says he loves that idea as much as me.

James pulls up in his Chevy truck and parks next to us. Walking past us, he gives a polite nod and moves on. We have some work to do if I'm to get this guy on my side as well.

"Let's hit the road, take in what goes on around this area. Also, we need to go check in with the Club, see if the guys have any new information."

"Aye", they both say. Stomping out my spoke in the dirt, we head over to our bikes, get on and crank the beasts on.

Out of The Black Rose's parking lot, we turn right and head up around the park, making our way up west on the freeway to the Truckee River. We end up riding for about forty-five minutes, longer than I initially planned. You really wouldn't think you would have found such a beautiful mountain ride so close to the city.

I didn't want to stop. I loved the open road, a new one to conquer. It called to the beast within me, and I kept going.

I can say that I love this area as much as Las Vegas, if not more. The scenery is definitely better and has a relaxing vibe.

Looking up ahead, I see there's a small diner with a truck stop right over the border into California. My stomach is protesting that it is time to grab some food before we head back to the clubhouse.

Pulling into the parking lot, we jump off our bikes to walk into the small building, when a truck pulls in. It has a painted devil on the side, *Hellfire Trucking, Inc* wrapped around the logo. Halting my hand from pulling the diner's door open, I nod toward the truck to direct Axl and Tank's attention that way.

"This can't be that fuckin' easy," Axl echoes my own stunned thoughts.

Motioning with my head for Axl and Tank to move with me, I step back behind the wall, grabbing my gun and tucking it into my cut. "We need to see and not be seen, stay back."

Tank, that pig headed motherfucker, tosses his cut and t-shirt at us, leaving his wife beater on. He picks up an empty coffee cup out of a trash can and starts walking out there, talking on his phone like he's checking in with his bitch.

"Yeah, babe, no worries, I'll be home in time for David's soccer game. Wait, you're breaking up." He pulls his phone down like he's trying to redial her back. After a couple of tries, he pockets his phone and nods to a few other truckers, saying stupid shit along the way. "Howdy... Good Afternoon... how's she haulin' today?"

He finally makes his way back over to us. Irritated, I whisper shout at him, "What the fuck was that?"

"Well, Prez, how else was I gonna get ugly dick pics for Spider and a license plate number? It really hurts my feelings when you doubt me like that." He frowns at me and pretends to wipe a tear away.

I flip him the bird, and so much for eating. Guess we should follow this truck till I can get a few men up here to help.

Taking my phone out, I pull up the contact number for the California chapter of the Battle Born Prez, Fuego. He's a Hispanic brother, and fuckin' fiery as hell when he's pissed off. I've only met him a handful of times. A demonic fucker and almost reminds me of the devil himself in appearance.

Stryker always dealt with the clubs up north in the past, while I was concentrating on my runs and crew in the south. Me being up this way was another strategy by my old man to strengthen our ties here. He also needed to be able to trust who was up here. He had offered the Prez position here to his VP and other members he trusted, but they didn't want it. They'd been with my old man for so long, none of them wanted to break up their crew.

I took about ten members total with me to Reno and wanted a fresh start to prove myself to the club that I could do this.

"Yeah," Fuego greets me with a gruff tone.

"Fuego, it's Blade. I ran into a Hellfire Trucking rig up here in Verdi. We need to keep eyes on it. Can you send some men this way to take over the tail? We're on our bikes, man. I don't want to spook this trucker."

"*Si*, they are on their way. I'll be in touch." The call is lost after he confirms his support. Paranoid fucker, I think to myself, pocketing my phone.

Axl and I both shrug it off and roll up our cuts. Walking over to our bikes, we stuff them into our saddle bags. He and Tank follow me up the road where we pull off to the side and wait. The trucker passes us, and we keep tabs on him from a short distance back deeper into the California. The tail gets easier the farther in we get, the heavy traffic helping us out.

Finally, after another hour on our bikes, a couple of cars pull up to us showing us their cuts and tossing them back down next to them. I nod in understanding and am relieved they got here to help. I hate California traffic, and, as soon as we can, we take the ramp off the freeway and head back to Nevada, thank fuck.

After a few too many hours on our bikes, I'm freezing my balls off from being up there in the mountains, with the higher altitudes and the fall chill. None of us dressed for a long ride, let alone a cold one.

As soon as our bikes are parked at the clubhouse, Tank, Axl and I jump off and haul ass inside the club for a hot shower. But first, we should check in if any progress has been made with the dick pics, courtesy of Tank.

We nod over to Spider who has CC, that stupid cunt hanger-on, giving him a BJ on her knees over in the booth. Fucking Spider. I'm cranky as fuck and don't have time for this shit.

Two other bitches are up on the table, licking each other's pussies in a sixty-nine, all you can eat buffet. I swear that bitch, CC, only gives the guys head. Stupid bitch is clueless as to why no man here would touch that pussy even when double wrapped. She's been passed around so many times that the guys have spread word from down at the old Mustang Ranch that their dicks itched, and she was fired. True or not, not a man alive wants to find out.

Spider grabs her hair and forces his hips forward, slamming the cunt's nose to his stomach. Her spit and tears hit the floor. He fucks her face unrelentingly, taking everything he wants from her. He knocks her back on her ass with a boot to her shoulder. Standing up, he jacks his cock off over the two other bitches on the table, then comes all over one's ass and the other bitch's face. He zips his pants up and walks back to my office where Tank and Axl are holding back a laugh at Spider's antics.

"Spider, you think CC's figured out her name yet?"

Spider shrugs back at me, "Don't know and don't care. If a man can't get that shit running down her face, making her Clarissa the Clown, then he isn't fucking her face hard enough." He shrugs like the true asshole that he is. "She fucking takes it, so why the fuck would I care?"

Axl looks up at him from his phone. "Jesus, dude, there's not a man in here that doesn't like his cock sucked, and sucked well, but she took a beating with what you were dishing out."

And with that, I'm done talking about this shit. I ask Spider, "So, what's up with the plate and pic Tank got for you?"

Spider sits down next to Tank, ready to start the meeting, but Tank jumps up to sit on the opposite side of him. A rumble of laughter pops out of me and my VP. Tank shouts, "I ain't sitting next to your jack off hand, dude. Seriously! Go wash your hands, fucker!" Tank's throwing his hands up towards the bathroom.

"Fine! Fuck you, you little pansy assed pussy!" Spider gets up to make a stop in the bathroom. Tank then turns to yell at us now, "Stop fucking laughing! I don't wanna sit next to, or be around, any man's hand that may or may not have jizz on it. Besides, don't you dumbasses wash your hands after you take a piss? This shit is not funny!"

"Okay, okay, Tank, yes I always wash my hands like a pansy assed pussy," I chuckle back.

Tank is rarely offended or serious which is making it even harder for us to stop laughing. Spider finally walks back in for the meeting and glares Tank's way who's still staring at us.

"Alright, Spider, what did you find?" I try to get this over with so I can get to my hot shower.

"Well, the plates are shit, of course they're stolen. They were originally registered in Las Vegas and reported stolen a week ago. So, I'm guessing these guys dump their plates for new ones every week. But we know they're heading north from Vegas, might be why Buck got caught up with these fuckers. Either he caught them in Texas or Las Vegas. I gave the pics you got today to Cuervo, and he's checking around for names. I'm working on the timelines of Buck's calls and death with this truck's timeline. Maybe he's the one that got him?"

Taking a deep breath, I rub my hands over my face and head. "We followed that truck up over into California where the chapter there finished the tail. We couldn't follow him long without him catching on. We'll see what the Cali chapter has for us in the morning. I'm fucking beat, we'll figure this shit out tomorrow."

Heading back to my room, exhausted, I finally get a hot shower and lie down. Grabbing my phone, I call my old man.

"Heard you were chasing tail up there in Reno," Stryker says in his way of a greeting.

"If by chasing tail, you mean that truck we followed into California, then yeah." I continue updating him on what happened today.

He hums along and says, "I'll call up Cuervo and give him an update. We'll see what Fuego's crew comes up with. I actually wasn't asking about that tail, though."

I must be hella tired because I'm lost. "What are you asking me, old man?" I'm impatient and loud in my response.

My dad just roars back a laugh. "Rough day, huh, kid? Well, I'll come out with it. Heard you have your dick set in on claiming a hot little firecracker who's giving you lip."

I can't see his face, but I know this asshole, and he's toying with me, so I don't respond.

"Silence says it all. Take care of her, son, it's about time. Your mom was a firecracker too, she sounds good for you. Don't fuck it up."

If he was here, I would be tempted to deck his ass. "Stryker, why the fuck would you tell me not to fuck it up?"

He takes a moment like he's thinking back on the past. "Blade, I wasn't always the best man to your mother when we were younger. I made choices that hurt her that I wish I could take back. She stuck by me though. Her love for me was stronger than the weak-minded choices I'd made. Be the man your mother and I raised you to be." My old man hangs up with that convoluted information.

I'm too tired to think on what he could possibly mean by all that, and fall asleep.

CHAPTER 6

Blade

Tank, Axl and I park around the back of Alessia's bar, then walk up to James who's manning the grill.

"What's up, shitheads?" James smirks our way. "You here to piss off the girls some more?" He asks us but doesn't look too happy that we're here.

"Nah, man, I'm looking to work out this business deal with Alessia." I try explaining, but his stance is telling me that something is off with him.

"Blade, just so you know, that woman in there has had enough shit from limp dicks in the past, so if you're serious, go on in. If not, leave her the fuck alone." James puts the lid down on the BBQ and squares his chest at me.

He's obviously dealt with some shit and is loyal to Alessia, but no fucker squares off with me. I step closer, facing James, looking him in the eyes.

"Look, James, don't judge me and make me look like the asshole you don't know me to be. So, fucking keep your big brother talks for the next fucker who gives a shit to listen to them."

Jesus. What's with James and Stryker telling me not to be a fuckup for?

"Just sayin', you're not here just for business, so don't sell me that shit either, just be upfront with her. Be the man she needs, or walk the fuck on and leave her alone."

James and I are still staring each other down when Jenn walks out with a plate in hand, stepping between us, her back to me.

She puts her hand on James' arm and rubs up and down. "James, those steaks done?"

"Yeah, they're done." He's looking at me when he says that, then turns toward her and the grill, placing his hand on her hip, kissing her head.

Taking a step back, I turn to go find Alessia, so I head toward her office. Deep laughter fills the air through the bar, and something about that laugh makes me want to smile. It calls to me. Helps me to relax a little after wanting to ram my fist down James' throat. I know he looks out for her, but I answer to only one man, and that's my Prez and old man.

Alessia spots me walking through her office and glares at me. "Do you walk through all offices like this and forget your manners?"

"Nah, babe, just yours." I smile at her, flipping a chair around to sit next to her, with my arms on the back of it.

Looking at her pretty blue eyes, I ask, "Did you look through the papers, how are we looking?"

"Pretty damn good." Axl snickers as he's pulling his chair out next to Dana's. She turns and looks at him like the little shit she would love to throat punch. The dipshit makes it worse by saying, "Brought some cherry pie..." Smiling a mile wide while sliding a boxed pie across the table for Dana.

She stands up and the chair scrapes across the floor when she punches the middle of the box, muttering, "Motherfucking, dickheaded asshole." Pissed off, she continues with her rant through the back office. Maybe James was right, and we *are* going to fuck this up.

Axl scoots in closer to the table. "She's in love with me, just doesn't know it yet." He's still smiling about it when he watches her walk back into the bar.

"Can we get real? Settle some business before you get us thrown out, asshole?" Now I'm glaring at my VP.

"Yeah, boss, all business from here on out," he replies in all mock seriousness.

Dana hands over the contracts to me, and then hands Alessia a plastic fork. I'm totally caught off guard at what the fuck is going on here. Are they going to eat the smashed pie?

Alessia pulls the box over, popping open the lid. She digs her fork in and starts eating right out of the box. Dana is right behind her, digging in too. Alessia has a smile in her eyes that I hadn't seen from her before.

Axl and I stare in fascination at this, neither one of us making a single move.

"Mmmm, so sweet." Dana salaciously licks her fork, and, for the life of me, I'm at a loss here and can't stop watching this train wreck.

Axl looks so lost in thought as he's staring at Dana who's eating the smashed pie, and my eyes are bouncing between all three of them.

I focus my eyes back on Alessia, and she playfully winks at me. Mind is blown, something is really off here. My instincts are screaming at me. I've been caught in some crazy situations, but this is a game I'm not sure of what is going on.

Dana asks Axl, "You want a bite?" All sweet and sultry. *Don't do it, brother, it's a fuckin' trap,* I think, but no, he goes for it.

Disappointment washes over me when Axl leans in closer and whispers back into her ear, "Yeah, princess, I want more than a bite." He backs up just a bit, gazing into her eyes.

Shit, he's not seeing this is a set up. Dana's sweet voice murmurs, "Mmmkay". She pokes her fork into the pie, turns it around, then flicks the cherries and crust all over his face. A stunned Axl flinches at the flying pie spattering across his face but recovers pretty well.

"Fuck, babe, I love your pie in my face," he tells Dana, then licks a piece off the side of his mouth. I think the tongue maneuver is supposed to be sexy, but he looks like a damn cow trying to catch flies.

Alessia is full on laughing with her head back, hands over her chest, and I can't help but laugh right along with them, shaking my head at Dana and Axl.

I can't help but to get a glimpse of the unabashed woman next to me. She is striking when she frees herself from expectations.

She grabs a few napkins and tosses them toward Axl. Dana's face gloats, mighty proud of her pie flicking aim, then she sits back, enjoying the mess she made. I have to agree that it was a kill shot, of the pie variety.

Tank, Jenn and James walk in and sit down with us.

"What the hell happened to the pie!"

Even though Jenn sounds upset at the condition of the dessert, she reaches over the bar to grab enough forks to pass around. She doesn't seem surprised, and, instead, joins in with no questions asked.

I decide to join in the crazy and grab Alessia's fork to take a bite out of the pie. I look deep into her blue eyes, wishing I could tell her all the dirty as sin thoughts I've had about her this week. My gut feeling tells me, though, that if I push her too fast, I'll end up pushing her completely away.

All of us sit in a comfortable silence, eating what's left of the dessert before Jenn asks, "Did Vegas go over the contracts with you?"

Feeling, once again, completely lost here. "Ahh, who would that be?"

Jenn answers with a point of her fork at Alessia. Alessia, or *Vegas*, steals my fork from my hand and piles the pie onto it. She doesn't get too far because I grab the hand that has the fork with pie on it and steal her bite, then release her.

"That's your road name, huh? This is a story I really wanna hear."

Apparently, I have the same affliction as my VP because I can't stop staring at Alessia like he can't stop staring at Dana. My hand rests on her knee, rubbing up and down the inside of her leggings. She doesn't move or flinch, and that is a good fucking sign.

Jenn jumps right in. "You see, Vegas here," she points at Alessia again, "quit her job, cashed out her retirement, and put it all down on this bar, bet it all on herself that she could make it work," Jenn waves her hand around the bar. "Right after she kicked that dumb... ow fuck!"

I feel Alessia's leg flex out from under my hand, and Jenn jumps back hitting her knee on the table.

"That's enough of that story." Alessia's warning clear. There is something personal in the other half of the story that wasn't told.

Jenn pouts over in Tank's direction. "She busted my toe, Tank! Look at it!" She lifts her foot up, taking her sandal off to show Tank, and he starts rubbing it.

"I'm sure it's fine, Jenn, put your foot down." A frustrated James storms off outback and slams the door after him.

My eyes warn Tank that I will end him if he keeps this shit up. He drops Jenn's foot like a hot brick and throws his hands up like he *'didn't do it'* gesture. Jenn is clueless, or pretending to be, at this drama she's creating by stringing these two dipshits along.

"Anyway," Alessia says pulling everyone's attention back to her, "We had Johnny, my lawyer, go over your offer, it's an agreeable amount. The only thing I had asked him to change is that if you decide to sell, the space comes back to me to re-buy within reasonable market value."

Rubbing my chin, I think on whether I like this change in the contract. Honestly, I didn't truly expect her to change anything. Though, this does impress me.

I look over at Axl and Tank to see what they think. They're both smiling at her. She just one upped me, and I'm finding this little power move really hot.

I pull my hand off her thigh, rubbing my head and pretending to be in deep thought over it, then decide to agree. "Okay, so if, or when, we decide to sell, I come to you first. That's a fare enough deal."

Jenn jumps up excited, shouting, "Oh, thank God!" She's mocking me like it's a huge relief. "Can we chill now or what?"

Alessia has a hellish smile for her. "Yeah, bitch, let loose. Hey, Blade, why don't you invite a few more of your brothers over? We have half a keg of beer they can have, anything else is on them." She finishes signing the papers and hands them back to me.

"Sounds good, I'll call Spider and a few others, tell them to head over."

We finish eating our steaks, macaroni salad and fruit when Alessia scoots in a little closer, snuggling into my side. My arm is stretched behind her chair. Together, we watch her friends dance and party with my brothers. She looks happy and more comfortable. I'm hoping she doesn't move or get up from our spot.

Some other members that weren't busy came over with their Ol' Ladies or bitches to drink with us. It's nice for a change to not worry, but to take a moment to relax.

Getting all these people together was a good idea. In these small moments, with Alessia at my side, I get why my dad leans so heavily on my mom for his peace.

Earlier, I sent Axl, Tank and Spider a text telling them to keep their eyes open. I need them watching the newer members for anything that looks shady. I don't need someone bringing this night down, but I also have to keep my eyes open for all the problems we've been having.

Axl has finally chilled the hell out and is not trying to piss Dana off any further. Jenn changes another track and yells across the floor, "As I promised the other night to play a real dirty song for you boys..."

We all stop and look at one another because what's coming out of those speakers isn't the kind of dirty we were thinking.

"What do you say? We get a little mud on the tires..."

Tank yells over to Jenn, "Are you fucking telling me this is your dirty song? A country, shit kicking, redneck song? Prez, we ain't moving in next door to a country bar, fuck no!"

Jenn laughs menacingly at the boys. "Too late, fuckers, your Prez already signed the papers!"

The girls and James are laughing hard, and my boys are glaring at me, so I can't help but laugh with them. It feels good to have fun with Alessia and her crazy as fuck crew.

Jenn sets them straight though. "Relax, fuckers, this ain't no hick bar, dumb shits." She laughs with one hand on her earphones and mixes in some G-Easy, *Lady Killers*. Jumping off the stage, she bows, and some guys glare, while others laugh. She proudly flips the whole room off with two middle fingers.

These crazy bitches, I can't quite figure out how, but they seem to blend in with these crazy as fuck assholes.

Alessia, or Vegas now, gets up, clearing the table we all ate at. Her hands full of plates and glasses that she collected, she turns to take them back to her small kitchen. Trailing right behind her is her black dog, his tail wagging back and forth.

Not wanting to miss a moment alone with her, I decide to help by picking up a few plates and glasses myself and follow her to the back.

She turns to look at me walking through the double swinging doors while she rinses glasses off, stacking them onto a tray. I place the rest of the dishes I was carrying into the sink when I feel her dog jumping up on my legs, and squat down to pet him. "Whoa there, boy, you pretty happy, aren't ya? What's his name?"

"Down, Tugg," Alessia reprimands him. "His name is Tugger. I found him when he was a puppy. He'll jump all over you if you let him," she advises me, but I get the sense she doesn't want me to allow him to do that.

Giving Tugger one final pat, I stand to help hand Alessia a few plates. "Thanks for all this tonight, Alessia. My boys haven't been relaxed since we moved up here, it's been a tough year for all of us. We haven't had too many good moments lately," I explain to her.

"I know, Blade, I can see the stress in your eyes. I love my bar, I enjoy bringing people together, and sometimes a change in scenery helps."

She peers down at her hands. I can see the forlorn sadness in her thoughts. My hands grab hers softly to pull her toward me, away from her task.

This feels so right, our hands touching, but also very foreign to me. I don't do intimacy with women. I don't hold hands. This gentle side of me, I have never experienced it before.

Gathering her to my chest, I hold them there for a minute, allowing our souls to connect through our gaze. Something in my concrete heart cracks open, a place I've never felt open before, letting a little of her seep inside of me.

Bringing her hands to my lips, I kiss them softly. Never wanting to let them go. Her eyes are opened wide at my actions. In that small period of time, I see her pain and feel her sadness or loneliness, I'm not exactly sure what it is, but I do know I want to protect her from it.

Alessia drops her arms and I feel her pulling back her true self from me. Small steps, I tell myself. And decide a better course is to get her to have more fun, for now.

"You want to dance with me?" A mischievous grin covers my face. I crave to see her smile and laugh again.

"Yeah, let's go dance." She smiles and leaves the rest of the dishes, backing away, then turning around. She glances at me over her shoulder, like I would miss this chance with her. Looking down at Tugger, I see that he's right behind her, out the door.

CHAPTER 7

Vegas

My heart is lodged in my throat as I stare up into Blade's deep, whiskey brown caramel eyes. There is a softness there, a feeling in his eyes that I haven't seen in a man before. This feeling terrifies me, but I don't pull my hands away, I don't back away from him.

Some place inside of me wonders if he can feel this too. But the last thing I want is to give a man my love or trust again. So, I don't. I can't let myself be open only to be the one destroyed again.

Thankfully, he has other ideas. "You want to dance with me?"

He looks very handsome when he smiles like that at me, when no one is around to see it. The softer side to his strong as stone one. It helps me to feel more comfortable around him when he opens small pieces of himself to me. Could he be trusted?

I can dance, I just can't do this feeling, not ever. "Yeah, let's go dance."

Walking out of the kitchen, I point to the small bed under the bar where Tugg jumps on to settle in. I smile when I see Dana, Jenn and the Battle Born boys all dancing and laughing.

Turning around and walking backwards, I grab Blade by his cut and lead us to the dance floor. I start bouncing to the beat as *Talk Dirty to Me* by Jason Derulo plays. I pull us to the middle of the group. I notice a couple of other chicks that must have just arrived while we were in the kitchen, but, if everyone keeps it mellow, that's okay with me.

Turning my body around, my hands are thrown up into the air, and I start moving to the beat. Blade grabs one hip tightly, squeezing me from behind. Tingles race up my spine from his strong hand. I feel his hard-muscled chest rub against my back. His head dips down to my ear and his hot breath fans across my neck. My hands skim back behind his head, running them up and down.

Mmm, I love the way his smooth skin feels in contrast to his prickly, short buzzed hair. Swaying my ass back and forth, I grind against his cock. I let my thoughts and feelings get lost in the songs.

Dance after dance, we all laugh, drink and enjoy the late-night hours, and, somehow, make it home before the sun comes up.

Blade

Watching Vegas move her body back and forth, it's killing me not to touch her. Especially when I spot Spider and a few others watching the same show I am. Oh, fuck that, I'm gonna make shit real clear.

I reach out and grab her hip, pulling her luscious ass to my dick. Bending over her, I want it to appear that I'm either talking to her or kissing her neck, either way, I'm staking a claim on her.

Taking a deep breath in, I inhale her scent, running my nose from her collarbone to under her ear. With one hand still firmly on her hip, the other wraps around her flat stomach. Alessia doesn't know this, but I never dance, so I know these assholes will damn well know better than to try and touch her now.

Her hot hands rub the back of my head, and damn, I want her small, soft hands all over my skin. Her touch alone ignites a hot wave of lust rippling down my body. I desperately want to continue making this burn hotter, but I know this is as far as it's going to go tonight.

When this woman is Alessia, she's open, sweet, caring and thoughtful. Piss her off or show her a good time, and my little vixen comes out to play as Vegas. Right now, all I want is a whole lot more of Vegas. Take her into her office and pin her to the wall to fuck her little pussy that has never been given a real dick to pound it till she comes for me.

She turns, flashing me a smile, running her hand up my body, pushing my cut back off my shoulders. Catching it in my hand, I toss it into Cowboy's face, his focus solely on the show we are giving him. Alessia's fingers begin to rub over my nipples. This little bitch is playing with me, getting herself off on the excitement.

My hands wrap around her waist, roaming up her sides till they hit her bra. She holds her breath, waiting and watching my eyes, daring me to finish what I started. Slowly I trace my thumbs up and over her hard tight nipples. I can feel the bumpy lace of her bra under her shirt, and fuck, I really want to see her tits in crimson red lace.

She throws her long hair back, wrapping a leg around my thigh, leaning backwards and forcing both of my hands to grab onto her hips to help her stay up. She's grinding her pussy against my dick to the beat. I start rubbing my dick hard against it, like I would if I had it in her.

She arches herself back up while biting her lip. She stares into my eyes, focused on the heat I'm showing her. She grabs my hips and drops herself low, with her legs open, popping up and down, swinging her wild hair back and forth. She finally comes back up after her bump and grind on the floor.

I'm about to attack her and make good on my fantasy of me and her against the office wall when hoots and hollers fill the air. Laughing, Alessia turns and grabs my shirt, pecking my lips and laughing some more.

Jenn gets on the speaker. "Down, you dirty ho, keep it clean for the ones who aren't getting laid tonight. For all of you who don't know, the ho's name is Vegas." Jenn points her fingers like she has six shooters instead of hands. Aiming at Vegas, she then blows off the barrels of her pistols, and holsters them with a wink.

We dance a few more songs, drinking a few beers in between. We cool it on the floor show for the rest of the night. Thank fuck.

Taking her hand, I pull her over to a table, sitting down and pulling her in my lap. Spider and Cowboy, being nosy little fucks, pull up a chair and sit with us.

"Hey, I'm Spider, this is Cowboy." Spider introduces himself, nodding toward Alessia and pointing at Cowboy with his thumb, which really surprises me because usually he's a dick, unless you're an Ol' Lady.

Alessia nods and bumps her fist with them both, which has even Spider cracking a barely there grin. Fuck, she made friends with Spider. This cannot be good, pairing these two up.

"So, you got his grumpy ass out on the dance floor," Cowboy laughs, looking at me, then at Alessia. "But I imagine that if he knew you were going to give that show, there's no way he wouldn't be there."

Alessia turns her focus in his direction, eyeing him curiously. "I don't know you, Cowboy, so I'm not going to pretend I get what the fuck you were just trying to say. Spell it out or shut the fuck up."

Spider scoots closer, eating this up, while I cough, trying to hold my laughter back.

Cowboy pops some Doritos in his mouth and chews, using one finger to push the brim of his hat up. Kicking his feet up on the open chair next to him, he says, "You're straight, so I'll give it to you straight. Blade doesn't fuck around with bitches on the dance floor, ever. So, he did that show for the rest of us. He's claiming who his woman is. Watcha think about that, honey? Are you going to claim Blade, or was that all to show off to these other bitches that you have the Prez?"

Alessia looks right at Cowboy, unwavering resolve in her voice. "Cowboy, I may be a bitch," she points to her chest, "I don't sit around in a sewing circle sharing my feelings. However, I don't run from shit that I want. As for the rest, you can fuck off."

She reaches over and grabs the bag of Doritos, which she is now sharing with Spider only.

Spider kicks Cowboy's feet off the chair, smiling. He shakes his head at him, not that Cowboy cares. I know my brothers are testing her to see if she's real.

In this life, we all prove we are strong enough to be in it.

Even though I am proud of her, I want to punch Cowboy for saying that shit so soon. I glare over his way to tell him to fuck off from fucking with my woman. Cowboy, in his dumbass hick hat, just smiles back. Fucker.

Alessia is focused back on the main floor, watching Jenn dance and laugh with James and Dana. She grabs her beer from the table to take a sip. Wrapping my hand around hers, I take her drink from her. I chug half of it, then set it back on the table.

She glares at me, grabs my shirt and pulls me to her, taking a hot, fast kiss and sitting back. While I wasn't paying attention, she grabbed her drink back. Lifting her head up, she chugs the rest. She slams the bottle onto the table and winks at me like I lost, and that causes me to grin in response.

She leans in, whispering in my ear, "I love the taste of beer on you."

It's those little things she does that get me to be a different person, one that no one else has seen. Wrapping a protective hand around her waist, I pull her tighter to me.

My job is twenty-four seven, never do I ever drink more than a couple of beers. It's my job to take care of the brothers. I'm enjoying seeing the softer side of Alessia, seeing her joy and excitement is my high.

She hiccups and yells out for the drunk crowd, "Last call was an hour ago, it's time to get the fuck out! You don't have to go home, but you sure as hell can't stay here!"

A resounding boo hits the walls in response. With a wave goodbye to the crowd, she wanders back to her office, shutting the door behind her.

I catch James' attention when I walk by. "Hey, James, the girls are pretty gone, you got Dana and Jenn?" I ask him.

"Yeah, dude, I'm going to take them home in Jenn's car. You mind carrying Vegas out to the car, too?" He wants to take Alessia home? Fuck no, that's not happening. I take care of her.

"Bro, you have two drunk chicks to stuff in that little ass car. I'm going to drop Alessia off, man, and before you give me massive shit, remember I'm not going to fuck her over. Two of my prospects dropped off a few SUV's. Let me help?" James nods warily in understanding right before he runs off to grab Jenn from one of the prospects.

Heading back behind the bar, I call Tugg on my way to the office. "Tugger, you ready? Let's go grab Alessia, boy." I pat my leg and he jumps up very happy to get home, too.

Peering inside Alessia's office, I see that she's passed out in her chair, arms folded on her desk, with her head resting on them. Making my way around the desk, I scoop up my little vixen, cradling her to my chest.

"Blade, why are you so soft with me?" Alessia asks and keeps mumbling on. "We can only be friends, my sexy man."

CHAPTER 8

Vegas

Oh shit, my head hurts. What was I thinking?! Well, I do know what I was thinking. And it had a lot to do with how crazy hot my body was burning for Blade's touch. I haven't been that drunk since my early twenties. Shit, never again.

Then, I hear something. Did my shower just turn off? Who stayed over last night? Who's in the shower? What the hell did I do last night?

My eyes are wildly moving around, trying to see if I can bring back the memories. The bathroom door opens, and I jerk my head to the right just as Blade steps out with a gray towel wrapped around his waist.

I openly watch him walk around to my side of the bed. The man is covered in sexy tattoos and has a body that he obviously takes good care of. I don't think you could fit another tattoo anywhere on his arms, chest or back. Holy shit, the man is fine.

Blade raises his eyebrows at me, "You loving on my body, Vegas? Because I'm really loving those pink panties I got a peek at."

I look down at my legs, and yep, I'm totally *not* covered, and sporting a hot pink thong. Well, shit, I've never been shy, so I shrug. "Nope, I was totally wondering if you could fit another tatt anywhere. Blade, you are not allowed to call me Vegas. And don't take this the wrong way, but why in the fuck *are* you here?"

Blade's eyes move over my legs to focus intently in on my face. "You and your girls were pretty ripped last night. I took you home, James took Jenn and Dana home. Before you ask, I slept on the couch." His face relaxes a bit as he continues, "Last night, you said we could only be friends. That means I can call you Vegas. After you shower, can you take me back to the bar so I can grab my bike?"

"Sure", I say, drawing out the rrr, because, really, what else could I say?

Blade leans over the bed and smacks my ass hard. "Get your sweet ass moving then," he says laughing.

Jumping up to get away from him I give him my best annoyed face, then head toward the bathroom and slam the door in his face. "Asshole!"

Laughing, he calls out, "Keep calling me that and I will show you asshole, Vegas," he yells through the door.

Ignoring the jerk, I step into the shower's hot water that helps to relax my stiff muscles and stinging ass.

I'm praying that it will wash the hangover away too. *Never again, Vegas*, I tell myself. Do not drink that much around this guy, or, really, *ever* again. Having turned twenty-eight, I just don't bounce back like I used to.

After my shower, I throw on my ripped jeans, white t-shirt and my favorite hoody. Deciding I'm too tired to make the effort of drying my hair, I walk back to the bathroom and start braiding it wet.

Blade walks in carrying a coffee which he sets down next to me. I drop my mascara and take a small sip. "Thank you." He eyes me strangely. Hasn't he ever seen a person enjoying their coffee?

"There's some eggs and toast, you done?" Blade points over his shoulder with his thumb.

Sighing, "Yeah, this is a hot mess today. It's as good as it's going to get. Wait, you made breakfast?" It's me now who looks at him strangely.

"I do know how to make scrambled eggs, Alessia." He grabs my hand and leads me to my kitchen. We plate our food and sit at the table.

Okay, this is so weird. After a few minutes of eating in awkward silence, I say the first thing that comes to mind. "Does everyone know your name is William Johnson?" I blurt it out remembering his name on the contracts.

I try to hold a straight face, but I crack a giggle. Except that Blade, or William, just dropped his coffee mug on the table. His eyes are telling me to drop it, and I should. Really, I should. Not everyone gets a kickass name like Alessia DeRosa.

We continue sitting in silence as we eat, but I can't help it. "Did you go by Willy Johnson as a kid?" Picking up more excitement, I laugh a little louder. "I bet you were picked on! Weren't ya, Willy boy?"

Blade's face is cold, with no hint of humor showing, eyes narrowed and dark. I'm really re-thinking teasing this hot biker, because, now, he's a *mad* hot biker. I blow on my coffee, fluttering my eyelashes at him. No, I'm not done yet, this is fun.

"C'mon, tell me, who knows? So we can laugh about it together. Who, *Bill*? Tell me, who–ahh eeks!"

Blade stands, and then he's darting around the table straight for me. I panic like a bear is coming for me and drop my coffee mug on the table before my mad dash to the door. I don't make it very far. His meaty, big hands I loved so much last night catch me by the arm, whipping me around and pulling me into his body. He tackles us to the couch in the living room and my legs wrap around him.

Tugger is up, barking and jumping around, thinking we're playing a game. Blade's eyes are piercing mine with a hard edge to them.

"You like to play games, don't you, Vegas? See how far you can take this before you break me? I'm a man, not one of those little boys you've been playing games with before. You will treat me like a man, you get me? Next time, I'll take my anger out on your ass."

His hands move down my back, squeezing my ass cheeks hard and grinding his rock-hard dick on my pussy. Fuuuck, I don't know who's breathing harder right now.

He smashes his lips against mine, pushing his tongue into my mouth, and I open to him. We dry fuck the hell out of each other for a few seconds until he is biting into my lower lip.

As quickly as he started it, he's done and popping himself up and off me. Man, he's fast, aggressive and hot when he's pissed.

Tugger nudges my arm to play with his nose. Pulling myself up, I pat my poor baby on the head. Adjusting my sweatshirt back down, I try to gain some sanity after being tackled into submission.

Blade walks over and stops by the door with his arms crossed while barking his orders at me. "Breakfast is over, grab your shoes and whatever shit you need."

I really want to tell him to shut it, but I'm not quite ready to find out what that look on his face means. Shoving on my black boots that are sitting by the door, I grab my keys and bag, then stomp my angry, frustrated and horny ass out the door.

Jumping in the driver's seat, I turn the Tahoe on. I can barely reach the pedal and have to move the seat forward. What the fuck? Oh, yeah, he drove us here last night.

I stare straight ahead with laser focus as the passenger door opens, then slams shut. Ripping the car in reverse, I peel out of my driveway and onto the road. And I do all of that just to get this controlling, dick-tease asshole out of my car!

The ride is quiet, and, soon enough, we pull up to the bar. Getting out, I slam my door behind me. I start speed walking inside, not wanting to look Blade in the eyes. Hopefully, he takes a hint, gets on his bike and gets the fuck out of here so I can calm down alone. I feel too damn much when he's around. He puts my thoughts and nerves on edge.

Walking around back, I storm through the back door and gun it to my office. Once I'm in, I throw my stuff on the desk and hear the tinkling sound of my keys hitting the floor. Shit! Now I'm going to have to find them! But, first, I need to check the damage from the chaos of the night before.

I kick my office door open with my boot and stomp into the bar area...

I'm completely taken aback and stop dead in my tracks. After last night, I was thinking it would take me half a day to clean up for sure. What I see, I was not expecting. It's all cleaned up. You would never know we had such a fun time in here last night.

Blade's gently pats my shoulder, and my hand grabs for my racing heart, startled at his soft touch. I never heard him walk through behind me.

"I asked the prospects to get this place picked up and cleaned. Don't worry, they locked up, everything should be where it was." He squeezes my shoulder, and the tenderness confuses me.

"Umm, okay, do I need to pay them?" This is making me uncomfortable, feeling like I owe him. I'm still pissed, so I can't, or rather won't, say thank you. Pride and all that won't let me turn around either.

"Nah, Alessia, it's part of what they do for the club." He pauses for a few moments, gently pulling me around to face him. "Hey, yesterday we didn't get a chance to look at the shop. Let's walk over and look at it now?"

Tilting my head, I see his face is relaxed and pleading for me to do... what? I feel so confused right now.

His fingers run along my jaw to the back of my neck. He draws me to him and hugs me, kissing the top of my head. I feel his voice vibrating against my cheek.

"Alessia, I'm not asking you to give me all of you today. But I'm asking you to give me a chance. Can you do that and not push me out before we even got started?"

I hug him a little closer, a little tighter to my body, not liking the idea of him leaving now. My heart feels safe when I'm in his arms. Have I ever felt protected by another man like this, other than my family? I really can't think of a time my heart fell this fast and this hard.

Giving myself a moment, I find the courage to talk. "That scares me most of all, Blade. It's not that you are asking for a part of me today. It's that you may eventually ask for all of me, then change your mind and throw it all away. I'm asking you that, if you don't think you want it all someday, to leave now."

But I don't let him go, because, somewhere deep down inside, I really hope that he does want it all with me.

Blade sighs and holds me tighter to him. "I don't know that in a week's time either of us knows for sure that we are the people we would ask the other to give it all to. I do know the thought of never knowing, never trying, I will regret that for the rest of my life.

I want to try and see if we can make it, to give every part of us to each other. I know I want to try and find out with you today," Blade tells me softly, never letting me go, and that, with his words, he gives me hope that he's real.

I look up at his face as he leans over and starts kissing me. A slow burn, sort of intense kind of kiss.

Stepping back, I smile up into his whiskey colored eyes, then go back for one more kiss, feeling happy with where we are at now.

I finally let him go and head toward my desk to grab the set of extra keys for his shop, tossing them to him on my way back. When I get to him, he grabs my hand and opens the front door for me.

We make our way over to his new shop. It's dusty and littered with boxes and old white sheets thrown around. Opening the blinds to see better, we both cough on the cloud of dust I stirred up.

Opening a window, I tell Blade, "Mac used this place for storage or never cleaned it up after whoever was here last left, and, with running the bar, I never did have time to clean this place up."

He just nods along, pulling his phone out. He dials while still looking around and waits until the other person answers.

"Tank, wake up, fucker, and grab some prospects, head over to the new shop. We have some work to do, bring the truck and cleaning shit." He pauses and frowns. "I'm here already, dipshit, and none of your goddamn business."

He hangs up the phone and slides it back into his pocket, all while watching me. God, his eyes are sexy as hell, he sees too much of me.

"Come over and I can make us some more coffee while you wait?" I suggest quietly.

He stalks toward me, grabs my hand and pulls me close to his chest. His other hand reaches up and tucks a stray piece of hair behind my ear, looking softly into my eyes. Leaning over, I touch my lips to his.

"Yeah, Alessia, that sounds good, I didn't get to finish my coffee this morning." His smirk has me chuckling back, and we walk out to make some coffee until the boys get here.

CHAPTER 9

Blade

I'm sitting at the bar on a stool, facing Alessia as she hands me my black coffee.

"So where are you from?" I'm curious to find out more about her, especially after she stomped on Jenn's foot to shut her up last night.

"Sacramento area, my parents still live there, although I spent a lot of time in Tahoe. My parents have a house up there. I moved here a few years back, started over, a change in scenery if you will." The mention of a house in Tahoe makes me wonder what kind of cash her old man is packing.

"Why would you pick Nevada and not stay somewhere close to your parents in California?" Odd that she would move so far away, unless she is running away from something?

"Nevada is different, the city and people here are different. California is too familiar, but, Blade, if you have a specific question, I'd rather you just asked me."

She's smarter than most bitches I come across. Most wouldn't have caught on my line of questioning yet.

"Okay, so why did you stomp on Jenn to shut her up last night?" I ask her, wondering how much she will tell.

"Are you telling me you didn't have one of your men dig up my past? I doubt that very much, Blade. Men like you, they look into everyone. I'm sure you know more about me at this point than I do you."

She has a point. "That's true, Alessia, and I haven't read it. I'm sure Spider already did that. He hasn't said anything, which does surprise me." I need to find out why Spider hasn't mentioned anything at all.

"Blade, do you always make friends this way? Or am I just special?" She's batting her eyes at me like a smartass, but decides to give me a little more.

"Things fell apart with my ex and I left. That's all I'm going to say about that, because that shit is going to stay in the past where that cocksucker, Derrick, belongs."

She raises her eyebrow at me in challenge, and if I wasn't so fired up over hearing his name, I would think she was being cute.

"What I was looking for was your business background, and personal. I don't want anything to bite me in the ass later if you have something you're running from. I'm just protecting my club," I say honestly.

"Blade, you don't have to deal with any of my shit, it's handled. And if anything does come back to bite *my* ass, *I*'ll handle it," she states annoyed.

The roar of the bikes hits my ears, ending this conversation. I'll store Derrick's name away for Spider.

"What are you doing for the rest of the day?" I ask her, hoping that she'll stick around for a bit. I know that with us being next door, I'll see her often, but I just don't want to walk away yet either right now.

"Hmm, I don't have much planned until I get back to the bar to work tonight," she says casually like heading home is a much better option.

"Jump up. Let's go grab some paint and boss those little bitches around next door."

Taking her hand, I tug her along behind me. I don't know when I turned into such a needy pussy, needing to have my hands on her all the time, but here I am. What can I do about it? I love the feel of her.

Outside, Tank, Spider and Axl show up, along with the other members and prospects who rode in trucks.

Axl is grinning from ear to ear as he and my two other brothers walk up to us. I pull her a little closer to my side because I don't want any of these fuckers touching her.

Vegas grins up at me and pinches my side before walking away to greet them.

"Morning, boys! Did you all get coffee? I can go grab some donuts on our way back after we look at paint?"

Tank lines up first with a devilish grin, tugging her close for a short hug.

"Morning, sweet stuff, I would love any sugar you wanted to give to me," he winks at her, and I feel my face starting to heat.

"Tank, quit," she slaps at his chest and steps back. "Coffee is in the bar and I'll bring you boys something back to snack on."

Axl butts in. "I'm good, but how about you bring Dana for my something sweet?"

Vegas rolls her eyes at him. "Axl, I dare you to go wake her up this early, see if she doesn't kick your ass."

Axl throws his hands up waving her off. "That's cool, my woman needs her beauty sleep."

Vegas chuckles back at him. "I don't think she knows she's your woman, though?"

"Oh, no doubt she will, Vegas. Soon, she will." Axl raises his eyebrows up and down.

The brothers and I walk into the shop and I start giving them orders on what to do while I'm out. Alessia is waiting for me outside, keys in hand, leaning with her hip against her car. Her face is beautiful, catching the morning rays. Every moment with her, I start feeling pieces of me soften, especially when I see her smile.

After I'm done organizing their tasks, I meet her outside. Leaning over, I snatch the keys from her.

"Hey, it's my car, I'll drive!"

"Nah, babe, I'm a man and you will not drive me around. Earlier this morning was a freebie. Get in and relax."

She stands still for a minute in a face-off with me, and I step into her space, making her look up at me. Relenting a little, I say, "Can I drive when we are together, Alessia? My mom would kick my ass if I didn't, and I want to."

Leaning forward slowly, I give her soft lips a quick peck.

All I know is that Axl had it right when he said about Dana, '*That's my woman and she just doesn't know it yet.*' I'm feeling the same way about Alessia.

As soon as I get her on my bike, she *will* be my woman.

We spend the next two hours picking out paint and buying supplies, along with a fuck ton of donuts and breakfast burritos that she ordered ahead of time. Which she then argued with me who would pay and ended up buying it all.

We unload the supplies and set up the food in the bar for the guys. She walks over and grabs the brothers to get them to come over to eat. Alessia's acting like a mother hen, doting on these assholes. I know I should be grateful, but, honestly, it's starting to piss me off and I wonder if I'm wasting my time with her.

"I see your mind has a lot going on in there. What's up, man?" Spider asks me.

"Nothing," I huff out.

"Seriously, don't pout like a pussy. Get that shit off your mind and do it quick. I'm not all that into your feelings and shit," the asshole says to me.

"Fine, fuck, I was just wondering if Vegas will ever really give me a chance or if I'm wasting my damn time trying at all." I feel like a pouty bitch because she doesn't dote over me that way.

"You know, Prez, she probably feels obligated to pay us back for cleaning the bar up after you left to take her home, and is showing us her gratitude. She's running around telling us all thank you. I personally like her bitchier side. Do you really want those bitches at the club? They spread their legs for any hard dick, will give you whatever you want without feelings. That right there," he nudges his chin in Vegas' direction, who's laughing with Tank, "is a woman who knows her value. You need to show her that she also has value at your side. You actually have to earn her trust. She sees you differently than the others, so it's harder for her to trust you. She can walk away from any of these assholes unscathed, but you she sees as a threat. She can't hand herself over to you and leave unaffected."

I'm fucking thrown by his words, who knew he could be this deep. "I need you to get me a file on Derrick, he was her ex."

"I already have it, but I think you need to build trust with her, let *her* tell you. She's not a job, man. If you want her for real, do the damn work. I'll let you know if there are any threats, but, from here forward, drop the business shit and be her man."

Spider's warning settles my mind on what I need to do. Be her fucking man.

CHAPTER 10

Vegas

"Babe, what are you doing out here?" Blade asks me, grabbing my waist and giving it a light squeeze. We spent most of the morning cleaning, and the shop looks good. I bet the boys will have it painted by tomorrow.

Glancing up from my phone, I say, "Looking for Halloween costumes. Every year we have a theme, and it's my year to pick them out, so I'm looking for something good."

Blade moves to grab my phone to look, but I pull it back. "Nah-ah, you want to find out, come to the bar on Halloween night. We come up with trick or treat games and it's a blast. But if you don't come in a costume, no entry," I shake my head in seriousness. Not everyone comes dressed up, but I'm not telling him that.

Blade moves in closer and wraps his arms around me, turning me to face him. Inhaling deeply, his scent is very intoxicating. I don't know what it is, but it's dangerous and sexy mixed with sweat.

Can't I have a little fun and not get burnt? Because, honestly, this feels too good to just throw completely away.

He rubs my back up and down. "How about I dress up like your man, is that scary enough?" His eyes are laughing at me.

"No one would know what that looks like, Blade," I mock him.

Blade crosses his arms over his chest. "How about we make a bet. I'll even let you pick what we bet on? If I win, you tell everyone I'm your man, and, if you win, I will wear whatever you pick for your party?"

I'm caught in a bind here, because, while this is tempting and fun, at the same time this isn't all fun and games. I release the breath I'm holding and tell him, "Okay, Blade, I'm always game to bet, but, before we start, let me lay this out for you. The guys in your world aren't faithful, they screw around with sluts. I'm not that way. I don't play with people or with emotions. You want a shot with me, you toe the line and be my man. You fuck with my trust, don't come back looking for second chances. We walk away, and we'll stay friends." Maybe.

Blade leans over and starts kissing my jaw to my ear. "You're going to lose, Vegas, and I'm going to make you deliver on our bet. Don't worry, I'll show you that you can trust me. I want a woman, not a slut or some bitches to warm my bed. I want *you*. And, when I finally have you, all of you, I'll never let you go."

My body shivers with his stubble scratching my skin, his lips on my jaw, and his strong hands rubbing my back.

"We'll see, hotshot, we'll see. How about a target contest?" I push back a little and ask him.

"Really? Do you even own a gun, princess?" Disbelief is lacing his tone at me.

"No faith in me, huh? Princess is worse than Vegas, don't call me that." I push him back farther from me, wanting to punch him more than kiss him right now.

That gives me about a week to practice before the bet. "Halloween night, it's on, and I'll bring your costume for when you lose. This also means that you'll be coming to the bar on Halloween," I can't help the mischievous grin.

"This, I can't wait to see."

I'm practically jumping in excitement to see these bikers come in all dressed up.

"Do *not* think I will accept you as bikers either, that will not be allowed." I point at his chest, then wrap my hand up around his neck and pull him closer to me. "I will pick it, and you will wear it."

Taking a step back, I shove my hand forward. "Let's shake on it?"

Blade grabs my hand and spins me till my back hits the wall, pressing his strong body against mine. "No, we'll kiss on it."

He smashes his lips to mine aggressively, making me open my mouth to his. Sliding his tongue around mine, he drags my bottom lip between his teeth, licking and kissing my lips and jaw, and then does it all over again. His leg slides between mine, rubbing my pussy against his strong muscles. My fingers wrap around the longer hair at the top of his head, then down to the back of his shaved head and neck.

His strong hold on my sweatshirt lightens. Needing more, his hands grab my ass, then lower around my thighs, lifting me up until I lock my legs around his back, rubbing myself up and down his hard dick. He groans, the feeling radiating through my chest, it's so deep.

Blade's hands sneak up under my clothes, his rough, cold fingertips touching my skin, and I shiver again. They trace up to my bra and squeeze my breast. Catcalls and whistles break the moment and I let go of his lip from between my teeth to look over his shoulder.

My eyes bug out at all of his men, along with Jenn and Dana, who are egging our scene on. I slowly slide my legs down his body and stand. Blade kisses my neck once more.

Standing straight up, he yells, "Get the fuck out of here." Most of them move, other than my girls, Axl and Tank.

Clearing my throat, I will my blood pressure to slow down. "I got to run home, check on Tugg and get ready for work."

Blade turns back to me. "Me too, babe, I got to run back and check on shit. I'll see you later, text me when you're home tonight. And, Alessia, you better get a hold of me this time. I don't like waiting around. Next time, I will spank your ass."

He leans forward to give me a quick kiss and swats me on the ass on his way over to his bike where his MC brothers are waiting for him already on their bikes.

Walking my way over to the girls, Dana and Jenn are so happy about catching me that it makes me a bit cranky.

"Vegas, that was the hottest make-out I have seen in the longest time. I think my panties need a change after watching you two." Dana starts fanning herself, sighs and continues, "It makes me miss having that kind of romance."

"Well, you'll get what you asked for. Axl has plans for you," I tell her sarcastically, feeling a bit better to rub it in.

"What", she shrieks.

"Settle in, princess, your prince will be storming your castle walls soon," Jenn wiggles her eyebrows.

"Nope, I'm not letting Axl anywhere near this castle, he's a little shit. Not. Happening," she stomps her foot.

Jenn and I look over and, sure enough, there's Axl with his eyes on his prize.

"You know you're just making this more fun for him, right? He loves this reaction from you, he's soaking it in," I tell her with a pointed look as if this was obvious.

Dana turns toward Axl and he's still smiling her way. "Fuck."

Her cheeks turn red and she bolts toward the front door, so I yell after her, "Be here in an hour!" She waves her hand in response and continues, not looking back at us.

Jenn asks, "You think she's hot for him, or really isn't into him?"

Gloating back at Jenn, I answer her. "I think so, she just said 'fuck.' She never cusses, he's getting to her. This little fire is a slow burn, and when she gives in, it will be like a wildfire was lit."

Jenn nods her head in agreement, walking in the same direction as Dana. "Heading in to setup, catch ya on the flip side, bitch."

We throw our hands up in the peace out sign, and both of us move on to the rest of the day.

Shutting the door and turning the car on, I hear the sounds of bikes filling the air. I glance up just as Blade throws one long leg over his bike and he catches me staring. He winks at me and starts his own bike.

Pulling out onto the highway, I'm shocked to see about twenty bikers behind me. Wouldn't they need to head in the other direction?

They follow me all the way to my driveway. I get out and watch them take off down the street to the next turn. "What the hell was that?", I whisper to no one at all.

My phone pings again with a message and I pull it out of my purse to see a text from Blade.

Blade: We are going to follow you home to make sure you're safe, have a good night.

My heart melted a little bit more from his sweetness.

I text back, **Who's going to protect me from you?**

CHAPTER 11

Blade

I had to tear myself away from that hot as fuck kiss. I was two seconds away from taking her into her office and fucking her. Good thing these assholes broke us up. It would have been hot as fuck, but I don't think Alessia is ready for that yet.

I pull my phone out and type a message to let her know I'm going to follow her home. Spider walks up to me and slaps my back. "Glad you're taking my advice seriously, she's not a girl to let go of so easily. By that display on the wall, she'll be the star of all our fantasies for a while now, that was so fucking hot."

Nodding my head in response, I'm not quite sure what to say. I'm not sharing shit about what just happened. We need to check in with the Las Vegas Chapter anyway.

"Let's head out, meet me at the clubhouse for Church."

Once I'm at the clubhouse, I go to take a hot shower. I relax under the feel of the hot water that's flowing down my back. My cock is still hard from my ride home. That bitch can make me fall to my knees and when I'm on my knees...

I start thinking of running my nose from her knee to her pink, soft pussy. Inhaling deep, I start imagining smelling her hot desire for me. Grabbing my dick, I pull back and forth, rubbing the head. Getting lost in my fantasy...

My tongue runs up and down her center, gathering her taste. Trailing my fingers up her sides, scraping my nails down her silky soft waist, I take soft, long strokes across her clit...

I'm breathing hard, in and out, and my hand is tighter, more aggressive with my cock.

She is close, I can fill her pussy starting to tighten around my fingers. I pick up the pace over her clit. Her juice is all over my hand when the orgasm flows over her. My tongue devours her soft, delicious lips, licking all her orgasm clean from her body.

My hand is in a tight fist now, pumping hard at my dick. My head is leaning against the wall. I come so hard in my own hand that I'm lost in my head thinking of that feisty woman and my fantasy about her. Long streams of cum spurt out, and I can't wait till I can sink my rock-hard cock in her pussy and make her crave my touch as much as she has tempted me with hers.

I rinse off and get out of the shower, then start drying off with a towel. I throw on a clean pair of jeans and black t-shirt with my cut over it. When I get to Church, the guys are waiting for me as I take a seat at the head of the table, with my VP to my right. "What do you have for me?"

Cowboy pipes up, "The tail we had on the truck from California, the one you ran into at the truck stop? Came out empty handed at his stop near Sacramento. Whatever he had, it was dropped off already. He sprayed his truck down and parked it inside a warehouse. That truck hasn't moved since, but another one pulled out last night and they have prospects following it."

"Spider, did you get the address and the name on the property?" Turning to Spider, I'm expecting more answers.

"Yeah, Prez, and it's under a dead old lady's. I'm looking through her background, see if, by a long shot, she has a greedy little shit in the family that used her name. Still putting it together, a timeline for the trucks and Buck. I should have something by the time the California Prez, Fuego, gets here tonight, and the other charters' Presidents will roll in shortly after in the next couple of days. They all wanted to meet here since it's central to all of our locations, and have a sit down."

I rub my head, hoping to God we pick up some more answers than questions soon. "Talking with Stryker earlier, he confirmed he'll haul up our equipment from Las Vegas to get the shop up and running. We need to finish painting and putting the new flooring down. With all of us working on it, except for Spider, I want it ready in two days. Tank, did you pull applications from the ad we posted online for the receptionist position?"

"I set up some interviews for tomorrow afternoon at the shop. We have about twenty that applied. I only scheduled about ten. We need someone who's worked in a shop before, the ones who didn't, I tossed," Tank confirms.

"Spider, start pulling some names of the dead old lady's family and hand those out, along with whatever information you have on everything else. Let's see if we can help you dig these assholes out of hiding. Go ahead and get started." I slam the gavel down. Church is over.

All the brothers file out, getting back to work. It will be a long night seeing if we can connect any of this, but the last thing I want is to come up empty handed by the time my old man, Stryker, gets here.

Checking my phone, I see there's a new text.

Alessia: Who's going to protect me from you?

Me: Not another man on this earth can.

I'm about to pocket my phone when my mom's name flashes across the screen. "Hey, Ma, how are you doing?" Instantly, I miss dinner at Mom's and seeing her around the clubhouse with my dad.

"Fine, love, you getting your place put together for your shop?" She continues excitedly, "Did you pick out paint yet?"

"Yeah, Ma, I picked it out earlier today." I can practically see her scrunch her nose up at me through the phone. "Don't worry, it will look good, Vegas picked it out."

"Must be a new prospect or member because I don't remember who that is. Anyway, I was calling to tell you something. The Ol' Ladies have been talking, and while they're happy, I don't think *you* will be..."

My father's voice booms into the background, "Woman, get off the damn phone and leave Blade the hell alone. He ain't your little boy anymore, he's a man. Let him deal with his own shit if there is a problem."

"I can tell my son whatever the hell I want, Bill!" There's a wrestling noise, then the phone goes dead. With my mom, that could mean a whole lot of things, but I'm sure she's coming up with him, so I'll find out then.

Hours later, we have a few ideas mapped out of what facts go together, when we all decide to drop this all and pick it up for another day. More members have piled in and there's a small party happening around the pool table. Getting closer, I realize it's some brothers from California. I shake hands with a few. One guy, who I vaguely remember from a few years back in passing, is all over one of our sluts.

I step over to talk to the Cali VP, Ghost. "Where's Fuego and the rest of your crew?" I am wondering why he didn't ride in with Ghost.

"He stopped in to check on his daughter and he'll bring the girls with him here in a few."

A beautiful, older blonde woman wraps her hand around his waist and shyly says, "Hi, I'm Katie."

Her Ol' Man, Ghost, tells her, "Katie, this is the Prez of the Reno Chapter, Blade, he's Stryker's son."

"Wow, you are pretty young to take over, good luck." She smiles at me. I nod to her in response when I hear the sound of more bikes picking up in the distance. Must be Fuego.

Making my way outside to catch them pulling up, I catch a glimpse of Fuego and his wife riding on the back of his bike, then his son, Snake. He looks just like his dad, Hispanic through and through, even though his mom is a gorgeous white lady who looks to be in her mid-fifties. Snake brought his woman as well, which, when she jumps off the bike, I'm having a very hard time keeping my eyes off her very fine ass.

She grabs her helmet and pulls it off her head, shaking out some silky, long, brunette hair. Who in the fuck is this? When she turns, my heart slams in my chest.

NO.

Fuego walks over to me, but my brain has stopped working, turning on to auto pilot. "This is Snake, my son, and this is..."

Cutting him off, I'm so pissed and yell in Vegas' face when I stop right in front of her. "What the motherfucking reason would you possibly give me that you are on another man's bike, Vegas!" I'm right on top of her and the little bitch doesn't look a bit scared right now. The anger is pumping so thick in my veins, I clench and unclench my fists trying to get control of this crazy feeling.

She just stares in my direction with both of her eyebrows hitting her hairline. Then she just says, "Hey, babe, I just rolled in with my *family*! Have you met my Papa, Fuego, and my *brother*, Snake? No? I didn't think so because you're acting like a *dumbass*!" She pats my chest and kisses my cheek, whispering, "Turn around, babe."

Looking over my shoulder, I see two very pissed off Mexican assholes behind me.

"Did you just yell at my daughter like that in front of my crew, Blade? If her old man tells her to jump on a bike with her brother, she'll goddamn do it." Fuego is really fucking pissed off at my outburst, understandably so.

"If Vegas had told me that her father was the Prez of the Cali chapter, I would have known this shit," I grind out.

"Why the fuck would my daughter tell you that for? So she can put a target on her back? Of course she didn't. *Santa Maria*, how long have you known her?" Fuego barks at me.

"Fuck, I don't know, about a week." Right about then, I realize that I just made myself look like the dumbass Vegas just called me.

"Take your shit and fix it in private, will you? Alessia, you and I will chat later, *que mierda, pinche niños*." Fuego hooks his arm around Vegas' amused mother, and they walk away.

Taking Vegas' hand, I storm through the club, heading to my room where I slam the door shut hard behind me. She just waltzes ahead of me, placing her hand on her hip, cocking it out. We stare at each other for a minute until I break, because we all know she's going to stand there all night unless I break. Fucking bitches.

Walking over to her, I grab her hips and spin her around till her hands hit the bed. I yank her jeans down her legs and almost stop. Almost, because my eyes are glued to her very nice ass and the blood red lace thong framing it. I run one finger over her right hipbone and back down around the bottom of her ass. My hand smooths over her cheek, then I raise it back and smack that fat, juicy ass.

She jerks her head up and moves to stand up. But I grab the hair at the back of her neck and hold her down. Her submission calms my nerves. Having her under my hands settles my rage, but it's not even close to being enough. My hand smacks her ass at least five more times. Her skin feels hot when I rub where I spanked her.

Our breathing is labored and heavy as I tell her, "We will talk this out, Alessia, but I'm too fucking angry right now. I never lose my shit, and I just lost it big time in front of a lot of men, so you're going to give me this right now and keep your fucking mouth shut."

I spank her again with a loud pop, and this time she moans. Pulling up the dark red string from between her ass cheeks, I run my finger under it, aiming for her center. This time, I groan when I feel her soft pussy lips hot and drenched for me.

"I love this shade of red on your skin. You like it when I pull your hair and spank you like the bad bitch you are, don't you, Vegas?" I tug her hair back some more to get a response.

"Fuck me, Blade, make me come." She pushes her hot pussy against my hand harder.

"Mmm. You'll come, Vegas, because you're being a good girl right now." Pumping my fingers in and out of her juicy cunt, I take her wetness to her little bud and stroke her softly. Alessia leans forward more and juts her ass out to get more from me.

"Fuck my fingers, Vegas. Make yourself come on my hand," I instruct her, and she does it unashamedly, just fucks my fingers. Letting go of her hair to give her more slaps on her ass, she shows me that she loves it by moving faster on my hand.

"Give me your dick, Blade," she moans out to me, pleading with me to fuck her till she comes. Oh, do I want to, but not today.

"You want my dick, Vegas? Then suck it," I tell her.

She stands up and toes off her pants and boots. She steps in front of me and places kisses on my neck as her hands undo my belt and zipper. She pushes my pants and boxers down my legs and uses her nails to scratch up my thighs. Holy mother of God, this little feisty cat.

She sinks to her knees and licks up the center of my dick, then licks around the head. "Stop playing with me, Vegas," I warn her, but my bad girl keeps at it, testing me. Grabbing her by the arms, I haul her up and bend her over the bed again, spanking her ass five times in quick succession. "You gonna play nice, Vegas, or are we gonna tease each other?"

My voice rises another octave and I growl at her, "You'll come when you submit to me. When we are together like this, you are my Alessia." Pulling her hair back more toward me, I bring her close and whisper menacingly into her ear, "Vegas doesn't show up, *ever,* when we are fucking." I force her back down onto the mattress and her body relaxes.

"Yes, Blade, your Alessia. Play nice with me," she says softly.

Lying down on my bed, I instruct her, "Ride my face, baby doll, and suck my dick."

She kneels on my bed, placing her leg over my head and slowly lowers her hips down. She grabs my dick in her hand and her hot, wet mouth devours it. Like my fantasy earlier, I run my nose from her thigh to her sweet pussy and smell my sweet Alessia, licking her just like how I've been wanting to.

Nice and slow at first, I speed up when she's close. I start pistoning my hips into her mouth. She's moaning around my dick, the sound vibrating down to my balls. I feel her pussy starting to quiver and, in two more thrusts, I blow my load down her throat. I finish licking my girl's cum from her pussy and turn her around to hold her. As I kiss her forehead, she wraps her hand around my chest and kisses my neck, humming in satisfaction.

Rubbing her ass, I start to worry. "Was I too rough with you, baby?" She sighs, causing me to hold my breath.

"No, Blade, that was just right." Thank fuck, I finally breathe out. I know our time's up for now and we have a whole club full of people here tonight.

"We gotta get dressed, baby doll. I need to go talk to your father." She laughs at me and gets up to walk into the bathroom. By the time she's back, I'm dressed, and my eyes can't stay away from watching her pull her panties and pants up.

After she's dressed, I tug her to me and tell her, "You should have called me to tell me where you were going and who you were with."

"Blade, I would've, but I didn't know Papa was going to drag me along at the last minute. By the time I figured out where they were headed and who with, I just went along with it. Really, what was I going to do? I didn't have time to call you and explain it all over the phone," she huffs out at me.

"We'll talk it out in the morning."

I grab her mouth in a passionate kiss and open the door to God only knows what else is going to happen tonight.

CHAPTER 12

Blade

Vegas and I are back in the main area with the rest of the group. My head is spinning with all these changes and my mind feels blown. I'm going to kick Spider's ass for not warning me.

Speaking of the devil, there he sits on the bar stool next to her father, the California chapter Prez, Fuego, tipping his beer back with a smirk, and next to him is Snake, her brother. Leading Alessia in front of me, we make our way around everyone. We reach Fuego, and he grunts looking us over.

"You two work that bullshit out and everyone is cooled off now?" Snake questions while staring at us.

"Yeah, man, I shouldn't have gone off like that. Alessia and I are still working all of our shit out, still getting to know each other. I obviously had no clue she's connected to the club or I would have gone about things differently. I meant no disrespect." Snake puts his fist up and we knuckle it out.

Fuego nods in agreement. "You better stay on top of Alessia or she'll run you around. If you aren't man enough to handle her ass, walk away now. She needs a firm hand. I raised her to be tough like the boys, so you'll have your work cut out for you. *Sí, mi querida hija*?"

Fuego puts his hand out to Alessia. She walks into his arms and he places a soft kiss on top of her head. "*Si*, Papa."

"Blade, you remember *mi hermosa esposa*, Cindy." Cindy steps out from her Ol' Man's side and I'm taken aback by how similar Alessia looks to her mother, except that Alessia's hair and skin are a couple shades darker. The deep blue eyes Alessia has are just the same as Cindy's.

"Hello, Blade, did you just move up here? I guess I'm a little surprised you and Alessia didn't know more about how much you two had in common?" Cindy's eyes move back and forth between us in question.

"No, ma'am, I've been back and forth between here and Las Vegas these last few years. I've just now settled in up here, and actually met Alessia when I went to buy the space next to her, that's how we met," I explain to her. Alessia moves back to my side and I place my arm around her shoulders.

"Cindy and I are going to head out to Alessia's house and crash, you kids have fun. Blade, I'll see you tomorrow, we'll sit down and go over business." Fuego looks me straight in the eye and heads out with Cindy by his side.

"Holy shit, is that Dana?" Snake asks and we all turn to the direction he's staring. And sure enough, there's Dana standing and laughing with Ghost and his O'l Lady, Katie.

"Yeah, bro, but I think you're too late. She may have crushed on you years ago, but all you had time for was those dirty club sluts," Alessia scowls her brother's way.

"Fuck me, she really has grown up these pasts few years up here." He takes off in Dana's direction, giving her a big hug and picking her up off the floor, which has Axl scowling at them.

"Don't worry, Dana got over her little crush years ago when she caught him getting head in the backyard from a club hanger-on. She moved on pretty quick." Vegas says this like it's no big deal. I'm still trying to wrap my head around everything else I learned about her tonight.

"Babe, I'm trying to catch up here, but who's Dana related to?"

Spider scoots over and answers for her. "Her Dad is Ghost, and that hot MILF is Katie. She also has a brother or two, but I don't see them running around here tonight."

"Spider, are you telling me you've done a background check on us?" Vegas points her finger at him.

"Yes, I did, it's my job. Now, if you'll excuse me, I have more shit to dig through tonight." He slides off the stool and heads back to his room.

I turn to Vegas. "Don't fucking look at me like that, Vegas, you know I don't know shit. I knew he had a file. *Everyone* is vetted. Spider said I should get to know you myself, build our trust together, so that's what I'm doing. Besides, you asked me if I had a background check on you, so you knew. The more I think on this, I'm really pissed at myself I didn't catch on this sooner. You had the upper hand the entire fucking time!"

Vegas rumbles out a hysterical laugh that has the whole room looking at her. Her eyes are watering with tears, and she can barely get her words out. "You were so lost, the look on your face when you figured out who I was! I knew who you were the whole time, but I was having fun waiting to see what you knew."

She stops to take in a deep breath. "But, seriously, Blade, the world I grew up in, the world *we* grew up in, people use us to get what they want. I know you know what that feels like. I have to be careful, like you are. I didn't mean to trick you, but I had to be sure you were in my bar for the right reasons. I was protecting myself, along with Dana and Jenn. You did show me trust by not reading my file, so I will give you the same. No more secrets." Vegas grabs my cut, pulling me forward and taking a kiss from my lips.

"I'm heading out, big guy. I'll be busy with my parents here." The feel of Vegas' hands on me is my version of heaven. Hearing her wanting to leave, though, irritates me, let alone, how the fuck is she getting home?

"Who the fuck is taking you home, Vegas?" Questioning her like a dick, my nerves are shot.

"Blade, you can ask me if you want to take me, or I can get Dana. She brought her car," she says while pushing her attitude my way. "You need to chill the fuck out."

She turns on her heel, and I watch her heading over to talk to Dana and Snake. Snake tosses some keys at her. She turns and nods my way, then takes off through the front door.

Tank and Axl are laughing while Snake and Dana are grinning like the assholes they are. I hear the rumble of a bike and sprint out front to see what the fuck is going on, followed by half of our crew. I make it in time to see Vegas whip the tail end of Snake's bike around with one foot planted on the ground, spraying dirt and rocks behind. Tucking her leg back in, she steps on the gas and speeds down the road.

My dick is hard, and I'm so fucking turned on, but so pissed off that she just peeled out of here like that.

Tank booms, "Holy fuck, that was hot, I think I'm in love!" Without warning, I turn and upper cut him right in his fucking big ass mouth.

"That bitch is mine, you all better watch what the fuck you say about her! Last warning to all you fuckers. Pick Tank up and throw him in his room."

The prospects grab the big fucker, dragging him to his room. Feeling exhausted and frustrated, I head to my room as well. This day sucked ass and I'm over it.

A few drinks later, I finally pass out, hoping tomorrow will be a better day.

Vegas

Just fuck him, is all I can think, *just watch, asshole! I don't need a keeper, I need a man, not a babysitter.* Walking over to Snake, I say, "Yo, bro, give me your keys. Dana can take you to my place, or wherever, I don't care."

Snake glares at me. "Do. Not. Fuck. With. My. Ride. I'm only doing this because I want to see his face." He tosses me his keys and I feel the adrenaline hit me like a junkie. I'm on a mission to score. On my way out, I raise my chin to Blade, thinking, *Eat shit, motherfucker, I already have a father.*

Picking up my pace once I hit the door, I throw the helmet on right as I get there. I toss my leg over one side, kicking up the kickstand. Turning the key, I hold the clutch, switch one gear up with my left foot and flip that switch. I feel the engine come alive, the beast roaring between my legs.

Cranking on the gas, I plant my right foot down and swing the bike around. Pure freaking high, it's been too long and I needed this, the open road and the freedom. I miss riding with my family. I haven't gone back, and I know a part of me was hiding and protecting myself. Not anymore, I'm letting it all out, I'm not holding back anymore.

There's a shadow above my head, but it's still early morning, eight maybe? "Momma, what's going on?" I mumble into my pillow.

"We are all getting up, going to go workout, get something to eat, and hang out, maybe go shopping?" She rambles out her list and continues, "Dana, Katie and Jenn will be here in a minute, so move it. I got you a coffee and a power bar." She heads out, shutting my door and yelling from the hallway, "Twenty minutes!"

I shower, then throw on my favorite workout clothes and head on out into the kitchen where Papa is sitting with Blade. That's halting my steps for a second, because Blade in my kitchen is catching me off guard. Picking up my pace, I decide that no man will affect me. Well, at least I tell myself that anyway because he's soooo freaky hot when he's mad and his hard eyes are on me just like the first night we met.

I'm so glad Mom wanted to work out because this sports bra and tank I'm wearing make my tits look phenomenal. "Morning, everyone! Where is Snake? Did he make it here last night?"

"Yeah, he's on the couch, still passed out. How did he even get here since you rode in on his bike?" Papa questions me with a smile in his eyes.

"I needed a ride," I shrug, smiling back at him. I have really missed him and my mom.

"You going to take a ride with your old man before I head back, *hija*?" I can see the hopeful question on his face.

"*Sí*, Papa, let me know your schedule." He hugs me and heads out of the kitchen, leaving me alone with Blade. Winking at him, I turn to grab my coffee and I feel him coming up behind me. His hands run up my ass that's covered by tight yoga pants. They go up around my tits as he grinds his hard dick against it.

"Where are you going in this outfit, Vegas?" He peppers kisses down my neck and back up while I say, "Gym."

"Mmmm. My bad girl is gonna text me when she's free, isn't she?" He questions while his hand is rubbing my pussy through my leggings.

"Yes, Blade..." I breathe out my words on a whisper.

"Good, don't leave me again like that, Alessia, show me you want me, or I'll spank your ass in front of everyone, and you won't come *or* like it." Blade spins me around and grabs my head taking my mouth hard, then, just as abruptly, he walks out.

"I like him." My mom points to where Blade just walked out. "He reminds me of your papa,"

"Sick, momma! Never ever, and I mean *never*, say that again!" She laughs and walks out saying, "You'll see, baby girl." She continues laughing down the hallway as she's heading to the spare room.

All of us girls make it on time into our class and start stretching before the instructor walks in. We all stare because this is the Killer Booty Burn Class, but this cute and muscled dude is most definitely *not* Veronica who usually teaches the class.

"Oh, yeah," we all mouth together and giggle as we're waiting for the class to start.

Soon enough, we are squatting, sweating, breathing hard, butts and thighs are cramping, and, Matt here, our instructor for the day, is saying, "Hold that squat there, ladies, and pulse, pulse, pulse, pulse, up and down, ladies, feel the burn."

Jenn giggles and says, "I don't know if I'm supposed to be feeling this kind of burn right now?"

"What's that from the back?" Matt yells over the room.

"Uh, nothing! Just that we all feel the burn?" Jenn's face actually goes red for once for being called out in class. Biting my lip, I try really hard not to laugh. Dana, Mom and Katie giggle at her.

After the intense workout, we take a shower and are drying off in the locker room. Dana, looking around for Jenn, says, "Where the hell did Jenn go?" Right then, Jenn finally appears, walking back in.

"What were you doing?" Katie asks.

"I was interested in hooking up with Matt, but he's totally gay. No score, struck out, swing and a miss." Jenn shrugs and pretends she has a bat in her hand and just missed the ball when taking a swing.

"How do you know?" Mom asks confused, scrunching her nose at Jenn.

"After class, I went to chit chat, he didn't even look at my boobs when I 'dropped' my water bottle, totally gay," Jenn explains, shrugging one shoulder like it's a no brainer.

"That makes him gay?" Katie laughs, shaking her head and not believing Jenn one bit.

"Yes, watch this." Jenn turns toward the door, holds it open, and yells out, "Matt, bring your man tonight to The Black Rose for a drink on us, yeah?"

"Really? I will tell him, thanks!" Matt waves bye, heading to the men's locker room.

"See, I knew it! I should have picked up on it earlier, but I'm burning so hot these days, only a man can cool me off. My gaydar is off." Katie and Mom are speechless and stare unblinking at the door. Probably also because they were only wearing towels when Jenn held it open.

"Jenn, you have options! Oh, I don't know, I think his name is James?" Dana deadpans.

"Ugh, not the James convo! We've been over this, he's taking girls home from the bar, and I do *not* want a hang-around at work if we don't work out." Jenn's eyes are popping out of her head, as if that makes her point better.

"Jenn, you are being a hypocrite, because James waited six months before he took any girl home while trying to snag you. You *still* lead him on with all your soft touches and moments, and then push him away when he gets too close. You need to decide and quit playing with him, he's not playing with you," I defend James because, hello, she's being unfair too.

"You can be a real bitch, Vegas." Jenn's pissed, but watching this back and forth between them is getting old.

"No, *the truth* is a bitch, and a friend will tell you the truth. Quit bitching and let's go grab lunch, I'm starving. You don't have time to shower, Jenn, since you used your time to 'chit chat.'" I pick up my workout bag, then pull out my jeans and t-shirt while standing there in my bra and thong.

Dana laughs, "You can be a real bitch, Vegas." Flipping her off, I show them that I disagree.

"Hurry up, bitch, and shower. We have food to get to, and that's top priority at the moment!"

Jenn smacks my bare ass cheek on the way to the showers, "Yes, ma'am!"

The best part about my family and friends is that we can tell each other the truth. Be pissed off at each other and be over it, all within five minutes. By the time everything is said, it's over and everyone is good.

Finally, Jenn is ready, and we head out to grab lunch. We all laugh and enjoy each other. Remembering I challenged Blade to a shooting contest, I need to practice. Which also reminds me of another reason we need to go shoot, so I drag all the girls with me.

CHAPTER 13

Blade

"What in the fuck is that?" I yell over to Spider and Axl. "Is someone shooting behind that old garage?" We pull our nine millimeters out of our waist bands and head out toward the garage, checking for cars or people on our way. The garage door is unlocked, so we take cover inside and head toward the back, looking through the old office blinds.

Spider whispers out, "Are the girls having a target shooting contest? I say we stay and watch."

"Hell yeah, they are, are they betting? They each put a twenty in a can. This is sexy as fuck, I can't wait to tell Tank what he missed," Axl grins enthusiastically.

After each round, Alessia and Cindy pull their targets and score them, tallying how many cans they hit. I watch Alessia taking aim. She's confident in her mark and moves just a hair above, breathes in and pulls the trigger. A miss. Why is she purposely missing her mark? She and Cindy pull all the score sheets again and they whisper back and forth while the other girls talk and laugh.

Vegas

"Mom, did you count the score sheets?" I look up at my mom and whisper softly so no one hears us.

"Yes, we were all close, but don't worry, Dana will win her boots, she'll think she won."

I'm happy because I know how much she wants those boots. She eyes them every time we walk into that store and will never spend four hundred bucks on a pair for herself.

"Your Papa gave me an extra forty that I snuck in there too when no one was looking, we have it covered." My mom is the best, I told her about the boots, and she was all in to help out.

Mom has the can in hand as I start to announce the scorings. "Katie shot a score of 25, Mom shot a 28, Jenn a 23, me a 29, and Dana shot the winning score of 32. Step forward and claim your prize, bitch!"

Dana jumps up and down and shouts, "Yeah!" Pumping a fist in the air like a champ, she runs forward and grabs the can, starting to count out the cash.

"What are we going to do now?" she asks, looking at all of us while stuffing the money in her pocket.

"We are going to the mall to buy those ugly Frye boots you love so much," I wink at her.

"No, we are not, I can't do that, I should really save this, and..."

"No, the fuck you are not! Get in the car, we are going to buy those boots and whatever other shit we find at the mall," I suggest, using my most serious face at her.

We start picking up and packing our stuff when Dana walks up to me and bumps my hip with hers. I stop and turn toward her under the window, leaning against the garage wall. Dana is looking at me with accusing eyes, "I know I didn't really win, no way, I counted my score in my head."

She is way too smart. I never count my score while I'm shooting. "You totally won, fair and square. I don't know what you're talking about. You probably didn't count it right. Anyway, I needed the practice."

"Why would you need target practice?" Dana looks at me like I lost my mind, but there is a good reason, and I tell one of my best friends all about the bet I'm going to win against Blade when I go against him after a couple more practices.

Today couldn't have been any better. I spent the whole day with my family. Even though Katie is not technically my aunt, she is, and Jenn and Danna are my sisters and always will be. After the mall, I ran home to change for work. I've missed Tugger so much these past few days that I'm really happy to take him to work with me. Tugg is sitting in the passenger seat next to me. Before I forget, I need to text Blade.

Me: Had a long day with all the girls. I'm heading to work, stop by if you have time.

The little dots pop up so I know he's typing me back and I wait, sitting outside of The Black Rose.

Blade: I'll try to make it

That's short, but I figure he must be working on something important, especially if Papa is here on business and not just a visit. I do what I always do, head into work and forget about it.

Blade

My head is pounding, the stress is getting heavier. We spent part of the day finishing the flooring for the shop. Equipment will be brought up by my old man, so that at least will be ready to be installed. We should have the place up and running in a week.

Earlier this afternoon, we interviewed for the receptionist position and hired a girl wanting to possibly apprentice to be a tattoo artist later. Thank God Tank picked some decent candidates, I was really worried who he had scheduled for interviews.

Sitting in our conference room, I'm waiting for the rest of the men to get here for a quick meeting. I wanted to pull Fuego and his closest members aside. Trust is still being earned, causing me to feel suspicious of who I can trust in my club.

Turning to the window, the deep red and orange rays of the sunset streak through the glass. The heat coming off it warms up my face. Along with the sun, my mind is ready to call it a day as well.

Grinning to myself, I'm reminded of earlier, catching Alessia and her family having a shooting contest. It brightens my sour mood just a bit. I need to get my work done so I can have more time with her.

Fuego walks in with his VP and a few others from his crew, and they all sit down across from me. Hopefully he can give me some ideas or information. Maybe he can see something we can't. "Fuego, Ghost, Snake," I nod at each of them.

Leaving the window, I turn to the table and settle in to get some work done. Following behind them are my closest men, Axl, Spider and Tank. Fuego scoots up to the oval table on the opposite end.

"How's the takeover going with the crew?" Fuego looks right at me and ignores the others.

"It's been a rough year, man, since we put their old Prez in the dirt, along with a most of thier members. The couple that wanted to stay were patched over. Building trust in these times is rough, especially since we are having conflict. Buck was shot and halfway buried down in Indian Springs. We think he was following a trucker that's been haulin' in our territory. The timelines fit, but we've got shit with his cell records. Stryker called in Cuervo to come help. Last I heard, he was starting in Texas and working his way up to us, hopefully bringing in some information. I have a feeling we have a rat, or a few. They are networking these drops no one can pin down, but they have enough connections to get the jobs done. We are thinking they are saving what they have and building some cash, guns and men for a takeover.

We are looking at another war if we don't stop this. The boys and I went up for a ride through Verdi, caught one of their haulers, but nothing was in it. The drop had already been made. We have a tail on another truck, but he ain't moving shit. The warehouse where the other truck has been parked belongs to a dead old lady, Evelyn Meyers. We have some names of relatives, no connections have been made there yet."

Fuego's cold stone killer gaze is focused on my words. He takes a few minutes thinking on the information given to him. "Blade, I agree, something is moving out from under our noses, but it's there. Have you looked at a map of the surrounding areas where you found these trucks? There will be something in common. Everything moves in a pattern, mistakes are made when we change from the plan, *no*?

So, keep watching, keep writing down everything you see. The snake will appear when we can track his pattern. I would suggest putting your crew at ease. Besides, those you know can be trusted. If you have an enemy in your ranks, he too will have a pattern, so watch for it. I would put out some false or misleading information to see if you can make them slip to your advantage. Tell them your killer has been found for Buck's murder and pin it on a dead man walking anyway. Find a way to bring in a load of Narcs from a new supplier, unknown, and have your new men just follow him, see what they report. That's where I would start."

"Fuego, you are one sly motherfucker. Stryker should be here tomorrow, and the Elko Prez, Ice, will be here too. I'm going to grab some maps and get to work."

Fuego and his guys stand up, but he stays while they head out. "Are you heading over to The Black Rose? I've got some bets placed. The World Series starts tonight, we're going to watch it over there. I'm sure you've met Vegas, *no*?" Fuego is obviously testing me again on my knowledge of his daughter.

"Yes, I have, are your bets with Vegas? If there is a way, she won't play fair." I'm amused her old man plays into her games.

He lights up at my observation. "Oh, yes, we bet many times, I've taught her over the years to look at all circumstances as opportunities. She just doesn't realize this yet, but she uses the same skills to protect and take care herself. One day perhaps, she will see this when she has her own *niños*. Blade, if you don't want *mi hija* for your *esposa*, you should walk away now. Or you could find an enemy in me. She's still young enough to make her dreams come true. She may fight and say she doesn't need a man, but she does. Alessia needs a family of her own. Look at her bar, every person in there, she treats them like family. *Niños* are very important to her. She needs a partner to compliment her, not a man to rule her. She has her own mind and ambitions. Share those with her and she will support your needs as well. *Comprendes*?"

"I don't know what the future holds for us, Fuego, but I am all in when it comes to Alessia. I want to see us through. What that means for us, I have no Idea." And I really don't, I've never thought of kids and having a family. Can I be the man my old man is?

"I can't ask more than that from you, other than be her man and be what she needs." Fuego heads out the door, not saying anything more.

My head and gut are telling me there is more going on with Alessia and there is definitely more to come with our MC problems. I just need the time and patience to see it all through.

Spider walks back in and places a stack of folders and maps on the table. "I need you all to think on what we want to tell the guys at Church, something soon. Tank and Axl, I need you both to find me a truck, unknown and unattached to us. Hire him to move a small load for us. Let's move on this, try and get ahead of our problem."

Axl and Tank nod in agreement, and Axl smiles wickedly. "I still have a few connections in California. I can ask and call in a favor. I'll get the truck moving and hand pick the crew we think could be ratting us out. Me and Tank will work on it, Prez, we got this." Tank and Axl fist bump me on their way out to get started.

Spider pulled out all his work from what information we have so far and is now spreading out each document on the table. "Prez, we need to see this information from a different angle. When we have a little more info, we'll be able to piece it together better. But let's see what theories we can come up with?"

"Roll out the maps, too. What was the route we know of so far?"

Spreading out the four by three-foot map, Spider gives me an update. "I looked, but couldn't find any concrete or clear reasoning. They've been avoiding all big suppliers or drop areas. I've just focused on the main roads from Texas, Nevada and California."

Spider has the three different routes highlighted, pointing out which is which. "The first truck route is short, but we are assuming still that he was headed north. Second line, we believe was still the first truck route that was followed north east, up to Elko. Third line is the truck you found in Verdi and parked in California. We'll map out the fourth when we hear the guys following that truck."

"All we have at this point is that we know they are moving south to north, possibly moving east or west as soon as they hit Highway 80. Up through Nevada, it's all desert. No one wants to truck or move through California. That's making Nevada a hot spot for transport. Every man that moves a truck through Nevada is on the old man's books. Pay your fee and the road is yours. So why not just pay your fee?" I wonder out loud.

"We need to see what's in the trucks. If we can't trust our guys a hundred percent, we need to call in some support. That's a whole lot of fucking highway and desert with no backup or cover," Spider reasons.

"No, we don't need the whole route covered. We need to place men at the intersections of the routes and follow them from there. Stryker can cover the south, Fuego the west, and Ice the east intersection. Fuck, bro, we are central. That war we had was over this location. This clubhouse didn't mean shit, man, it had to do with location." It's like a lightbulb went off in my head.

"Fuck, Blade, if you are right, we need to put these fuckers down. If they gain this territory, they will go after the next clubhouse. This was always the starting point. Take out the biggest target and spread out from there. This fucker is cancer, we all thought it was over their old Prez not wanting to pay road fees, he was being paid off, there's someone bigger."

"That we both agree on. Spider, this is a long-term end game. No doubt we'll catch this fucker. Or fuckers."

We wrap up some more notes, feeling a little better where we are today than where we were yesterday. At least we have a starting point. The last thing I want is to hand over nothing to the other Presidents tomorrow. I will show they all voted me as President of this chapter for a reason, and failure is not an option.

CHAPTER 14

Vegas

"Papa, Momma, Snake, I saved you a table over by the big screen. Momma, you look hot!" I run around the bar and hug my Papa and brother but hold my mom at an arm's length. Even though she's in her fifties, she could pass for my sister. "Jesus, Momma! I need to borrow those stripper heels, and those pants are hot as fuck!"

"*Mija*! Do not talk to your *madre* like one of your friends." Papa barks at me because he's still somewhat old school when it comes to my mom. He smiles only really for her, and kisses her lips, stealing her back from me because she's his and so precious to him. Seeing them together gives me a small hope that I can have that too. Deep down I want that so much, so unique and rare.

Snake, ever the gentlemen in front of our *padre*, pulls out a chair for our mother, and pushes her in.

"Vegas, can you grab Pops and me a draft and a red wine for Mom?" he asks. I secretly love how he always takes care of her as much as our Papa does. Papa would beat his ass if he wasn't polite to the women in the club or our family.

The feeling of having them around and being protected when they are here is an indescribable calmness. "*Sí*, bro, I'll go grab our drinks and be right back. James will help behind the bar tonight, so I can sit with you guys."

More of Papa's crew filter into the bar and look around to find seats. On a tray, I line up all of our drinks and take them to the table to set them down in front of everyone.

Taking a seat next to my brother, I look at the tv and see that the World Series just started. I'm so excited. Earlier, I had James do some intel with a few loan sharks he knows from out there around the casinos. He brought me back the stats for the game tonight. It's a sure bet that I'll kick their asses.

Papa and Snake love baseball as much as I do, if not more. When I was a little girl, he would take all of us to the Dodger games, memories I will always treasure. Snake was so good, he almost made it to the Little League World Series a couple of times, but, as he got older, priorities of the club became his life.

"*Mija*, your man just struck out swinging for the fences. You can just pay me the hundred now, your team is going to clam up after that," Papa smirks at me, thinking he is going to win.

"Hell no, I am not! There are five more innings left, one batting error? That means nothing yet. What about your shortstop? Don't think I didn't notice his routine grounding fielding error that could have given your team a double play? The team who makes the least amount of fielding errors will win this game. Our bats are still going strong." Like I was saying, I did my homework and prepped to win.

We spend the next few hours chatting and laughing. Surprisingly, we are packed, with the game on and several bikers from Cali and Reno charters here rooting the game on. Some bet on players, while others bet on point spreads, the cash is piling on the tabletops by the minute. Shit talk fills the space along with laughs and clanking glasses.

The moment we all have been waiting for has us on the edge of our seats. The Dodgers have the field, bottom of the ninth inning, score is 7 to 9. My team, the Astros, are two runs behind. We have two guys on third and first base. Guess who comes up to bat? You would be right, it's the big hitter who struck out before. Papa tries, but fails, not to gloat, with a smirk he can't wipe off if he tried. One out is all they need, and Dodgers win the World Series.

My face remains impassive. Hiding my anxiety from my opponents. The batter steps up to the plate. He digs his feet into the dirt, kicking some back. *Confidence is everything*, I tell him in my head. But I cannot hold it in, "Make something happen, man!" The pitcher stares the batter down, rocks back, and fires down a fast ball. Strike!

"Fuck! Get in the game, dickhead!" I scream at the tv along with many others. Papa grins at me but says nothing. "Focus, man, focus!" I yell at the tv again.

The pitcher rocks back, letting go a wicked drop ball. The batter drops his shoulder pushing his weight forward and sends that fucking ball over the fence!

Jumping out of my seat, I start screaming at the table, "Yeah, motherfucker! Fuck, yes! We won! The Astros won with a home run! Pay up, Papa! I won! The Astros won!"

I can tell he'd love to send me to my room with my language to him, but he can't, so, yeah, I own it, bad behavior and all, even though he raised me better.

"*Mija*, here's your hundred," he hands me my hard-earned cash. Somewhere along the way, Snake got cocky with Papa and bet against me, so he pulls out a hundred and passes it over to me, too.

"Thanks, bro, your money is the best, I love taking your cash," I say folding it and sticking it into my back pocket. Hugs and fist bumps are passed around the tables, along with more shit talk.

Looking over to the right, my heart hits my stomach, completely taking my win to a low. No. Why would Papa and Snake bring *him* here?

At the opposite side of the room sits a man with dark eyes who I really didn't want to see ever again. I'm pretty sure I had made that clear. Derrick must have been tracking me all night, I can tell by the haunted look in his gaze for me.

Standing, he strides toward me, and I'm rooted to my spot on the floor. The man I once pictured as my future is standing in front of me, looking over my face with a yearning that scares me.

"Alessia, you look happy, and this place is incredible." He says it but doesn't sell it. "Can we talk for a minute? Alone?"

This is not what I wanted. I never wanted him to touch my place. Papa says to me in Spanish, which I know Derrick won't understand, "*Mija*, take care of your past, whatever future you choose or *who* you choose, it needs to be dealt with. You should have talked this out a long time ago, it's time. Lay your demons to rest, baby girl."

Taking Papa's advice, Derrick, my ex, and I walk through the bar, back to my office. All I feel is a thousand eyes on my back.

Shit, Blade will hear of this. I just hope he'll hear me out later.

Blade

Spider and I just wrapped club business for tonight, getting our books balanced and our phone calls done, when a call comes in from Cowboy. "Prez, did you meet all of Fuego's men?"

"No, why would that be a problem? And get to the fucking point, what is going on?"

"Vegas has her family here with her, the bar has been packed watching the game. She's too into the game to notice this fucker, Hawk, sitting in the corner, and he's been watching her all night. Like I thought, he was just going to make his move after the game, and he did. Hawk walked right up to her, man, and she froze like she saw a ghost. Her father didn't look very happy about it, but Vegas and Hawk headed to her office. Alone. What do you want me to do?"

"Not a goddamn thing." Tossing my phone on the table, with my head down, I feel my heart trying to jump out of my chest. I try to calm the fuck down before I head over there and make another fool of myself.

"Hawk is her ex, bro, she hasn't spoken to him in two years. I heard him asking about her around the club recently. I put Cowboy on him. It's Derrick." Spider knew, and I get he's trying to let us do our thing and get to know each other, but fuck.

"A heads up would've been nice, dickhead! Derrick, that fucker, is only here to get her back. Word was going around about me and Vegas. Fuck, man, get your shit on, we are riding over there. She's mine, she belongs at my side."

"Fuck, yeah, Prez, let's go claim your Ol' Lady." Spider follows me out, and, soon, we're on the road to The Black Rose.

Vegas

The door shuts as soon as I sit down at my desk. Derrick and I haven't been alone or even talked since that day when I left California. The air in here is suffocating with the ghosts of the past.

He stands at the door watching me and waiting for me to talk first. I'll wait him out. This is my place, and I have the upper hand here.

"Alessia, where can I start?" He sighs and runs a hand through his hair. "Say I'm sorry? We both know you could care less about an apology. What I want to tell you is that a part of me left the day you did. A piece of me broke when I broke your trust. I want you back. I'll transfer up here to the local chapter, do what I need to do to show you I am ready to be the man you wanted then. I want it all back, Alessia. Every kiss, every time we came together. I miss your touch, your heart, I miss my best friend. Can we try to get us back?" He pleads with me, and, to my surprise, I believe him, he really does want me back.

"Derick, you had it all when we were married for six years. I gave you my trust and my future. It wasn't enough then, and it's supposed to be enough now? Your hopeful words won't get me to give into your pleading of a bright future now. Did you really fight for me when I left? You sure as fuck didn't. That says it all, Derrick, says a whole lot about Jenn's little sister, Ashley, doesn't it?"

"What does it say, Alessia? Tell me!" Derrick angry voice booms off the walls. He never could handle my mouth or confidence. This man always wanted a good girl who would just stay at home and be submissive to him.

"You fucked her more than once, you were probably giving her the hopes and dreams every woman wants to hear. *My* hopes and dreams, asshole, the ones you had already promised to give *me*. You were setting up your life to leave me behind. Why didn't you have the balls to go through with it? I'll tell you why. Because we both know my Papa and brother would have buried your ass six feet deep for betraying and disrespecting me. Consider it a parting gift the fact that I never told a soul about who you were with that day." The longer I talk about this, the anger pours out thicker with each word.

"Really? Is that what you think? No, I wasn't giving her the love I GAVE you. Ever! I'm not going to lie and say we didn't fuck around, because we did. You and I were so young, Alessia. We'd known each other since high school. Hooked up, and I couldn't control you. You were a force I couldn't let go of. You are so bright and beautiful, I felt like I was a shadow compared to you. When Ashley started hanging around the club, just back home from college, she looked at me like I looked at you. I fucked her to feel better about myself. It made me feel like the man I never could feel around you. I didn't have the confidence you did, okay?"

He expresses the same guilt and anguish he did all those years ago. "That's on me now, I learned that shit the hard way. I thought it was your love in me lacking, not my confidence in me, in us." Dropping his head in his hands, Derrick grabs his hair and looks back up at me with glossy eyes. Pleading for my love and forgiveness.

"Don't you think I needed all of you too, Derrick? I needed your trust, love and respect. I also needed your damn words. We were best friends. At some point, you stopped talking to me about your fears, hopes and dreams. You pulled yourself away from me. I gave you your space, Derrick, thinking you would come back to me. You used that space to fuck new pussy, to make yourself feel better!"

I can't stand the look on his face at my words, but he will hear and feel them. Like the pain I felt at his betrayal. "That broke my heart and us. You walked out on us. Instead of coming to me, your friend, your wife, you went to another woman. I can't forget that, not ever. Say, we did get back together? You end up in another low situation, I will never believe you won't go to another woman for strength. You should've come to me. I was your backup. You forgot that part from your vows to me."

Courage is what I feel right now. I will rip every piece of me apart to get this over with. Time apart has given me courage to face this man again.

"That's just it, Alessia, how do you go to the woman you think is better than you and ask for strength?" Derrick stands, his voice rising with his emotions, stepping in front of me, hitting his chest with a fist. "That made me feel worse! I see the fool I was, what I was lacking back then. I see you now, Alessia! I see the woman that always wanted to be free, but also be special to the man she lies with. I didn't know how to let you go, be as bright as the confidence inside you, and at the same time keep you close. I am sorry! I want you back. I want us back, Alessia, please?"

Derrick's voice drops with his sincerity. He moves from the door. Stepping closer, he removes the few feet that separate us and crouches next to me, practically on his knees for me.

For a few seconds, I look at the person who used to be my best friend. The one that I remember. The man I married. For a short moment in time, I mourn him for the last time.

"Life is crazy. One day you think you can have it all, the next it all can be gone. We weren't good enough for each other, Derrick. Not just you, but me too. I see that now. I should have pulled you to me, consumed you with my love. I didn't do that, did I? You resented me for who I was. I do think now, even if you wouldn't have done what you did, that we would have split eventually. You're right. I needed the freedom to grow, and, instead of you feeling a part of it, you felt left out. I thought you needed time to deal with your thoughts, I let you hang yourself. Then I blamed it all on you."

I sigh at the realization that I am as much to blame, not for his cheating but for us growing apart.

"Derrick, we were friends once who found comfort in each other. We let our feelings of lust and friendship be blinded by what we thought was love. You don't know me now, and I don't really know you. We are just two old friends. The woman you see today isn't the same girl from then. I think you see what we were never going to be. You need to find that woman who really is your future. Someone who compliments and understands you better than I can."

Standing up, I feel done. I faced what I never wanted to, that I was part to blame. Derrick stands next to me, devastated, but also resigned.

I jump when there is a loud knock at the door. At the same time, we both turn our heads in that direction. "Come in."

Blade opens the door, and Spider is standing at the bar, arms crossed over his chest behind him. My breath catches, because I'm scared. What will Blade think? *Please let him hear me out on this*, I keep saying over and over to myself. He stays by the door, and that terrifies me. *Please come stand by me*, I call out to him.

Derrick breaks me away from my thoughts with his words, but not my eyes, which stay on Blade. "I see the man who stands by that door is the man you already chose."

Blade grunts, and I can tell he's about to explode, but tries to keep it reeled in. Derrick storms out, slamming the door fiercely on the past, on us. Finally, I feel free of the pain we were holding onto.

My voice sounds small and shaky, "Blade, that was Derrick."

"I know who that was, and I know why he was here. The only thing I want to hear from you is what do you want, Alessia?" He sounds more like the fearless Prez, and less like my Blade.

"You, Blade, that's all I want, just you." I pray that he can feel the truth.

"Did you work out your past, is it over?" Blade asks a little less defensive.

"Yes, it is all over." I pause, then ask, "Do you want me to tell you about it?"

Blade steps away from the door and comes to stands in front of me. His fingers trail up my arm, tracing the roses, like he did the first night we met. "Nah, babe, I just need to feel you right now." His hand continues up my neck, touching my cheek, then in the back of my head. I can't help but to get lost in his honey whiskey colored eyes.

His lips touch mine reverently, then his forehead rests on mine. "Grab your coat, Alessia, we are going for a ride to your place," he softly whispers.

Grabbing my jacket, I pull it over my arms and zip it up. Together, we head out the back door to his bike. Taking his outstretched hand, I swing my leg over and slide in close behind him.

An unspoken promise is made between us. His bike is sacred and when I got on for the ride, it was forever.

The night air chills me down to my core on our ride home. My arms snake up under his jacket, crossing my forearms across his stomach and making an "X". Scooting in so close that my body feels welded tightly to his. Blade guides us through the starry night. We turn together, our bodies in sync with one another.

I pray to the stars above to please make this one right, make this man be my new beginning.

CHAPTER 15

Blade

Beautiful. Pulling Alessia close to my body, I unzip her leather jacket and let it hit the bedroom floor. My hands start skimming her sides, taking her shirt off over her head and tossing it somewhere behind me. Kissing along the side of her neck, I inhale her scent. Her head drops to the side and then back when I remove her bra, kissing down the middle of her chest.

I place one long kiss right over this woman's heart, the heart that fits mine. My match. Trailing kisses down to her toned stomach, she giggles, and my lips stretch in a smile. My Alessia is ticklish. I pull her pants down, taking one boot off at a time. Undressing her until all that's left is her in her dark blue silk G-string.

On my knees, I turn her around so that her back is facing me. Starting at her knees, my hands flow up to the curve of her ass. Kissing each of her cheeks, my fingers hook and pull her underwear off. I drop kisses up her back, until I am standing behind her, and press my chest to her back.

Reaching my hands around her, I cup her tits and whisper in her ear, "I can't share any part of you, Alessia... I'm selfish when it comes to you, I want to consume all of you. Tie you to my side forever. I never realized someone could mean as much to me as you do." I hug her to me, tightly, so that I can make her feel my words.

Alessia turns in my arms, holding my face in her small hands. "I want you to take all of me, Blade, consume my heart, thoughts and world with you. Make me yours, destroy me for all others. I want to consume every part of your life too." She takes her hands from my face to undo my belt and unzip my pants, pushing my boxers down with them.

Grabbing her face, I kiss her, sealing our words in a promise to each other. That we will consume the other, destroying the chance of there ever being anyone else. Kicking off my pants and shoes, I grab my shirt at the back with one hand, ridding it with the rest of our clothes thrown around. I step forward, and Alessia follows my lead by stepping back to her bed, lying down in the middle. I look at her naked and open to me, burning her in my soul and memory forever.

Alessia smiles brightly up at me through the shadows. Holding her hand up, she calls me to her. Picking up her legs I open her wide for me.

"I'm ready, Blade, I want you inside of me, claim me as yours." She touches my cheek with her fingertips when I near. She relaxes her body and lifts both of her hands over her head, reaching back until she grabs the iron of her headboard, submitting her body to me.

Kneeling before her on the bed, my hand glides down the smooth skin of her leg until I touch her silky pussy with my fingers, pumping two fingers in her. Her breathing picks up and her legs open a little more. Scooting back, I give it one slow lick up the middle, tasting her. My woman.

Lying the rest of my body on top of hers, my dick is anxious to claim her. My hands fist her thick hair at the same time my lips find hers in a dominating kiss. She whimpers for more beneath me, grinding her wet pussy against my cock. One hand stills her hip, and, thrusting my dick forward, I claim the rest of her. Marking her, taking her body as mine.

Our kisses devour each other's breaths and taste. Her hands run through my hair and scratch down my back. My thrusts are measured and steady, getting us both drunk on lust. Alessia wraps both legs around me, content with the pace I set. Both of us wanting this to last.

My fingers pull at one nipple, then the other. Her back arches, begging me for more, and I can't hold back from her desire. Thrusting harder, faster, her breaths pick up quicker. I pull away from her lips and feather kisses down her cheek and neck. Fulfilling my need to hear her pleads of ecstasy.

Pumping in and out of her, the sounds of our bodies colliding echo off the walls. The only two people in this room, in the world, are in this bed. She gasps for air, coming hard around my dick. The sounds she makes and seeing her come have me blow my cum inside her pussy. The thought of me and her coming together is too much to hold back.

She takes my face and licks across my lips, opening me for her. Our tongues dance around each other, hands running over each other's bodies, not ready to let go of this moment. I keep my dick inside of her as far and for as long as possible.

The pull we have to each other is intense. It's beautiful.

Vegas

We haven't stirred from our spot on the bed, too lazy to move after that intense orgasm. Picking up my head, I rest my chin on my hand that's on his chest. "Blade?"

"Hmm?" He hums out in response cracking open one eye, but keeps running one hand through my hair.

"Are you not worried about knocking me up? Or other things? We didn't wrap you up," I point out, feeling a little stressed over it.

"Alessia, I would not put my dick in you if I thought for second it would give you something. You are the only woman I have ever gone without a condom into. Second, if I knocked you up, would it be so bad? I figured if you didn't want a baby, you would have stopped me."

I *would* have stopped him. Thinking on his words for a minute, I wonder, do I want a baby now? It's too much to consider so soon, I know that much.

"Blade, I have had an IUD for a while, no babies will be made tonight, big guy," I pat his chest to let him down easy.

"Doesn't matter to me when it happens, Alessia, it will happen, when you want it to. You'll tell me when you're ready. I trust you, so I didn't ask, I didn't need to." Kissing his chest, I lay my head back down, my arm across his strong abs.

Roaming his fingers across my roses, he asks me again, "Who did these roses for you? The lines are clean, and the shading is perfect. The black with deep red shading is artistic."

"She is a cousin of mine, lives in California, does a lot of tatts for the members. I started them a few years ago and would add a few more when she would come to visit. Wild times. That's when we started our Wednesday girls' night. Except for Dana."

I start to laugh behind my words as I continue, "She would never get one. Sometimes she would think that, yeah, she should or could get a small one. As soon as the needles came out, she would freak. Just like Phoebe in that episode of *Friends*."

I look up at him. "If you don't know *Friends*, then I'm sorry, we cannot be together. You should know this now before we go on any further. Non-negotiable. I draw the line," I cut my hand through the air.

Blade just lays there, listening to my story, amusement written across his features.

"Anyway, I got them for the obvious reason of my last name, DeRosa, but, also, roses are strong and can outlive most plants with little care. Gorgeous flower with the silkiest petals and pretty smell. I love the thorns the most though, like the armor we all have, to warn off others to stay away. When I had them done, they were my armor. To keep me strong, keep me going, remind me that I am beautiful to me. My brother came with me one time and got a few roses done too, matching ones. He said to me, *'You are never alone, Alessia, we are always family till we die'*. I think he did it to support me, remind me he'd always have my back."

"Did your family not know what you went through?" His face is concerned, his hand stops running through my hair, resting his hand on my back.

"We never talked about it. We never said the details. Long story short, Papa and my brother had to know.

Being who Papa was, he set me free in a way he knew I needed to grow and let me work it out myself. My mom wanted me to talk to her about it, but I wouldn't. I wanted to start over, not dwell on what I couldn't change. They all knew but let me go to get better or be stronger. I needed that, the support, not the talks."

Feeling done and not really wanting to go further into that ordeal, I roll onto my back, pulling the covers over us, feeling the breeze fall over me, cooling my skin. Blade rolls over onto his side and pulls me back to him and up against his chest. Kissing my shoulder, we fall into a deep, restful sleep.

Vegas

Something wet pokes my face. Eww, for the love of all things holy, what *was* that? It pokes me again, then snorts bad breath up my nose. "Tugger! Don't poke my face, dude, that's so rude. Take yourself outside!"

Pulling the blankets over my head, I cover my face from his doggy kisses. "Uhmf, get off the bed, Tugg! Jesus, fine I'll take you out. God forbid you use the doggy door, dumbass."

Frustrated because the floors are cold and I'm still naked, I stomp to the bathroom to pee, and, on my way out, I grab Blade's shirt and jacket, along with my boots.

"Alessia, you mad at Tugger, babe?" He's laughing at me, which only pisses me off more. "I'll take him out, you're only half dressed and it's cold out."

"Whatever, I'm dressed, I'll take him out. Start the shower, I'll be there in a second." Slamming the door on my way out, I follow Tugger. For some reason, he always makes me take him out first thing in the morning. Probably because when he was a puppy, that was our routine. Why isn't he past that?

After Tugg does his business, I get a hot, sexy shower, and a happy ending in there. Blade is the man of my dreams. He feeds me breakfast too before he leaving to get to the clubhouse to do whatever the Prez does all day. I can say I am very satisfied this morning.

Right on time, the sound of two, no, actually four, car doors shut. Tugger sits by the door, wagging his cute tail back and forth, waiting for the girls to walk in. He's so damn cute, but annoying first thing in the morning.

In walk Dana, Jenn, Mom and Katie. "Well, hello, ladies, what a surprise! You all came to visit me? How sweet." Pulling my hands up together up under my chin, I fake smile for them.

My mom snickers. "Morning, baby girl," she says, then kisses my cheek. "Get your bag, you're coming with us to breakfast, because we all are hungry, and we all want the story of what happened last night. We waited for you, but one of the guys, Spider, he said you two had taken off for the night. Your Papa had me take your Tahoe to a hotel last night." She raises both brows, "I brought it back this morning with me and Katie."

Grabbing my purse and jacket, I follow my girl crew while listening to my momma talk on and on. Even all the way to the diner, and while they order their food. I know she's excited and happy for me. Seriously though, does she always talk this much?

"Momma, cool it and slow down, no one else has even had a chance to get a word in. I'll tell you all about it," I explain to her softly and squeeze her hand.

"Sorry, sweetie, we just had such a great night, it's been a long time since I've seen you light up like that."

"I know, Momma." Jenn and Dana look a little worried. They know this was a big night for me.

"Vegas, when I was rounding the tables, I noticed Derrick later on, about halfway through the game. I didn't know if he was just there waiting for you or waiting to leave. He never ordered a drink from me. Did he go to the bar at all, Dana?" Jenn asks her as she's lifting her cup and taking a drink of her coffee.

"No, like you said, I noticed him off to the side. I thought the same as you. Next thing I know, I look over and you two are shutting the door to your office. It was a busy night at the bar. We were packed, which was good. What happened? What did he say?" Dana sounds distressed. Great, she probably didn't sleep well. I never thought about texting them either.

"I see that look, don't worry. Axl told me you took care of it, and Blade and you were happy. Now details. Go," she waves her hand for me to start my story.

"I was pretty blindsided and felt a little ambushed. One minute I'm collecting my winnings in my victorious sweep of the World Series. Next thing I know, Derrick is standing right in front of me. One extreme to the other. One minute I'm crazed with a win, the next I'm being pulled down into a low reality. We talked in the office. He wanted to try again."

Waiting all this time, my mom deserves to hear it all. I do feel a little bad when I tell her about the other woman. She gasps and her face gets bright red. To give her credit, she does not say a word, which I'm sure she'll unload on Papa, poor guy. I never mention Ashley though, because that ties her to Jenn. Besides, I'm sure she's still around.

"After all these years, I realize my part in it. Don't get me wrong, he was way wrong for what he did, and that was what broke us apart eventually. But I just realized that, in my own way, I knew I was giving him too much space and didn't protect our relationship like I should have. In my way, I was letting him go. I knew we didn't fit. We didn't love each other that way. We did love and that's why his betrayal did hurt. We were friends turned into lovers stemmed from convenience and circumstance. I forgave him a long time ago, but, seeing him last night, I had to forgive myself. I just didn't know that was my missing piece that I had left in the past. Forgiving the younger version of myself. I was protecting her."

Taking in a full breath and letting it out, I feel whole again. As if my family was a priest and I absolved myself of my sins. The waitress delivers our food and one glance at my mom has her take off as fast as her feet would carry her.

Except, I feel bad because my momma is crying and that makes me feel awful. "Momma, don't cry, it's a good thing." I start rubbing her back and she pulls me in for a hug.

"Baby girl, I waited years to hear that story, and it's so sad and so uplifting. Please finish your story. These damn hormones got me emotional. Please finish the rest. I ordered extra food because I know you'll pick off my plate." That gives me watery eyes. Damn, this woman knows me too well.

Katie laughs at her. "One day you'll get what she is saying. It's hard for a mom to let go. Not be involved in your life and not help you fix it. It's what mothers do, we worry, or we fix it. Plus, menopause is karma's fucked up cousin."

All of us laugh because Katie is sweet and kind and, when she says something that off from her character, it's priceless.

Taking a moment to collect ourselves, I continue the story. "Right about the time I tell Derrick there is nothing between us like there should be, Blade knocks on my door and walks in. I swear Spider stood behind the door like an enforcer to scare the shit out of me. Standing there all badass, with his arms crossed. Derrick got the hint that Blade was there for me. He had nothing else to say at that point and walked out. Blade asked me if it was over. I said yes, it was so over. He asked what I wanted, and I said all I wanted was him. We took off after that short conversation. We went to my house where he stayed the night for the first time. It was really amazing, never have I ever experienced a night like that." The memories from last night with Blade come rushing back and have my face reddening.

"Wow, so you guys are together, no more bullshit from now on?" Jenn is very perky, even for her.

"Yes, no more pissing each other off and flirting around it. We agreed to give it a real shot."

Betting on us and betting on forever.

After breakfast, I head home, and Mom comes with me. We spend the afternoon watching old movies and relaxing together. Knowing that Papa stays busy, I make a mental note to invite her to stay more often. I just miss her being around. Besides, she cleans, so yeah, definitely inviting her to come more often. Later, she comes to work with me, along with Katie, and when we aren't too busy, we have mini dance parties, which is such a blast. How many people get to dance while at work, unless you're a stripper? Not many, I know that.

All of us girls had a great day, just like we used to. Papa picks her up around eight and they head over to my house to crash. She takes pity on Tugger and takes him with her. It's almost closing time now and I decide to see if Blade is at the clubhouse.

Me: Did you get dinner? How does a hamburger sound? At the clubhouse?

Blade: No, I didn't. Get your ass here with food. Yes, at the clubhouse.

Me: On it, and on my way.

"Yo, Dana, let's close this up for the night!" I yell over the floor to her.

"What do you think I was doing picking up these chairs and putting them on the tables for?" she deadpans, the smartass.

"Har-har, I'll start cleaning up the bar after I order some food. You want a hamburger? I'm heading over to the clubhouse. You wanna come with me?"

"Yes, on the burger, I'm starving! And, yeah, I'll head over to the club with you." She gave in easily, which makes me a little suspicious. But then, her dad could be there still.

We work together, and, within ten minutes, we're on the road. I break the speed limit to get there, I am so hungry. We walk in and hear Guns N' Roses' *Paradise City* playing loud on the speakers. Dana and I both turn and say at the same, "Ghost." If that song plays, better watch out because that's his drinking fight song. That means he's drunk and is looking to fight. Through the crowd near the bar, we see Tank, Axl, Spider and Blade all sitting at a table.

Blade spots me, and, when I'm close enough, he pulls me down to sit in his lap. Happy to have my hands on him, my lips find his for a big kiss.

"Hey, we brought you dinner and a few extra hamburgers, I figured you had your boys here still." Blade looks stressed out and tired. Maybe I can get him to leave, and get some sleep that he really needs.

Axl shoves Tank over, giving Dana a seat next to me and Blade, but also placing her in the seat next to him. "Where's *my* kiss, princess?" She just rolls her eyes at him. "Then I want that burger," he points to the bags of food.

"Here, and I am *not* your princess." Dana drops the bag in front of Axl, like a brick on the table.

"Yes, you are my princess, Dana. I'm too wiped out to fight you right now. We'll have to pick this up tomorrow." Dana rolls her eyes again, but it's a little less angry than normal, or she is just as tired.

"You tired?" I ask Blade, tracing my thumbs over the bags under his eyes. He closes his eyes, leaning deeper into my touch. Kissing his forehead, I put my head back against his. Poor guy is exhausted.

I'm betting with all these men here, they are working on something big. I know he won't tell me unless he can or needs to. I will be his resting place, his home to come to when he needs me. The rest doesn't matter to me, only him.

"Thanks, babe." Blade kisses me again. I hand him the burger and fries from the bag, and he starts cramming food into his mouth, then ends up eating all of his and most of my fries.

CHAPTER 16

Blade

I'm tired, hungry and worn out. I would have headed out of here already, but since the Elko Prez, Ice, showed up, we've been hanging around the clubhouse catching up with his crew.

Sitting around for the last few hours, I've been observing the guys, looking for possible leads for a rat. This is putting me on edge and in an even worse mood.

Vegas and Dana brought us food after they closed the bar. Looking over at the VP, you can tell that, even though they aren't anything yet, he's happy with both the food and Dana being here. I lean in and give my woman a kiss that I'm sure I needed more than she did. I need to relax more in my world.

We settle into eating a late, or really early, depending on how you look at it, dinner, enjoying the food with no nonsense conversation. Rubbing the skin under her shirt with my thumb, I start relaxing with her body warming mine. My thoughts, though, stay focused on my tasks. Taking on this club as my own, and now Alessia, it's a solace I crave and need. Failing is not an option. I will take these fuckers who are threatening me and my family on. I will protect them with my life. If not for my future, I will be successful for theirs.

I tense instantly when I see Tanya walking through the door, strutting her stripper red shoes. Displeasure is replacing the calm I just had. She is a fucking hot woman, always would fuck or suck my cock when I needed it. That fucking cunt rode up here with the crew from Las Vegas. She did that knowing that, when I left, I made it clear we were done. Stupid slut thought I would make her used pussy my Ol' Lady. Tired of my old life, I wanted new shit, better shit for me. Her looks don't phase me and I'm tired of seeing her ugly, bitchy personality.

Pulling my gun out and blasting her brains on the wall would satisfy me. Fucking club sluts are not a complication I want or need right now when I'm starting to get the shit I want. Tanya is pushing the demon to rise within me. The wicked thought of her dead and decaying corpse is a fantasy I could get hard to. I'm not going to make a scene though, hoping she'll mind her own goddamn business. I'll make sure they take her back to Las Vegas when they leave. That way I don't have to explain to Alessia why that cunt is here, and why I don't want her here. Tilting my chin toward the floor, I keep my eyes away from hers. Here's to hoping the dumb cunt takes a clue.

Alessia's spine straightens and her muscles tense. And I know that bitch is standing right there. Shit makes me smile, and, glancing up, I see the challenge in Tanya's face. She thinks my smile is for her. Tanya is so fucking wrong about that. *Challenge my woman, bitch.* I know Vegas will and can handle her own. If there was ever a time I regretted fucking Tanya, that time would be right now.

"Well, who's the new bitch on your lap, Blade? I thought you were saving me a spot? I'm here now, so you can find another dick to ride," Tanya flicks her hand, dismissing Vegas. "That man is mine and has been mine for a while." Vegas drops her burger, staring Tanya dead in her soulless eyes.

She lowers her voice, crisp and clear, and it's on. "Let's clear shit up right now. I don't know you, so don't ever feel you can call me a bitch. Don't *you* act like a bitch and ruin my dinner, shit is downright fucking rude. Mind your goddamn manners in this clubhouse. And lastly, I don't pick random dicks to ride for the night. Know who you're talking to before you open your mouth. You look stupid." Vegas leans back against my chest, waiting on the dumb cunt to leave.

"Honey, you may have him for right now, but they all fuck around. I'll have his dick again," Tanya sneers, and I want to grab her by her hair and kick her out myself.

Vegas stands, pulling her keys and phone out of her hoody pocket, handing them to Dana next to her.

Leaning over the table, she says to Tanya, "Kick rocks, crazy, I won't cat fight over a man, but I won't hesitate to kick a bitch's ass either."

I've had enough, and the demon is out. Bitch needs to know she's in my club. Pushing myself out of the chair, I pace around the table and stand right next to Tanya, placing my gun to her head, cocking the hammer back. The room goes quiet. Tanya brings her terrified, tear-filled face up to me, at least as much as she can with my nine pushing against her skull.

"Dumb cunt, do not come into my club like you are somebody here. You are some trashy ass pussy I used, get that through your skull or my bullet will. The next time you disrespect my Ol' Lady will be your last. Get the fuck out, and do not come into my club again. Move!" My voice booms across the room.

Damn terrified, the stupid cunt takes off crying and twisting her ankle on the way out. Fucking dumb bitch. Sitting back in my chair, I pull Vegas to sit back down with me. I wrap my arm around her waist and hug her back to me where she belongs. On my side, as my Ol' Lady. Conversations pick back up, men start moving back to what they were doing.

Picking up my whiskey, I slam the rest back and drop the glass down. I turn my head and catch Hawk watching my every move. Glaring back at him, I'm thinking that I could blow his brains out too. Instead, I feel like playing with the dirty fucker inside of me. A cold stone face, filled with dominance slips over my face, my mask. I slip my hand up Vegas' shirt, pinching her nipple hard and she gasps in surprise. I take her lips punishing her with my rage. She submits to my mood.

Hawk glares, and, unable to stand the sight of her in my arms, he takes off down the hall to one of the rooms. Good, motherfucker, message received. What you let go, I took, so fuck off.

Standing, I pull Vegas across the floor to our Church meeting room, slamming and locking the door shut. I place my gun on the table right next to us. If someone does get through, they will catch a bullet to the head.

Vegas beams with pride and lust at my demonic side. She knows I need her body as much as she needs me claiming her to the club. She pulls her sweatshirt and shirt over her head, leaving her lacy, black bra on. Her hands travel down to her pants unbuckling and pushing them, along with her G-string, down to her knees.

She bends over the table and my control is dissipating at the sight of her plump ass and bare pussy. Pushing my own pants down, I thrust my stiff cock in her in one quick move. Deep inside of her, I moan at the feel of her silky hot cunt. I squeeze and then slap her ass three times. She's wild with her lust for me, for my crazy murderous side, claiming her as my bitch.

Wrapping her hair in my fist, I pull just enough to arch her more. Holding onto her hip with my other hand, I smoothly slide my dick out and slam it back inside her, punishing her pussy. I punch my dick in and out, releasing my stress with her body.

Every thrust is pushing her body forward and she takes it all for me. She's arching her ass back into me, excited for more. My balls draw up and I come inside of my pussy, because yeah, it's mine, slowly rubbing and caressing it with my dick.

I release my strong hold on her hair, running my fingers down the middle of her back, all the way to her front where I rub her clit till she releases her cum on me. On my dick. On my hand.

Pulling out, I draw her back up to me. I turn her head and take her mouth while sticking my fingers back inside her pussy, feeling our releases mix together. Fucking perfect mess.

After we straighten and clean ourselves up, we head back out. I spot my old man at the table I just left and lead us in that direction.

"I never thought the day would come when I would have missed your ugly ass, yet here I stand happy to see it?" I shrug my shoulders and throw my hand in his direction.

Stryker moves around the table and we give each other a half hug, complete with man back slaps. "Once a little shit, always a little shit. Plus, you look like my ugly ass."

Seeing Vegas off to my side, he forgets all about me and goes to pick her up in a big hug. "How have you been, Vegas? Where's your old man at?" he asks her as if they are old friends. Just what the fuck? My old man *knows* her?

Setting her back down on her feet, she laughs saying back to him, "Papa and Momma took off to my house to crash for the night, but Snake is probably causing problems around here somewhere." She looks around the room but is not able to spot her brother.

"Blade!" Spinning my head to the right, my mom is headed over our way, giving me a hug. "Oh, this is the Alessia you were talking about!" She moves to grab her from my dad. "Hey, sweetie! Oh, Dana is here too. Did Cindy and Katie come too?"

My mom pushes the girls over where hugs and animated conversation are happening. My mom loves these two girls and knows them well. Once again, I feel completely out of the loop here.

Staring at Stryker, I state very calmly compared to how I'm feeling, "Just. What. The. Fuck." My old man and Spider throw their heads back, laughing. I'm going to kill Spider.

Stryker starts to fill me in. "You know all those shopping trips your mom would go on with the Ol' ladies from Cali? Meet the Cali Ol' ladies' daughters. None of you little fuckers seen them years ago. No way would their fathers parade them around club houses when they were so young. Your mom and I have known them for years, she was a sweet kid your mom loved. I stopped in Vegas' bar here and there over the years to check in on her and the girls. When I knew she was ready, I sent you over there to open your shop.

At the very least, I knew she could be trusted. You two hooking up? I just guessed she was a good match for you. I knew you needed a woman to watch your back. This life gets lonely as the Prez if you don't have the right woman to back you up," he explains as if it's all just that simple.

I expect this revelation from my old man, but Spider? "Fuck you, Spider, you cock sucking asshole. I'm reading that file now. 'Get to know her', you said. 'Earn her trust', you said. That shit blows, I know enough now. Fuck that getting to know each other. I'm reading that file tomorrow." Spider knows I'm mad enough to deck his ass.

"Blade," Stryker says, "Grow the fuck up and quit being a pussy over it. It's done. Spider didn't know that we knew her as much as we do. Her father would shoot me himself if I betrayed his trust and talked about her before now. It's a good thing though, yeah? Your mom and I trust her like family," Stryker states while telling me to let the shit go.

Spider leans forward across the table. "Besides, you know I'm right, because you didn't read her file, she at least respected you or trusted you more for it. Watching all this drama unfold was just a bonus for the rest of us. She brings out the fun, man. You've been a corpse walking around, she's kickstarted you back to life. You're fucking welcome, too." Sitting down, I resign to what it is, not really giving a fuck either way.

Ghost heads over to us. "About fucking time some older dicks got here, these young cocks listen to some dude named G-Easy. Sounds like a stripper to me. Had to blow this joint up with the classics, Guns N' Roses. How was the ride, man?"

Ghost and Stryker start catching up on life. Stryker signals for us to move into the room for Church. For the next twenty minutes, Spider and I spend some time catching Stryker up on what our current plans are, and show him the maps and possible routes.

Stryker nods along in agreement. "Tomorrow we'll have Church, tell all the members that Cuervo is on his way here with Buck's killer. We'll torture the little fucker that was stealing from us, and pin Buck's murder on him. Put all the men's minds to rest that we think this shit is settled. Get our rat laid back and wait for him to make a mistake."

Ghost listens intently, with haunted eyes. The desire to spill blood is evident. "Aye, Stryker, we'll hunt these fuckers down, bring them to their knees, one by one, when we catch them. No one fucks with the Battle Born brotherhood, no one."

"Agreed, no more one on one meetings after this. It's all business as usual," I agree, backing the other Presidents up.

No one says a word after that, knowing this threat is real, but also knowing we kill to keep what is ours. It's late and we are all ready to deal with this shit later. Heading back out to the main room, we find our women right where we left them.

"Mom, you and Dad take my room, I'll stay with Vegas at her house." My mom scrunches her face at me. "What the hell is that look for?"

"Blade, I don't want to sleep on those sheets, you know what I'm saying." She leans forward, raising her brows at me like I should've thought of this. My old man laughs from behind her.

"Mom, I have not had any club bitches in there at all. Besides that, they're new sheets." She's shocked at my admission.

"They're new and you haven't had any girls in there?" She's making a damn scene over this.

Axl laughs and takes pity on my mom. "No, Moxie, our boy here was saving himself for Vegas since we moved up here. Now that he has her, they've been fucking at her house, so you're good." That was fucking cool, telling my mom that. I roll my eyes and shake my head at his dumb ass.

"No worries, Moxie, we can christen his bed for him. Move that ass, woman, your man is tired and wants his woman." My old man leans over kissing my mom on the lips and rubbing her ass. Not wanting to watch that shit, I turn my head toward Vegas and Dana who are both openly watching my parents, along with Spider.

"God, they are so sweet," Vegas says quietly to Dana.

"I know, I want what they have. Sexy and strong." They both sigh in sync together.

Spider leans in telling them both, "Moxie is a MILF, man. Damn, has been since we were kids."

Stryker snaps his attention to Spider. "*My* MILF, fucker, keep your eyes on a woman you can fuck without catching a bullet to your head."

"Sound advice, Stryker, on my way to find my own pussy." Spider takes off to a group of club bitches.

"Blade, we'll haul your equipment to the shop at eight tomorrow. Go grab your shit from your room, a couple days' worth," my sly old man suggests. He knows that any excuse I have to stay in Vegas' bed, I'll take it.

Grabbing a bag and a week's worth of clothes and other crap, I hug my mom while she and Vegas make plans to hang out tomorrow. Vegas makes her promise to stay for Halloween with her devilish grin. Of course she agrees while Stryker drags her down the hall, telling her they'll talk tomorrow.

Vegas and I walk out to her Tahoe, and she hands me her keys as she yawns and sits in the passenger seat. Driving us to her place feels comfortable, as if we've done this a hundred times already.

"Alessia, that slutty ass bitch, Tanya, from earlier..." I pause, lost in what to say or explain about who or what she is.

"Blade, I for real do not want to talk about that un-classy bitch, ever. I get what the men do at the clubhouse, have seen it and lived it. I get it, getting easy bitches was what you did for a while. I really don't want to talk about her or any other ones. As long as you keep yourself real to me, no need to know all the details. Besides that, do you want to hear about all the dicks I had before you?" she questions me in a mocking voice.

"Fuck no!" Now I'm wondering how many guys she's fucked. That just pisses me off more, thinking of other men touching her.

"Don't go there, Blade, no good will come from knowing all those details. What matters is the future." Alessia stops and turns to me. "What we are together, what we can be together, no one has had from either of us. That's what I want, something unique and beautiful. Strong and withstanding."

Grabbing Alessia's hand from her lap, I raise it to my lips, kissing the back of it. "I want all of those things too. I want to be the thorns on your roses for you." Setting our hands in my lap, I squeeze her hand and continue, "Protect you from the world. I want to be the man to protect your heart."

Alessia closes her shining, deep blue eyes, swallowing back her fears. She breathes in and out and squeezes my hand back.

CHAPTER 17

Blade

In the next few days, we all fall into a rhythm of work and sleep. We have the shop set up and will be open for business soon. The guys and I are excited to get back to work. Vegas and her girls, along with the Ol' Ladies, have helped us with cleaning and organizing. Dana worked with Axl, setting up accounting software that is easy and efficient. Axl acts stupid and keeps asking her questions, so she'll talk to him more. I know that asshole knows what he's doing. Vegas does too but plays along with him. Secretly, I think Vegas wants those two to hookup.

The bell rings above the door, signaling the arrival of Vegas and her girls into the Battle Born Brothers Tattoos. She whistles low, "Wow, got to hand it to myself, I made this place... the bomb!" I hear what she's saying, but the three of them are dressed in some slutty cheerleader costumes. Their tits are pushed up higher, popping out of all their tops. And fuck, they are wearing fishnet tights with combat boots and short fucking skirts.

Vegas keeps talking, but me, Axl, Tank and Spider are having the dirtiest fucking daydreams.

"The gray with navy really looks good in here. Holy shit! Who drew the wolf?" Vegas strides over to the center wall that's painted gray and starts examining the painting, her hand outreached like she wants to touch the wet paint.

"I did, babe." Walking up behind her, I hold onto her waist with one hand, my other one wrapping around hers, leaving her pointer finger out. I trace her finger through the wolf's fur, leaving pieces of my Alessia in the painting with me. After a few more strokes, I wipe her finger off on my pants. I then lean forward and kiss her soft, plump, red lips.

"That painting is gorgeous! It's the same one on your back, except this one has deep blue eyes and a blue moon. I love it," she tells me.

"Speaking of gorgeous, so is this outfit. This must be your Halloween costume, huh?" Leaning forward, I whisper, "We are fucking in your office later, with you in this costume, then later at home. You hear me?"

She breathes, "Fuck, yes, I hear you, loud and clear, big guy."

Jenn laughs and says, "We can *all* hear you."

Dana has her hand over her mouth, stifling her laugh. "Be quiet though, we do have paying customers tonight."

"Fine," Vegas sighs. "We do have a bet to settle, Blade. Don't think I forgot." Vegas grabs the plastic bag that Jenn is holding. "If I win, you wear this all night long." Reaching in, she pulls out a football jersey and pads.

Tank, Spider and Axl laugh at the back that says, *My Man Lost*, and, in the middle, at the bottom, *#1 Loser*.

"Feeling cocky, are you, Vegas? Let's get it on. I'm holding out my surprise till after I win the bet." Playing along with her game, I upped it and she doesn't know about it yet. I figured she owes me after all the shit she's put me through.

"It's hot you came out full throttle to play, Blade. Let's go get it on then."

"Ladies first, babe." I hold the door open for Vegas and the girls. But my hand 'slips' and the door shuts in Tank's face. Spider and Axl laugh while Tank flips me off before walking through and locking the door.

Vegas and the girls walk to her Tahoe, grabbing their targets and cans from the back. Vegas grabs a small metal case and pulls out her gun, tucking her Smith & Wesson in Titanium in her cheerleading skirt. Fuck the bet, there are better things to do with our time. But I do want to teach her a lesson in fucking with me.

"We need more targets?" Tank questions which has all of our heads whipping around at his comment. That dumb fucker gave Vegas a clue, and the look on her face proves it. Her head is tilted, eyeing Tank, then slowly directs her gaze at me. I harden my features. I won't give more away. She just nods her head, closes the back of her ride and moves on.

The girls are a team and walk ahead of us to make a statement. Axl says, "This is the best Halloween I have ever had. I can't wait to see what I get to unwrap for Christmas." His eyes are focused on Dana. Jenn and Vegas laugh while Dana keeps walking.

"Santa is bringing you blue balls instead of coal, Axl. Sorry, you haven't been a good boy." Dana keeps strutting to the back of the garage where all three of them come to a screeching halt once they round the corner. They gape openly at what I had waiting for them.

That's right, baby, I'm ahead of you this time. There, in place of her made up target range, I had the prospects up here early this morning, setting up a more tactical range. I also had them add fifteen more yards to make the shot more difficult. So, while she was sleeping in, I was making plans for a victory.

I had Solo, my number one prospect, follow her all week. Solo measured the distance she was practicing at, and, naturally, I increased it to the yards I practiced at. He also saw the jersey in her office. I took Fuego's advice seriously. She does need a man to watch her.

Vegas zeros in on Solo with a glare that promises payback. "You little snitch, I saw you everywhere all week." She drops her targets into the dirt and points directly at him. "You will pay, not today, but you will pay, fucker."

"Come on, Vegas, I was doing what I was told," Solo raises both palms up in defeat.

"You entered the game, you stay over there by the wall where I can see you. Don't touch anything." She snarls at Solo and points to the garage. Poor guy stalks backward till his back hits the wall.

Vegas directs her anger and surprise at me, glaring. We all have the face of the devil painted across our faces. Ready for war. Crossing my arms over my chest, I'm enjoying the feisty kitten side of her. It reminds me of the first day we met.

"You dirty assholes! How did you know this was where the bet would be?" She's mad and flustered. Right where I want her. She walks over to me, this time, pointing her finger at my face.

"Vegas likes to play games, so I jumped on it. You need to know when you play with me, Vegas, I will win at all costs. I remember telling you to finish what you started. This is me finishing what you started. Dirty games with you is becoming my favorite pastime." Not moving, I just stare right back at her stunning, heated face.

Vegas steps back like she's been smacked, realizing she gave in to the game. She got lazy. Her shoulders relax, then says too calmly, "What tipped you off,

Blade?" And when I don't reply quick enough, "Answer my question," she barks out.

"The day the boys and I were at the shop cleaning, you didn't check for our bikes," I shrug at her. "We heard gunshots and went looking to figure out what was going on. Then we stumbled on all of you girls having your contest right here. That whole time, Axl, Spider and I watched from that window," I nod towards the office window of the old garage behind us.

Vegas purses her lips together. "You heard it all, everything I said to Dana about the bet. Fuck, man! Well, the bet isn't over yet. You may have rigged this setup to your advantage. We'll split the targets. You pick one of the shots, and I'll pick the other. Also, Dana will score my points and you can pick one of your brothers to score yours." Vegas is back into winning mode at full force.

"Deal, sweet cheeks. Axl and Dana will score them together. Keep it honest, they can check each other's work." She knows my meaning, and Jenn and Dana chuckle behind her.

"Let's begin, and ladies first, *bro*," Vegas smarts off.

"Vegas, watch your fucking mouth. I will spank your ass in front of everyone in that tiny as fuck skirt you have on, and I bet there ain't hardly shit of what you wear as panties on underneath there. Last warning, you hear me?" Hard as stone, I stare at her. My woman will respect me.

"Shit, Vegas, he's hot as fuck when he's mad. But I really don't want to see your ass any more than I already have," Jenn states, her comment intriguing me and the guys. We all turn with eager expressions, so she clarifies. "Oh God, you know, gym showers, trying on clothes when we're shopping. Girly shit, you perverts," she bats her hand at us.

"I'm definitely hanging with these chicks at the gym," Tank affirms.

"Not without me!" Axl complains. "I'm going, too. Dana, give me your class schedule," he demands from her.

Dana shakes her head '*no*' at him, and Axl grins, "Okay, princess, play it your way. Solo will get me all of your schedules."

We hear a loud thud and we turn to look toward the sound. Solo must have hit his head on the garage wall because it looks like he's praying up at the sky.

Frustrated with these two dipshits, I bring it back to the bet. "As Vegas said, ladies first. Pick your target, then Dana and Axl will keep score."

Vegas grabs three full beer cans with red tape around the middle. She walks over and hands them to Jenn who, in turn, walks over to the old fence against the mountain and sets one on each large pole of the fence, making three different distances.

Vegas bends over and grabs a stick. Her skirt rises to the bottom of her ass cheeks. The wind picks it up, giving us all a flash of yes, a very bare ass. That little bitch just turns and says, "Oopsie."

Tossing the stick in front of her, she draws her gun and points it at the dirt, flipping the safety off. Standing with one foot in front of the other, she squares her body with her targets.

She turns to face us and tells us the rules. "As soon as you take aim, the time starts, an extra two points for the fastest time. But you must hit all three cans in the red tape." Jenn drops a timer on a string from her hand. "Did Solo report that to you?" Vegas smiles, showing the white teeth of a predator, just like the wolf on our club patch.

From the other side of the barn, I hear steps and see Ghost, Fuego, Snake and Stryker walking over. My mouth wants to drop open, but I reign in my features.

"What was it you said, Blade? Oh, yeah, finish what I started, right, honey? I recruited Ghost. You know he's a sniper, right? You didn't think I knew Solo was on my tail? Of course I did. I only let him see what I wanted him to see."

Stryker, my old man, walks over and takes the timer from Jenn, grinning at me in fascination, then watches Vegas who's looking really unhinged. She turns to focus on her targets, closes her eyes, takes a deep steadying breath and opens them back up. She raises her handgun and pulls the trigger three times in quick succession, nailing all three cans.

"Fuckin A," I say out loud, not sure if I can beat that. Fuego beams with pride at his daughter, and Snake fist bumps his sister.

Walking over to the stick, I pull my nine from behind my back. I take a deep breath as well, aim and pull the trigger three times. I hit all three cans and am damn happy about that.

Dana brings Vegas' cans and Axl brings mine. Dana shows us Vegas hit all three cans in the red tape, time is four seconds. Her score is five. Axl pulls mine, and I too hit all the cans in the red tape, my old man tells us my time was five seconds. She wins the first round with two points ahead.

Walking over to Vegas, I haul her to me and smack her lips with a big kiss. "That was hot, babe, but you got to win the next round, too. Or you'll wear my tatt. What other way are you going to tell everyone I'm your Ol' Man if you're not wearing my ink, baby?"

Vegas stills, her eyes bugging out at me. Seeing her father behind her, he nods his head my way, approving. That gives me a little more confidence to win this bet, so I step over to one of the more difficult targets I had set up.

"Okay, Vegas, this one is not timed, but at fifty yards. Every circle you hit in the bullseye is three points, the outer center is one point." Vegas nods back to me in agreement.

Stepping over behind a rock, I take aim at the target. Pulling the trigger, I hit all five circles. Each time one is hit, the circle drops back, leaving the others propped up. Axl grabs mine and scores them, handing them to Dana to double check. She agrees and says, "Blade hit a score of sixteen." Dana looks over to Vegas who pulls together her determination to win.

She walks over to the rock where I'm standing. Moving to the side, I block the view to everyone else. Running my hand up her skirt, I palm her ass and lean over to whisper, "Good luck, Alessia." Then I kiss her temple and back away, allowing her to get set up.

Standing right behind her, I watch her confidently aim and shoot the first two in the center. Perfect bullseye, each one. She aims at the third target, takes a deep breath and moves off center just a hair. What the fuck is she doing? In the corner of my eye, I see Stryker hand Fuego a hundred.

What. The. Fuck.

Vegas

I truly hope that Blade is in this relationship for real, because I'm taking the biggest risk of my life. Betting on a permanent tattoo is no joke. Neither are my emotions.

Blade will really fuck me over if he isn't serious about us. So, I do what I have to do. I'm going to take a dive for the man I love. Yeah, I can't believe this either. So, here I am, staring at my last target, and I blow it. I hit the outer circle on purpose. I am *that* good, but I want Blade more than I want to win.

Dana is grinning when she counts out my score. "Vegas unfortunately lost the last round with a score of thirteen, total score of eighteen to Blade's score of nineteen. Step forward, Prez, and claim your prize, you lucky bastard."

Blade struts his very fine ass my way. A devilish look is plastered across his goatee, handsome face. "Doesn't matter to me how we got here, Vegas, as long as we got here. Come on, I have something special for you in the shop."

"You have the stencil ready already?" I ask in disbelief, because, when did he have time to do all this?

"Yeah, babe, it wasn't hard to draw it out, you inspire the hell out of me. Move your cute ass, I've got work to do." Inside of the shop, he takes me to his workstation in the back corner. Everyone files in, wanting to see what Blade drew for me.

"Out, you can see it when it's done. The first person to see it will be Vegas. We'll head over to the bar when we're done." Blade stands firm at the doorway to his station, with his arms crossed.

Dana and Jenn pout, mumbling on their way out that Blade is no fun. "Fine, we'll go to work then, sheesh" they complain, leaving to go to the bar.

Blade yells out to Axl, "Yo, bro, lock the door on your way out, yeah?" effectively dismissing him and the rest who are still standing around.

"Yeah, Prez, we'll see you next door. I got a cheerleader to make out with anyway." Axl locks the door behind them, arguing with Dana that he's helping her bartend tonight.

Blade sets up his supplies, then rolls his stool over to me, sitting me in what looks like a massage chair. "Alessia, I know you blew the last round of the bet. Why did you do it?" he asks, his face full of worry.

"I could have hit that mark, and part of me really wanted to. Blade, I wanted to bet on you more than I wanted the winning bragging rights. It all hit me at once. I could win either way. The biggest payoff was the one with the biggest risk. I want it all, Blade. What our parents have is priceless in this world. I bet on you, I'm all in this with you." I start running my hand up his arm, stopping at his elbow.

Blade leans forward and pulls my shirt over my head, leaving my bra in place. "I was hoping that was what you were doing. I love how hard you show love to others around you. When I saw you rig the first bet against Dana, so she would win, I think you seeped in a little deeper. When you make or bring me dinner, a little deeper. When you kiss and touch me, a whole lot deeper."

Blade grabs one of my pigtails and tugs on the curly end. "I really love these things, too." He smiles, reaching for the sides of my face and pulling me close until our lips meet. Devouring me with everything he has.

Softly, he pushes me back and gazes into my eyes, before rasping out, "Not having all of you would crush me, Alessia. I need you as much, if not more, than I need everything else. You needed to protect your heart, I needed you to soften mine up. You have the magic touch to reach me, baby." He pecks my lips, then bends down to kiss my chest, making my heart speed up with his passion.

"I love your heart, the soft, the bold, the tough, every piece that makes you, *you*. I love you, Alessia."

My hands reach for his face, pulling him back to my lips for a searing kiss. "I love all of you, Blade. The strong, determined, powerful and the soft side you have just for me. I love every part of you. Always."

Leaning toward him, he backs up enough for me to unzip his pants. He helps shoving them off along with his boxers. His hand meets mine and guides me to stroke his hard cock. His rough fingertips run up the back of my thighs, reaching my thong under my short skirt, taking them down until they hit the floor. Stepping out of them, my hand guides him to sit back into the chair I was just in. I straddle him and slowly fill my body with his.

Looking up at his face, I can see into his soul. Obsessed with the love in his heart. I bare my feelings to him by giving myself and my trust. My hands wrap around his head, messaging, before he moves down my torso. He tenderly kisses the tops of my breasts and unclasps my bra. His thumbs start caressing my nipples, making me arch my back, wanting and craving more from him. He loses control and his teeth graze my tits, then sucks them into his mouth. But it is still not enough. I beg him, "Come inside me, please."

Blade lifts me slowly up and down on his dick. I memorize everything, taking in his arms and chest that flex and move under my body. Needing more, wanting more, my hips aggressively move back and forth, grinding harder on his cock. Blade's deep moan vibrates through his body into mine, somehow connecting us even closer. I place kisses from his shoulder and up to his ear and whisper to him, "I love you, Blade, promise me forever, promise me everything."

"I promise you, baby, as long as I breathe, my life is your life. I promise you all of me is yours. Forever."

Quickening the pace, I fuck him harder up and down. My swollen clit rubs against him, but it is not enough yet. Blade pushes me back a bit, forcing me to rest my hands behind me on the chair. He licks his thumb and rubs my clit while bucking his hips harder into me. Unrelenting, hard and quick thrusts. His thumb pushes down, circling quicker.

I come around his dick, exploding my release and screaming his name, "Blade!" I can feel my heart bursting with the exertion. He roars out his release right behind me. We breathe heavily, relaxing into the comforting feeling of our chests rising and falling together.

"I thought for sure I would fuck you in your office before mine," he murmurs in my neck.

His blunt thought makes me laugh and I hug him tighter. "Ruined your sex plans for tonight, did I?"

"Nah, never ruined. I'll get you in there. I wanted you to be the first I gave a tattoo to in here. Now I will love this shop even more, but we better get to work, babe." He swats my ass, getting me to move off him.

After I've cleaned up, I grab my underwear and bra off the floor, then, with them back in place, I ask, "Where do you want me? I assume, since you already drew it, you know where you want to put it?"

"You would be right about that. Sit in the chair the opposite way, straddling it, with your back to me."

Moving to how and where he said, I sit down. Blade undoes my bra again and cleans the middle of my back between my shoulder blades, from shoulder-to-shoulder. He slowly places the stencil on my back. He takes his time to look it over, drawing in some areas. Then starts up his gun, tracing the outline. Over the next several hours, we talk and laugh while he lets me play songs off my phone on the small speakers he has in here.

"Okay, babe, I think we're done. I'll touch up a few spots after it heals, but you're done for today." Blade rubs ointment into my skin, then takes a picture with his phone and hands it to me.

"Oh my God, Blade! It's so pretty! I really love what you did, it's so different. I thought I was getting what the Ol' Ladies usually get. This is much more badass!"

Racing to the full-length, double mirrors, I turn sideways to look at it over my shoulder. Right in the middle of my back is the face of a black wolf with gray shading and a touch of blue eyes. The roses on my right side fade from the black and red to just black and gray around the wolf, then fading into black and gray with blue over to the left shoulder.

"Can we add more blue roses later?" I ask eagerly, wishing we could do it now. Blade hands me a strapless bra and cami that he must've taken from my dresser this morning.

"Whenever you want it, we can. Come back over here and let me wrap that."

He tapes plastic over the tattoo, helping me slide the bra over and the black cami over my head and body. Pulling my pigtails out, he places a kiss on the back of my neck.

Smiling, he questions, "You ready to head over there and show the rest of them?"

"Hell yeah! Let's go."

Blade holds the door open for me, letting me walk into the bar first. We maneuver around the crowd and I falter a few steps in. Playing on the loud speakers is *Cherry Pie* by Warrant. Axl is up on stage, dancing around in the football jersey I had made for Blade. On the stage, Dana is sitting in a chair, letting Axl give her a lap dance in front of everyone. He even painted black lines under his eyes. He's taking his task very seriously.

Walking over to my mom and Papa at the bar, I yell and point, "What the hell is going on?"

Mom giggles and explains, "Well, Dana told Axl to get lost, that he probably has other girls here anyway. He tells her, there are no other girls. She said there's no way to prove it, and she was still pissed over whatever he did before. He grabs her hand, hauls her up there and starts making a fool of himself for her. I sure miss you girls. I've been so bored without all of you around."

Papa rolls his eyes at her, clearly not enjoying the show. "Why she likes for you girls to fall all over these shitheads is beyond me," he grumbles, watching Axl toss his Jersey on Dana. Dana laughs, picks it up with two fingers, pretending to smell it like it stinks, then dropping it to the floor.

"This shit is stupid," Snake agrees and turns around back to the bar, signaling Solo to hand him a beer.

"Aww, is big brother mad that Dana found someone and moved on? I think he's jealous," I taunt him.

Snake moves over, cornering me against the bar. "Did someone just get a fresh tatt? Did anyone set it for you yet, Vegas?" The sly little fucker snickers at me. He raises his hand, ready to strike. Cringing, I close my eyes. I'm ready for impact, then... nothing.

Cracking an eye open, I look around, wondering what happened. Blade has a solid grip on Snake's wrist, not allowing him to touch me. My mouth pops wide open in surprise that's replaced with a dirty 'Can't fuck with me' smirk crossing my face.

"Why the fuck does it look like you're about to smack my woman, Snake?" Blade drops his wrist, and I laugh at Snake which makes him glare at me.

"Fuck, Blade, we are just fucking around. We've had this game for a while now. If we ever catch the other with a fresh tatt, we smack it because it hurts like a bitch." He tosses his hand at me like I started it. Well, I did, a very long time ago.

Blade moves closer to my side and wraps his arm around my waist. Snake glares at me and mouths 'Later', then goes back to his beer.

"Baby girl?" My mom calls and comes closer, getting off her stool to look at my tattoo. "Did you do this?" she questions Blade.

"Yes, ma'am, I did. Do you like it?"

"Blade, unless you want Fuego to kick your ass, do not call me that again. Call me Cindy. This is beautiful."

Mom lightly runs her fingers over the plastic, tracing the lines. "It is stunning, you are very talented.

Will you copy one of these roses for me? This means so much to me, Blade, you have no idea."

Mom hugs me with tears in her eyes. "My baby girl is finally in love, isn't she?" I can't answer but I do hug her back. Then she surprises me by giving Blade a big hug too.

By that time, Stryker, Moxie, Jenn and Dana spotted us, and join our group. A happy Stryker asks, "Let's see my son's work."

Feeling a little anxious, I turn to show the group and I hear the girls gasp. Blade antagonizes me by asking, "Who's your man, baby?"

Huffing at his enjoyment, I say as plain as possible, "Blade is my man."

"That's right, you're my Ol' Lady."

"Okay, okay, I told everyone, the bet is over." Blade gives me a smacking kiss, then whispers, "Now it's over."

CHAPTER 18

Blade

Spider, Tank and Cowboy follow me out of Vegas' office and through the back door for a smoke. First, we check around the building that no one is listening. Lighting up my smoke, I take drag in and blow out a long puff. "Got any updates?"

Tank nods, "Yeah, the trucks Axl set up for the brothers to follow worked out well. One brother didn't report back that he found anything or anyone hauling, even though he followed him all the way to his drop in Wells, Nevada. He shanked the driver and tossed him in the dumpster. He made a call we couldn't trace. He's our rat. It's one of the old President's men, Skid. I've kept eyes on him. He hasn't made any moves yet."

"That old fucker followed him then dumped him and took off, then reported it to whoever he works with now." I pull in another drag that my nerves crave. "We need to get his phone and see what's on there. We can't let him meet with whoever he's working with. Who's with him now?"

Spider laughs, "I've got Fawn and CC getting that old horny dick liquored up with a roofie. As soon as he passes out, I'm heading back to the club house to open his phone. Stupid fucker uses his thumb print to open the screen. If he's smart, he would have erased everything. But I have a plan. I can't believe I didn't think of this before a crazy bitch did." Spider shakes his head kicking dirt. "The other day when I was sitting at the bar, I heard this woman telling the girls how she caught her boyfriend cheating. She logged onto his Apple account, copied his login name and password. She goes into her phone account, changes her cloud account to match his. Not only does she get her own text messages but his too. I went and bought a new phone. As soon as he falls asleep, I'll use his thumb to unlock the screen, his password will be saved automatically on the cloud. I'll log in, get the info and log out. Add the account to my new phone and I'll be able to track his texts, who's in his contacts, and track his whereabouts with the Find My Phone app."

"Fuck, man, I can't say I'm surprised that a crazy bitch thought that scenario out, they are relentless cunts when they're onto something."

We hear the rumble of a bike park out front. Striding in that direction to check who it is, I'm relieved to see Cuervo's finally made it. The crazy fucking nomad tracks down shit you never thought you could resurrect off the grid.

"Fuck, brother, you made it." Slapping Cuervo on the back, I watch him kicking out the kickstand, then shaking hands with the rest of the brothers.

Cowboy tells him, "You haven't changed at all in a decade, brother. Same long black hair in a ponytail, same old devil stash. I think you have the same black vaquero boots from the eighties." Cowboy would be right. Cuervo looks the traditional Mexican he always has.

Cuervo spits his chew down by Cowboy's boot, and, with his gravely deep voice, asks, "What? I'm not pretty like my brother, Fuego, that crazy fire-starting motherfucker." Cuervo assesses me, "Heard you tatted his daughter up, Blade. Better treat her right, brother, or you'll see what the end of my machete in your skull feels like. No shit, I love Vegas like she's my own. Don't fuck with her."

"I hear you, Cuervo." I nod and blow out a long drag, like I give a shit what this asshole has to say about it.

"GOOD." Cuervo stares me down with his weathered, scarred up face. If I wasn't who I was, I would think twice before fucking around with this psycho.

Stryker and Fuego come through the back door to greet Cuervo as well. Fuego, the devil lookalike himself, hugs his brother. Stryker, who holds out his fist for a bump, asks first, "Where's the bitch we have to get the info from?"

"That whiny, little pussy is tied up at Arrowhead, the abandoned mineral mine in the hills. We'll need to grab the trucks to get up there, though. I'll be waiting at the clubhouse. Let's move, I need sleep." With that, Cuervo cranks his bike and leaves the rest of us in his dust.

"Moody asshole," Cowboy stares in the direction of where Cuervo took off.

"You would be, too, *cabrón*, if your only son and wife were stabbed and bled out for days. Never talk shit about Cuervo, unless you desire to join the dead," Fuego slaps Cowboy on the back on his way to his bike. "You heard him, let's move."

"Meet you all there, I'll be a minute behind you. Gonna go grab Axl." Tank, Cowboy and Stryker take off with Fuego. Walking into the bar, I spot Axl hanging behind the bar with Dana and Vegas.

"Axl, we got work at the clubhouse, we gotta head out, brother." Axl nods and tells the girls bye. Vegas stiffens a bit at my words, but doesn't comment. I know she knows there is a whole lot more going on.

Walking up behind her, I use my weight to pin her to the bar. "Babe, I gotta work tonight. I don't know when I'll be back, so I'll crash at the club." Kissing her cheek, I turn to head out.

Vegas' hand catches my forearm just before I exit the back door. "Blade, let's get some things straight. You will come home to me every night, unless there is a damn good reason you can't. The other is, when you go to work, kiss me goodbye like it's your last. Did you or did you not tattoo my back? You hear me?" Vegas stands there with her hand on her cocked hip, piercing my soul with her words and angry eyes.

"Yeah, babe, heard every word. I'll be home later." Grabbing Vegas' waist, I pull her into my arms and kiss her sweet mouth. "Behave, Vegas," I slap her ass in warning.

"Later, love," she waves her hand, and I watch her hot ass walk back behind the bar.

Blade

Swinging open the old steel mine plant doors, the smell of musk and dust, along with blood, hits my nose. "Cuervo, got this party started," I sneer, that greedy asshole.

Axl and Tank are at my back and follow me inside. This is our show and he will learn that right now. Shadows appear around the corner from the only light in the main room.

Quickly striding into the open plant room, Cuervo has our informer on his knees, with his arms tied behind his back. Blood drips from his nose and mouth. His head is tilted forward, realizing he isn't getting out of this. Cuervo raises his fist to rain down more punishing hits. Tank grabs Cuervo's other arm, not a physical match for Tank, but he's a quick killer.

Cuervo grabs at the knife in the leather sheath that's tied around his leg, spinning around and holding it at Tank's neck. Tank's eyes narrow as he steps into the sharp blade. "Pulling a knife on me, Cuervo?" he holds back his impatience while ignoring Cuervo's psychotic state. Cuervo pulls back a bit and drops his knife back into its sheath.

"Not today, *cabrón*, not today." He drops his head to the side and waits for Tank's next move. Pushing Cuervo back a step, they both eye the other, animosity in their eyes for each other's blood.

Interrupting their standoff, I step in. "Cuervo, I'm the fucking Prez of this chapter, that's my Road Captain, get your shit together. Or did you forget that?"

Cuervo turns his body to face the rest of us. "*Sí*, Prez. Just getting this fucker warmed up for you. I did haul his ass all the way up here, *no?*"

"Yeah, Cuervo, I see that and appreciate your work, but don't forget that we are your brothers too, *or* your place."

My face is stone, but this prick is conjuring the rage out from within. Looking weak in front of my men is not an option. Cuervo gives me a smile I know he doesn't mean, and it's on only to keep pushing me. Fuego grabs Cuervo by the shoulder, but he tugs out of his hold and walks to the far wall in the dark, out of sight. Crazy asshole. Looking at Axl, he catches my stare, knowing I mean for him to keep eyes on the nomad.

Walking over to an old dirty, dusty table, I drop my tools down that I carried in a heavy, black metal case, rolling the dial and unlocking the combination. I pop the top open, flipping the lid over. A cloud of dust settles around me. On each side of the box there is a variety of knives or pokers. I run my finger along my favorite, a combat tactical blade, all black, twelve inches long, with a saw on the opposite side of the blade.

Pulling it out, my heart races with enthusiasm to let out the stress. To kill this man, show to the others who are standing in here that if they cross our club, I won't hesitate to throw a knife into their back. No, my first choice is never a bullet.

Facing the dead man on his knees before me, I ask, "What's your name?" The man snarls and spits out blood, hitting my boot with it. I hold the knife tighter, roll my head, the lust for his blood pouring from my pores, soothing me, calming me.

The wolf pacing inside of us all howls in our minds, waiting to be freed. We all laugh out loud to each other. I nod toward Tank and he picks up the rope at his feet. Tank likes to play with his ropes. Pulling it taught between his hands, he walks toward our prisoner, feeling its strength and bite on his skin.

Tank turns his body sideways to the man, kicking his size thirteen boot right in the center of his chest.

The man's head cracks like a melon on the old concrete floor. He's struggling to breathe, so I'm certain he knocked the wind out of him and worse.

Tank tosses the loop end around a steel hook above, tying the other end to the man's feet. Flipping a switch on the old machine, he turns it on. He pushes a button and pulls the man up and off his feet. We watch his face scrape along the dirty concrete floor.

Stepping closer, I grab his shirt, cutting it open from the collar down, opening his chest to me. "You see, Dan Robertson, I knew who you were coming in here. The question is, what else do I know?"

I start slicing into his skin, and he screams, fueling my thirst for his pain. I continue by slicing the right side of his body from his thigh down to his ankle, then move to his left side. "I know about your wife, Julie, and your two kids."

"Fuck you, asshole, I still ain't telling you shit," Dan yells back at me. There is a code among these thieves and thugs. One rule is that we don't mess with each other's families.

Walking calmly to my case, I'm done with this fucker. "Okay, so let's not waste time. Tell me what I want to know, and you die quicker. Fuck around with my time, the longer I make you suffer here. Tell me, is your blood pounding in your head yet?" Still not looking at Dan, I find what I'm looking for. "I wonder if you'll go into a seizure if I nicked your artery? Or, do you think you'll feel a deep euphoria at your blood draining from your body?" I ask, seriously wondering what that would feel like.

Grabbing my daggers from my case, I take six steps, turn, and one by one throw them at Dan like he's a dartboard, sticking them into each thigh and bicep. Hollers erupt from his vocal cords, making him bow forward.

"Start talking, Dan, this will only get worse for you," I warn and step back to him, "because the next knife I throw will be deeper." Waiting on Dan through his gasps of air, I light up a smoke and pull in a few deep lung-fulls.

Dan stutters out, "I-I-I-I... was paid to haul trucks, keep it on the down low. I never got to see what was in the trucks. D-d-d-drive the trucks, wait till I got a text and m-m-move out. When I delivered in Sacramento, I dropped the truck. N-n-n-never unloaded." Frustration booms inside of me because that tells me shit.

Nodding at Stryker, he places two fingers to his teeth and whistles loud. Cowboy carries in a kicking and screaming slut, tossing her to the ground like trash. Dan's eyes are bloodshot and pop out at the sight of his girlfriend, or whore. Not sure which, and don't care either.

Reaching over, I grab a fist-full of her ratty hair and pull the bitch up to stand. "Say goodbye to Dan."

"No!" The little bitch screams, gurgling on my blade. Stabbing the bitch in the side of her throat, I rip it back out. Her blood splatters my face and pours down my hand. The wolf inside of me feels satisfied, and I toss the kill onto the floor.

She twitches before Dan, reaching for him, then drops her hand. Dying with her eyes open.

Dan sees death in her stare, and he knows she died because of him. She was going to be dead tonight, no matter what. He just tortured himself as far as I'm concerned. Dan snivels, tears tracking down his eyes, mixing with the blood. He closes them, unable to look at her anymore.

The broken man speaks. "Johnny Carmine. He paid me to haul. G-gave me the burner p-p-phone with addresses and t-t-times. It's in m-m-y truck's glove box where that c-c-crazy Mexican fucker g-g-rabbed me. I still don't know what I was hauling, j-j-just, he just left c-c-cash for me." Dan finishes on a whisper, with a wish of death in his voice. The wish to go back and do it differently.

Stryker, Fuego and I all stop at his words. The air just got sucked out of my lungs. Fuck.

"And Buck, who killed him in Indian Springs?" I question him, maybe he does know more?

"Another t-t-trucker on the p-p-payroll, I t-t-took over his route, t-they moved him, so you couldn't f-f-find him. I just seen him in p-p-passing, middle a-a-ge guy," Dan moans, his voice shaking from all the blood loss. Pulling my knives out from his body, his jeans soak up the blood before deep crimson coats a puddle on the floor around the dead bitch. Placing my knives into a garbage bag, I hand it over to Solo, then turn and look for the man as in love with knives as me. "Cuervo," is all I say and stay put.

A swishing, twirling noise filters through the air before a splitting sound stops it. Cuervo threw his machete, hitting Dan in the heart. Breaking through his rib cage, Dan never saw it coming.

The sickening sucking sound of flesh separating back and forth from the movement of the heavy knife is echoing through the room. The force of it is swaying his dead body, making it swing back and forth.

CHAPTER 19

Vegas

It's late and I'm trying to sleep, but not able to. I'm almost under, when I hear two sets of heavy feet lightly stepping across the floor. Reaching down into my bag, I pull out the handgun from my purse.

Blinking a few times to wake myself up, I take aim at the door. I hear the guest room open, then shut. Tugg is wagging his tail by my door. Relaxing a bit, I realize it must be Papa and, hopefully, Blade. The door swings open and a very tired Blade steps in looking at what is in my hand.

"Blade, you should have a code like, 'Hey, babe' when it's all clear, and 'Honey, I'm home' when shit has hit the fan, because if I didn't catch on that it was you, I would have blown a hole right through your handsome face."

Blade just huffs out humor at my logic. Placing my gun on my nightstand, I flick the light on, looking him over. He still has blood coated all over him.

I run to the kitchen and grab two trash bags. I knock on the guest room door first on my way back, handing one to Papa. "*Gracias, mija.*" He takes the bag and shuts the door.

I get back to my room and see that Blade has already taken his blood-soaked clothes off. Taking them from his hands, I shove the soiled clothes into the bag and toss it onto the floor for now.

"Long night, babe?" I ask him, using his nickname for me on him, and grin. I take my phone from the dresser, grab Blade's hand and lead him to the bathroom.

"Yeah," he cracks just a bit from the dark place he just came from.

"Hmmm, let's get your mind off it, okay?" Not really expecting him to answer, I turn on some mellow tracks on a playlist labeled 'Chill' from my phone. Turning toward the tub, Blade pulls back the shower curtain and steps into the hot, inviting water.

He places his hands on the wall in front of him, allowing the water to massage his back. I pull out a sugar scrub along with a washcloth and stretch my arm in to wash his back. Hearing him moan when he feels my hands on him brings me joy. Taking the washcloth from me and putting more sugar scrub on it, Blade washes his chest, arms and then his face.

He's about to turn the water off, when I pull back the shower curtain to stop him, and bend down to flip the stopper on for the bathtub to fill up. Wrapping my hair up in a bun and securing it with a clip, I remove my panties and sleep tank. Stepping in behind him, I pull him down in front of me. I wrap my arms around him and let his weight rest on my chest.

We sit in the hot steamy bath, letting the music relax both of us as the water fills the tub. Minutes pass as I hold him against me, slowly feeling his tense muscles loosen up. Blade takes my feet in his hands and crosses them over his stomach, massaging the arches, and this time it's me who moans in pleasure.

"Why didn't you get into the shower with me?" Blade questions, not sounding really curious, just more of a thought.

"That would be because this really hot biker put a tatt on my back, and I can't get it wet. I guess I'm stuck in this tub now until it heals," I answer, kissing his neck and biting his earlobe. Blade groans, rubbing his hands up and down my legs.

He turns toward me, lowering his body down on top of mine, kissing my mouth and thrusting his tongue inside. Running his hand from my leg to my pussy, he starts rubbing my clit, then pulls his lips back from mine. "I love your soft pussy, Alessia. Give it to me," he demands in a low voice.

Using my hands, I gently push him back and stand, wrapping a towel around me and handing him two. Wrapping one around his waist, he quickly towels off his body and follows me to our bed. He grabs my phone and changes the song to *Today* by the Smashing Pumpkins.

Smiling, I sing the words and watch the amusement on his face. He leans down to my naked body and starts singing along too, pulling me to the end of the bed, then he flips me over so that I'm face down. Grabbing my hips, he pulls me up to my knees, resting on the edge of the bed. He kneels behind me, kissing my ass cheeks one by one, then my pussy.

He glides his large hands up my back and around my front. Cupping my tits, he pinches and tugs at my nipples. "Give me more, Blade," I moan, "Make it intense and fast."

Scratching his nails into my sides and up to my hips, he answers, "Yeah, babe, I want that, too."

I feel him giving me one lick up my center to my asshole and back down to my clit. He gives no mercy, licking quickly, with hard pressure. Then I feel him pumping his fingers in and out. I can feel my climax coming already just as he takes one finger coated in the wetness from my pussy to circle my asshole.

"Blade!" I screech into the sheets, trying not to be loud.

"Shut it, Alessia, you'll like it, and you'll take whatever I want you to," he demands. Blade continues to play with my ass and lick my clit, bringing me right back to where I was, on the verge of coming.

He licks and sucks my pussy lips, devouring them with his mouth, his tongue flows up to lick and suck my clit. His index finger protrudes slightly into my ass, then backs it out, in, then out until he is using his whole finger, all while licking my clit. He finger fucks my ass while eating my pussy and I love it. I call out his name, "Blade, fuck, yes! Make me come, do not stop, make me come, big guy!" And he does. I come hard, fast and intensely on his face and fingers.

Blade, still on his knees, worships my pussy, licking up all my cum, moaning into my cunt as it still contracts from my orgasm. I fall down and lay on my left side. He stands, leaving my left leg between his, placing my right one across his stomach and around his right hip. Gripping his dick, he runs the head through my pussy, wrapping what's left of my come around it. He jerks his hips forward, thrusting hard and impaling me on him, chasing his own orgasm. Him taking what he wants turns me on all over again. He leans forward, placing his fists on the mattress, making his thrusts stronger.

Reaching up, I stick my fingers into his mouth and he sucks them greedily. Taking them out and to my pussy, I rub my clit to chase after another orgasm for him. This time, when Blade smiles, I see only the predator inside of him, the hungry wolf.

Closing my eyes, I think of him inside of my body and our sex earlier at the shop. Him undressing me. His hands and mouth all over my body. I moan out loudly and come, taking him over with me, and I feel him coating me with his release. He continues thrusting himself back and forth slowly, taking deep breaths, trying to calm down.

Finally pulling out, he crawls and settles in next to me, then pulls my back close to his chest. Resting his hand on my tit, he hugs me closer to him. "Tell me that someday, someday soon, you'll give me babies, Alessia?"

Bubbles of light laughter burst up my throat. "Babies, huh, like a little pack of them?" I tease back.

"That's what I want, you with my babies. It was hot as fuck to think of me getting you knocked up with my babies. I want to tie you to me every way possible."

With that last idea said, we drift off to sleep next to each other, possibly dreaming of the future, about the babies we both want.

A life with love and laughter between the hard times.

Waking up to the smell of bacon, I feel rested and completely happy. I dress in black leggings and a t-shirt. After I brush my teeth, I find the reason to the aroma of food.

Blade is standing at the stove, flipping eggs, shirtless. Hugging him from behind, I kiss his back, because this is my fantasy come to life.

Snake's voice startles me from the hallway, "No 'big guy' shit till after I eat breakfast. I almost had to leave last night," he smirks his evil at me.

"God, that's so gross, Snake!" I dig my face into Blade's back.

"No worries, it's payback for all the skin slapping you had to listen to growing up while sleeping next to my bedroom," Snake shrugs and states simply, making Blade chuckle.

"Shut up, bro, I really don't want to talk about you and all those sluts, I really don't." Filling my mug with coffee, I mix in my coconut creamer.

"Some of them were your friends, they weren't all sluts. It was easy, too. I would sit on the couch watching tv, waiting for them to come out of your room. I would invite them to sit. It was a slaughter, man. That's how Papa gave me my road name," his sly grin comes out, again. "Well, that and other things. But, speaking of friends, what's up with Dana?" Snake asks way too curiously.

"Dana and Axl are together. I wouldn't go there, Axl claimed that. You're about a month shy trying to get with her." Damn, that makes me happy to rub it in.

"I don't see her patched, I don't see her riding his bike, explain that," he protests.

"Axl is working on her, Snake. Dana needs a little time to come to terms with it. He found out about the *Cherry Pie*, and he made a scene. A funny one, but she was pissed. So, Axl has a little extra work to do. Are you for real, though? That if you went for it with her, you would go balls to the wall and want to claim her yourself?" I ask while observing him. "Because she needs a lover, Snake, not a fuck buddy."

"Okay, Vegas, I hear you," he concedes and drops it.

Papa and Momma meet us in the kitchen, bringing their bags with them. "Snake, help your *madre* with these bags, pack them onto the bikes." Snake stands and grabs the bags from Papa.

Momma gives me a big hug, holding me tightly. "Hey, baby girl, no goodbyes. We are going to see you in Tahoe for Thanksgiving. We can stay in for the whole week. I'll see you soon." She holds me close, not wanting to let go.

"I'll call you later and tell you about everything, we'll talk more, Momma." Holding her just as tight, I wish I hadn't pushed her away for as long as I did.

"Yes, you will." She playfully scolds and reminds me, "Keep an eye on Jenn and Dana, too." Finally, she lets go of me to say goodbye to Blade. She gives him a kiss on the cheek and a hug, and, on the way out, she reminds him, "Take care of my baby girl. See you both soon!" She waves and shuts her cheery cheeked face behind the door.

"Alessia," Papa calls for my attention. "I'll see you at the clubhouse in an hour," he says to me in all his take-no-prisoners business voice.

"*Sí, Papa, en una hora*," I nod my head in understanding. So, shit really hit the fan last night, huh.

With that done, we finish eating, dress and haul ass over to the clubhouse on Blade's bike. Neither one of us wants to have the bosses waiting for us. Walking into the meeting room for Church, I'm surprised to see Tank, Axl, Stryker, Snake, Ghost, Spider and Papa sitting and waiting for us.

"Morning, brothers, you all look like shit," Blade insults them all in the process. Hauling me along to sit in his chair at the head of the table, he pulls me to sit in his lap and wraps his arms around my waist.

Tank and Axl huff. Axl smarts back, "Asshole, we didn't get to wrap ourselves around a beautiful woman and head to bed like you." He looks around and shakes his head at the other guys.

Looking at Blade, I question what happened. "They had to stay up all night working, baby." Turning his attention back to the brothers, he asks, "Did we get his phone?"

Spider sits back and starts talking. "Yeah, I just got it an hour ago, I'll get you all the info here soon."

Papa interrupts, cutting to the chase. "Vegas, you're here because last night we had a source tell us that he was working with Johnny Carmine, said that Johnny is up to some bad shit. We know he's been working with you and your friends. We are worried about what he may know or be up to. What's up with him?" Papa looks worried, more about what I could be involved in and not know it.

"We met when I first moved here. We worked together on the purchase of The Black Rose. He never knew a whole lot about me personally, because I never had the same last name as you. Last year I bumped into him at the Nugget Casino. We started hanging out and became closer. As friends." Glancing around, I see that all the men have their haggard eyes on me.

"Then he started asking shady questions. Asking if I heard of or knew of who could haul cargo. It was around a time the club came to visit. He'd seen all of you at the bar one night and questioned how I knew you. Acting stupid, I said all the dumb things, like, 'Oh, are you starting a shipping company?'. I think he bought it and dropped it. Wanting to see what else he was dealing in, we invited him to the bar a few more times. Liquored him up, till he cracked just a little. He said 'I have big opportunities coming up moving shit, and I know people who can make people disappear or make people up. It's the who you know in politics. You want to play in politics?', he asked me. I cut off my ties with him later, saying I wasn't interested in dating, and he took off." I take a deep breath to gather my thoughts, then continue.

"And bring it to the last month when the Battle Born MC walked in asking for an appointment. He became more curious. I never planned to use him as a lawyer again after the shady shit he started asking after the sale of The Black Rose. He recently called me up, thinking he had an in, asking me more questions about Blade's crew. I sent him some fake documents to test him, some papers for a month to month lease. My name was written in, Blade's name was not. Well, not his real name anyway," I say holding back a smile.

"What name did you use, Vegas?" Stryker questions interested.

"Richard Dickerson?" I shrug and tell them hesitantly. Out of the corner of my eye, I see by Blade's killer expression, that he doesn't find it as funny as me.

"Dick Dickerson, Vegas? Really?" he shakes his head.

Tank finds it funny and so does everyone else, since they're all laughing. "You were a dick those first few days! Anyway, I take Johnny the fake rental agreement. I tell him that my ex-husband has been poking around my bar lately, too. That I was scared he would take alimony from me. What should I do!

"A couple of days later, he offers me a side deal and brings me the rental agreement with revisions added to it. The side deal is, a contact contingent that I get him Blade's partnership. I needed to be his connection for a reference, and, in return, he would give me his contact. This government contact he has can file a grievance where I can get a fake identity to protect me. They use a fake name to claim a hardship. My ex would never find me on any documentation of ownership," I finish explaining.

Blade's eyes have gone dark again, but contains himself and calmly asks, "How would he know I'd use you as a reference?"

"He didn't, he was willing to use me in any way he could. You see, Johnny said the contract he brought for the fake identity, if I signed it, it would protect me. What the contract also had was that I bequeathed my business to him in the event of my death. If I didn't follow through with you, he was going to kill me. Then he'd have had a win over you, but you wouldn't have known of it because of the fake name." I pause again, thinking back to that day.

"We ended up getting a different lawyer to draw up the sale for the building for Blade, and also for The Black Rose. I've already sold the majority of the business to Dana and Jenn. I'm just a teeny tiny shareholder on paper. They bought me out for a dollar each.

"Dana pays me a very generous salary for bartending, on a monthly basis. I'm just a regular employee with a 'tiny' cash monthly bonus. He doesn't know I sold the bar. I don't own the controlling portion of the property for him to take as he documented. I explained to Johnny that the ex took off and that I didn't need his contact anymore. His focus was always on you."

I shrug like it's no big deal, and it really isn't. I was going to sell the bar to the girls anyway. As for Johnny, James has been watching him.

Blade

I knew Vegas was badass, but I just never realized at how far she was willing to go to play. I feel mind fucked by that story. Really fucking pisses me off that she's playing in a game where I'm not even a hundred percent sure who the players are. I open my mouth to rip her ass open, but her old man beats me to it.

"*Mija*, you should call me when dirty fuckers are playing games like this. I'm proud as fuck of you. But just because it doesn't seem to you to affect club business, you don't tell me? We are *familia*, *comprendes*? If you weren't so fucking stubborn like me..." Fuego stops, taking a deep breath in. "For fuck's sake, *niña*, talk to your *familia*! *Sí*?" Fuego thunders, equally proud and pissed off at her.

The connections would have become clear had she just finished following through. My old man looks like he wants to congratulate her on a job well done. Spider, along with Tank and Axl couldn't be any fucking prouder of her. Snake just shakes his head and says, "And they gave me the road name Snake." He lifts his chin at her, giving her props.

Squeezing her thigh, I grab her attention. "Vegas, baby, we got to go over that fucked up story you just told. We have club business to discuss now. Take my truck back to the bar, get the keys from Solo. If you see Johnny, stay the fuck away. If you hear from him, you don't do shit we all don't agree on. Right?" Piercing my eyes into hers, I give her my most menacing stare because she needs to feel how serious this is.

"Yeah, love, I hear you loud and clear. No fun and games, don't play around with thieves today, got it." Vegas stands up straight, mock saluting the table and hitting her boots together.

Tank salutes her back like a general, trying to hold his laugh back. "At ease, soldier."

Bending over, she kisses my lips, "See ya on the flip side, big guy."

Snake groans in disgust as I slap her ass on her way out and shut the door. Jumping out of his seat, Axl exclaims, "What the fuck, dude! Just what... the.... fuck," and starts pacing back and forth.

The room quiets down, the officers of the MC contemplating what we have learned and what we need to do. Coming to a conclusion, I voice my thoughts. "First off, Johnny needs to die. When, we all are going to have to agree on. I think we need to go back and ask Johnny for help. We need his contact if we are going to figure out who owns that warehouse in Sac Town." I rub my face with my hands.

"Blade," my old man speaks up. "Who is going to go ask Johnny for his contact? I don't think any of us would be a smart move."

"I agree, that's why we have to let Hawk stick around, and we have to get Vegas do it."

Fuego's fists hit the table, leaning toward me. "My daughter is not your puppet to get this resolved, *pendejo.* She will not get hurt. She's not fucking getting any more involved." Fuego is on fire, and he's right, Vegas shouldn't be involved.

"Fuego, I hear you, man, but there ain't no way we can snoop around those offices in time to get ahead with the information we need. Could we do it if we had time, yeah, but we are putting everyone at more risk the longer we wait. Johnny could put a hit out on Vegas as soon as he figures out who her family is and the bullshit she did." Fuego's face looks resigned as he sits back and stares at me.

"You trust James and Hawk?" I look between Snake and Fuego.

"James, he's had her back since she's been up here," Snake starts. "Hawk, he'll look after Vegas, too, either one has to be with her at all times. No prospects riding around with her, and, for now, you either. She has to appear to be alone and like she needs the help."

Stryker sits back and releases a long breath, worried. "You claimed Vegas yesterday, the whole club knows and saw you two together. That means, when Skid wakes up, those little club bitches, they'll tell him everything, eventually. We have to move him, for now."

"Tank, I need you to put a crew together, go out on a long run. Take Skid with you, tell the men he is 'the run' and keep me in the loop. Take him down south in California, to our sister chapter."

Taking out my smokes, I light one up, fear snaking up my spine along with anger as I exhale. Even though Vegas and I are in a solid place, I'm dreading not being able to be with her openly till this whole freaking mess is taken care of.

"Axl, pull Church together after Tank leaves, so we can update the men, and get me all the info you can on Skid's phone by then." Frustration booms in my chest, the need for space to calm down is tearing through my skin.

Nodding at the men, I stand and push my chair back so hard that I hear it banging against the wall behind me. Walking through my clubhouse to the front lot where all our bikes are, I stand and let the mid-morning sun warm my face. The door opens and shuts behind me. Not long after, I feel a hand grasping my shoulder and then letting go. He takes the pack from my hand and lights up as well.

"Son, we'll figure this shit all out." Stryker blows out his smoke next to me. "Vegas will be safe, she's strong and a perfect match for you. In these moments, you'll have each other to lean on. Being the Prez isn't easy and can be fucking lonely. Go to her when you need to let all this go, then come back fighting stronger. This is just the beginning, let her be strong for you when you need it."

Standing side by side, I can't help but feel proud of my old man. This life would be so much harder if I didn't have him in it. Soon, others start coming out, revving their bikes, getting ready for the long ride home. Finishing our smokes and stomping them out, we say our goodbyes, and they all go, leaving me and Axl outside.

"Bro, we've got to take a quick ride to talk to Vegas and the girls. Grab your gear, let's ride over to the bar." Waiting for Axl to get ready, I text Vegas.

Me: I'm on my way to chat with you and your crew. Can you have them all meet us there in ten minutes?

Alessia: Sure thing.

Walking in through the back office of the bar, Tugg jumps up from under Vegas' desk, running and sitting at my feet, waiting for me to pet him. Vegas' beautiful smile has my attention while I crouch down to reach Tugg.

"Hey, Tugg, what are you working on, Vegas?" I ask just as Axl walks past us and into the bar area to get the others to join us in the office.

"Some invoices to pay, nothing big, but later I have some good news. You okay, baby?" She tilts her head up to look at me. Giving Tugg one more pat on the head, I walk over to her, pulling her up and out of the chair, then sitting and placing her back down in my lap. I hold her to me and smell the skin on her neck, pecking my way up to her ear. "Everything will be fine... God, you smell good."

Axl walks in with a grumbling Dana. "I really hope it's important that I hauled my ass here so early, Vegas! Axl, quit laughing, damn it!" All that is being followed by a sleepy Jenn, and, finally, James. Jenn and Dana take the two open chairs opposite Vegas and me.

"You guys all know of Johnny..."

"Yeah...?" Dana and Jenn say in unison, interrupting me and looking too interested.

"This isn't a girl chat, so please shut it." My patience's worn thin and I bark at the girls, which earns me a scowl from both James and Axl. Dana's head snaps back offended and Jenn rolls her eyes at me.

Vegas rubs my back. "Blade, they aren't the boys, and they don't know how stressed out you are." She helps calm me down and telling them what I can't. "Girls, he has some important stuff to say, let's hear him out, okay?" Dana tips her head at me, signaling to move along.

Closing my eyes and letting Vegas' hands calm my nerves, I continue. "Johnny's got his hands into some crooked shit. He wants to get into my business using Vegas if he can."

I continue telling them what they need to know, what Vegas told us at the club this morning. "We can't talk about Vegas and me to anyone. As far as you guys know of us, it's just all business, no attachments.

Dana, you and Axl need to put your flirting on ice too for now."

Dana gives me a wicked glare, like I accused her of flirting. Fuck, she needs a wakeup call. "We can't have any real personal anything, Dana. He may read more into it than what we want it to be for now, okay? Until we get a handle on Johnny, life is to appear as all business to others looking in. I need James to stay around Vegas twenty-four seven, and, because part of Vegas' scheme involved Hawk, he's sticking around too, but only call him by Derrick."

Vegas tenses, "What exactly does that mean, Blade? Spill it, there is more, isn't there?"

"That means he's going to appear to be harassing you when I set up Johnny to stop by, and you are going to lure Johnny in with your helplessness and make that deal he offered you before so we can figure out who's working for him. That's all I'm telling you for now. You two," I look back at an open mouthed Dana and Jenn, "Are going to act like you work for Vegas still, and do not say anything to anyone about anything. And if it is a MUST to respond, be as vague and blond as possible. Hand your phones over to Axl, he's putting his number in there. Call him with any problems or questions. I do mean *anything* that looks strange or makes you uncomfortable."

A stunned Jenn and Dana look at Vegas and then to each other. Vegas stands and grins mischievously. "We have some prep work, girls. We need to sync our conversation in front of Johnny when he comes. Are you bringing him to the bar, Blade?" Excitement lights up her eyes.

"Yeah, I'll get Johnny here to walk in, so he can see the show, you just got to sell it, Vegas."

"Oh, this will be fun!" She claps her hands in excitement. "When is this going down?" Vegas is practically dancing from foot to foot.

"Don't worry, she's a complete maniac when it comes to a bet, or, in this case, running a scam. She's an adrenaline junkie," Jenn states, as if this is normal behavior for a chick. I guess, in Vegas' case, it is.

Vegas claps her hands again, "Alright, boys, you got to get out of here." She throws a thumb over her shoulder. "Bring me my sucker to bait. Me and the girls are going to prep."

CHAPTER 20

Vegas

Dana tilts her body closer so I can hear her whispering, while she pulls the handle to the margarita machine back. "Did Spider really use that crazy ass chick's idea to catch her boyfriend cheating, to get Johnny here tonight? How?"

Leaning back over the bar, she hands the cute twenty-something girl her margarita. She smiles and takes the customer's money to the cash register. Dollar Margarita Night brings in the younger crowd from the local college. Battle Born Tattoos has been tattooing butterflies all night. I spot a new one on the shoulder blade of the girl who just walked away.

Laughing, I answer, "Because when you have the same iCloud ID, you receive all of that person's texts sent to your device. Tank has been telling Skid info to get back to Johnny. So, Tank is manipulating their conversations, being able to receive everything. He told Johnny that Derrick has been harassing me again. Since Skid has been on the road doing what the club or

Johnny have asked him to, he doesn't really know what's been going on, or who Derrick is. Blade has had a tail on Johnny. He'll alert us when he's on his way here. Johnny wants the Battle Born's territory, he'll come."

"Giving my number to Axl was the worst idea ever. He's been texting me non-stop all day for the past two days. I haven't been able to sleep with all this stress. The first time he texted me, I didn't even know who it was," Dana holds up her phone, reading the sender's name as Roger Rabbit to Jessica Rabbit. I laugh at how cute Axl really is with her.

"The man is certifiable, Vegas, he thinks we need code names for our 'Framing Johnny Carmine' operation", she shakes her head at me. "I slipped and said, *roger that*, agreeing with him and he hasn't dropped it since. It's only made it worse. He sent me a link to trucker terms, Vegas! Who has time for that! He was talking about installing a CB radio in my car.... OMG! I just figured out where the rabbit idea came from! I call my car Rabbit, she's my little rabbit, damn it!"

Right then, her phone pings with a new alert from none other than Roger Rabbit himself.

Roger Rabbit: The Bear is on the MOVE, COPY???

Jessica Rabbit: Roger that

"Who is the Bear and why is he on the move?" I ask since Axl didn't send the rest of us the trucker code.

"Bear means law enforcement, that means Johnny is on his way here." Dana looks a little worried how this all will play out. Right on cue, my phone beeps with a message.

Blade: Johnny is headed your way. Be ready, I have eyes on you.

Me: I got this, Blade xo

Jenn puts her music on a playlist. She and James must have received the same message since they both come over to the bar, Jenn grabbing a soda with ice. James heads into the kitchen area behind the bar where the crowd won't be in his way if he needs to get to me.

Derrick heads in from the back of the office where he's been waiting all night, a crazed look in his eyes. I would believe he's a psycho by the way he walks straight over to me forcing me to step back against the shelves lined with alcohol. Towering over my short height, he places each hand on either side of me, trapping me on the spot.

His threatening appearance sends a hush falling over the partiers. "Vegas, I always thought you to be a smart girl," he growls loudly. "Not a stupid one. I know you make some money cashing in on selling booze. We are still married, so what's yours is mine."

Derrick winks at me before grabbing my arm and dragging me closer to his face. I can see Johnny standing back in the crowd, closer to the door. Pulling my face all the way to the right, I clinch my eyes shut. Derrick's breath breezes across my skin. "Don't," he jerks me hard at him, "Make me mad, Vegas."

My sweet little Tugger starts growling at Derrick, warning him to back off. "Derrick, leave Vegas a..lone!" Dana sounds panicked and upset, but I think it's all nerves because she chokes on the end.

She steps forward to push Derrick back, when, to my surprise, he flies back. Johnny was the one to grab Derrick, slamming him against the bottles on the shelf that go crashing down, several of them breaking.

"It's time you left, asshole, and don't come back looking for a handout." Johnny shoves Derrick forward toward the front door. Almost tripping on his feet from the forceful shove, Derrick storms out.

Taking the next step of the plan, I purposely bite my lower lip with a deep inhale and run out the back door. I have to get Johnny alone to get the information we need. I'm counting on him following me.

It's cold as hell out here, which helps me to shake for real. Leaving my back to the door, I wrap my arms tightly around me. I hear the door behind closing and I drop my head in mock shame.

Johnny's wraps his arm around my shoulders, causing me to shiver more from his touch than the cold. "Why didn't you come to me sooner, Vegas?" He pulls me in close to him, trying to warm me up.

I want to shove the douche bag off me but try to stop myself from moving. "I couldn't go back and ask you again, I'd turned you away already. I-I-I didn't think you would want to talk to me again. I was just so scared, Johnny, it's hard for me to trust again."

Johnny wraps his other arm around me. "Sweetie, I know it's hard being a scared woman, you should know a man is what you need to help you take care of this. This is not what you are capable of dealing with."

He tries to soothe me, but, instead, it makes me want to kill the bastard right here on the spot. "Sign the agreements I sent you and I'll take care of this for you. I even have a man off the radar who will take care of Derrick for you. You'll get used to coming to me for everything, and I'll do all the work. You'll see, we'll work all this out." Rubbing his hands up and down my back, it's all I can take not to puke on his shoes.

Stepping back out of his hold, I jump when he touches my face. "Don't flinch from me, sweetie, I'll show you how good having a good man behind you can be." God, that double entendre really has me gagging back a *fuck you* and *never gonna happen. Ever.*

"How does this work? How do you keep Derrick from taking money from me?" I ask softly, still looking down.

"I'll file a hardship with the court. Laurie files those for me, sweetie. All I need is for you to do what I say." Johnny runs both hands across my jaw, forcing me to tilt my head up to his. Oh shit. No, no, no.

Jenn slams the back door open, hollering, "Vegas, we need you in here ASAP! Big crowd just walked in." Thank God that distracted Johnny from moving any closer. His look skewers Jenn on the spot.

I walk away, praising Johnny, "Thank you so much for saving me. I will have James bring the papers to you first thing in the morning." Half heartily waving, I close the door, locking it behind me.

Jenn lets a shaky laugh out. "You owe me big for keeping you from locking lips with that sleazy dick, just gross. I wanted to puke just listening to the whole thing. Spider is sly, I watched the whole thing from my phone. It was really cool."

"I just hope this whole situation gets resolved soon because I will never let that guy ever touch me again. I was literally shaking from his touch." Just to prove my point, my body shivers in response. Noise at the door startles us with three hard bangs.

Jenn and I jump back before cracking it open, only for Blade to barge through and slam the door in Axl's face. He grabs me by my ass, and my legs wrap around his waist. I pull his face to mine and kiss him so hard. I've missed him so much, not seeing him for two days. Jenn laughs while locking my office door on her way out back to the bar.

Kissing down my throat to the tops of my breasts, he growls when he meets my off the shoulder sweater. "I don't like that he touched any part of you, this is all mine, Alessia," he says as he's nipping my skin with his teeth. "Never again."

Blade sits me on the desk and kisses my forehead, pulling me to him and hugging me tightly. "I'm coming home tonight, and I'm never leaving. I don't care what Axl says."

Humor laces my tone, "What do you mean, 'what Axl says'?" I pull back a little to look at his handsome face.

"I've been a grouchy fucker. Tonight I was at my fucking limit with those damn chicks, swear to you. I made the last three cry when I said I wouldn't tattoo another damn heart or fuckin' butterfly on another bitch tonight. Then Axl had his limit with me and the girls, and we shut down for the night. I'm going to paint a sign that says, 'No Shoes, No Shirt, No Problem. Just No Damn Butterflies or Pansies Will Be Tatted Here.'"

"My man is tired and grumpy," I say while giving him a soft kiss. "Let's take off. Dana and Jenn are going to close soon anyway." Getting off the desk, I grab my stuff.

I open the door and whistle for Tugger, who barrels forward and jumps into my arms. Laughing, I drop him to the floor and tell everyone goodnight.

"Were you worried, Tugg?" He whines and puts his paw on my leg. "It's okay, Tugg. Sorry I scared you, poor guy." I kiss the top of his head and he settles down.

The three of us walk out the back door, and I'm shocked to see my Tahoe parked right there. Blade's hands wrap around my waist. "We are going to your parents' house in Tahoe. Fuego said you had a key. Don't want you anywhere near here till we get all the information from Johnny." Kissing my forehead, he opens the door. Tugger jumps in, thinking it's for him.

"Sit in the back, Tugg!" I scold him, and he jumps back to the bench seat, landing on his blanket.

On the drive up there, I can't stop worrying. It just feels like we are missing something.

CHAPTER 21

Blade

The day after, Alessia and I eat lunch in a small café up in this hipster little part of town. Not my crowd of people but I ain't gonna complain. She seems to fit in well as she's able to start up a conversation with just about anyone. Our waitress, who has long dreads down her back, is telling her about a few hiking trails and a few stores she can stop in and pick up some shit.

I have no idea what they're talking about. My mind is distracted because I haven't heard any progress from the MC yet. Whatever she plans for the day, I'll just follow along.

Taking a drink of my coffee, I grunt when I feel Alessia's boot hitting my shin. Looking back up to her, I give her a 'what the fuck are you kicking me for, woman' look, when she starts bitching.

"Jesus, Blade! The girl was asking you a few questions and you completely ignored her. Did you even hear her? She just walked off when you wouldn't bother answering even after I called your name," she glares back at me.

"Chill, babe, I was just letting you get your girl talk in. Not my place to interject my thoughts, I wasn't listening. Doesn't matter anyway, you done with your bagel? What are we doing next?" I question, hoping that she will drop it.

Her face scrunches a little, which is really cute on her. It's like fighting with a puppy. The thought makes me laugh out loud. Alessia's face turns bright red and she grinds her teeth together. Throwing her napkin on her plate, she huffs out and storms out the door. Now I'm chasing her quick angry strides down the sidewalk.

Catching up to the little firecracker, I pull her off the sidewalk to me and give her a big, wet kiss, then kiss her nose. "Sorry, baby, I just zoned out. I didn't mean anything by it. Let it go, yeah?" What her problem is, I don't know, I'm freaking lost on that one. It just felt like the right thing to say. Look at me being a good boyfriend and shit.

I grab her hand. "So, where are we walking to, being the car is about three blocks back." She abruptly stops, turns and glares at me, pulling her shades over her eyes.

"Blade," she shakes her head, placing her hands on her hips, drawing my focus to those black leggings that are fucking hot. The greatest pants these girls started wearing.

"The waitress back there was telling me where I could pick up some jewelry that I know both our moms would love. We could buy them for their Christmas presents since we are up here, you nodded and said sure. I really can't even deal with you right now." She finishes and picks up her ringing phone from her pocket. "Hey, James." She listens for a moment. "You told Johnny I was out of town shopping with my mom? No, that's good... K... thanks, bye."

Putting her phone back into her pocket, she continues to the place she must have just been talking about. "Business taken care of, now let's go exploring." Or not. Slapping her fine, firm ass, I follow along.

We spend the day sightseeing. I can't even remember the last time I walked around a city. Alessia meets and talks to all kinds of different people. We finally find the jewelry store that is custom art of whatever these girls die over, which is really just overpriced shit to me.

Except, there's this one piece of jewelry that catches my eye.

Alessia is on the other side of the store, talking animatedly to the owner, I guess they know each other.

Silently signaling the sales guy over, I point to the ring. I hand him five hundred bucks out of my wallet and say quietly, "Hold that under the name William Johnson, I'll be in touch with the rest of the details."

Snatching the business card from the counter, I say his name, "Stan Smith," then tuck it into my wallet.

"Yes, sir," he stammers out. "I'll wait for your call." Stan takes the ring out of the case, moving quickly to the back of the store and never coming back out.

Alessia picks out two necklaces that I pay for, and a pair of earrings that I caught her ogling while I was paying. She was so excited that, as soon as we stepped out of the store, she took the silver hoops that had a hundred little diamonds wrapped around them out of the box, placing them in her ears, and thanked me with promises of dirty deeds.

It just makes me happy seeing her happy. Which is a strange feeling. New, but it's a good kind of new.

Sitting down on a bench with hot coffee cups in our hands, we watch the snowflakes fall. "Blade, if our families were so close, why didn't you ever come up here with your parents for a visit? There are so many parties or vacations I can remember your parents being at, but never did they bring you, why?"

I think back to what I can remember and what Stryker told me. "From what I know, your old man didn't want any boys around all you girls. Kept you girls a secret as best as he could. Not only from boys around your age or the club, but also to protect you from people that would use you to get to him. Since I'm about nine years older, I don't think time caught up with us till recently. I had a lot of work to take care of before I got to where I am. I think our timing is just about right. Had I known or met you a few years ago, I don't think it would have been the right time."

"Yeah, I don't think it would have been the right time either." Alessia snuggles in a little closer to my side. She lifts my arm and scoots in even closer to rest her head on my shoulder. "Our lives crossed right when we were least expecting it," she muses. "You were so arrogant. Hot, but arrogant. I wanted to punch you as much as I wanted to climb on top of you."

"Arrogant, huh? You were sexy as fuck with that attitude you were throwing my way. I wanted to smack your ass and ride you hard to shut you up. We were a time bomb, baby. Eventually, we were going to detonate."

Alessia's deep laugh reverberates through my chest, causing me to laugh along with her. She has a way of drawing me to her that no one else ever could. Even when I'm right next to her, I want more, it's never enough. More laughs, more love, just a whole lot more of it all.

"That was the best *worst* line ever!" Alessia kisses my neck. She is sending shivers down my spine from her cold lips. "Blade, I wanted to tell you about a business idea I had in mind. I'm taking the money I made off the sale of the building from you to build a brewery."

She stops, and her face alights with mischief. "You can invest as much as you want, be a silent partner, or an active one. We can see how it goes and employ a few members. I already got the business permits and contracting plans. I'm going to start remodeling the shop out back behind the bar soon. If any of the brothers can build, I'll let them build it. Take time to think about it. If you are interested, I'll have the contracts drawn up for you to look over."

"Alessia, that's a really big project, I'll have to run it by the club. We will see where it takes us?"

"It will be a challenging project. I'm really excited about it, but yeah, I'm not in a big rush. I want it to be right. Come on, big guy, let's grab some food and head home where it's warm."

Driving through the winding snowy roads and endless pine trees, we finally make it back to her parents' two-story vacation home. Building a fire in the fireplace in the living-room, we grab our food, then go to sit on the couch, eating and warming up in front of the fire.

That's how we spend the evening, wrapped up in each other, then again the next day, and the day after that.

Feeling rested with Alessia in my arms, I've been lying here watching the snow fall from the sky, waiting for her to wake. The last few days have been so relaxing. I could keep her here in peace forever. I understand why Fuego bought this home for his family.

Tugg gets up from his bed on the floor, excited to wake Alessia up. I glare at the little fucker and he tucks tail and takes off through the doggy door I installed yesterday. Fuego's probably going to be pissed, but that little cock blocker needed to start taking care of himself and going outside to piss alone.

My phone vibrates from the side table and I pick it up to answer Spider's call. "Yeah." Grabbing the white down comforter, I start turning to get out of the bed, not wanting to wake Alessia, but she rolls over and wraps her naked body around mine.

I hear her mumbling, "Don't move, I'm awake." So, I lie on my back as she settles into my side. It's not distracting at all to have her tits pressed into my ribs or the feel of her bare pussy on my leg. Nope, not distracting at all.

Spider continues, "I figured out why they were hauling on that timeline. Johnny has them using the trains to do most of their transport. From what I dug out from the text messages to the times and locations of the meetings, they were the exact same as when the trains were pulling through. What they were haulin' from the south, they were dropping off in Reno. That takes the train clear across the States. They are haulin' probably nationwide. They have a meet scheduled for tonight. Tank says they were almost back, a few hours out. We will stake out the meeting, let Skid head over there, keep eyes on him. After the meeting, I'm thinking we are going to take him up to the mine?" Spider questions.

"Yeah, after the meetup, Skid is taking a ride up to the mine. I'll be at the clubhouse in a few hours." Hanging up the phone, I place it back on the nightstand and run my cold hand back under the covers where I feel Alessia shivering. Running my fingers over her soft, smooth skin on her side, her goose bumps pop up. I reach her hip and push a little to get her to lay on her back.

Moving my body between her legs, I hold my weight just enough off her, but enough to hold her right where I want her, underneath me. "We have to leave soon, but not till I've had a little more of you."

Alessia brings her legs up, opening wide and wrapping them around my back. I drop my body lower into hers and start rocking my hardening dick through her slick pussy. Pumping a few slow strokes through her softness, I pull out and move back to sit before my beautiful woman. Roaming my eyes over her face and curves, I save this image right here forever.

I kneel forward and lick up her pussy, loving her smell and taste. I could spend my days worshipping her body. Sucking her lips into my mouth, I get back to work by licking her clit around in circles, knowing I won't be getting her off this way. I just want to build her up so high that she'll crash hard when she comes.

I go back and forth from licking to sucking her pussy, bringing her close, only to stop. She pants out her frustration and I know she's ready. Finally, I plunge my dick inside of her and slowly start rocking into her. "Mmm," she moans for me. "Your dick was made for me," she whispers with her eyes still closed.

"Yeah, baby, this soft pussy was made for me."

I suck on her bottom lip, then scrap it between my teeth. Pulling my cock back out, I scoot back to lick her pussy more till she's close. She breathes rapidly and moans out her pain from the torture. Slowly, my cock rocks back inside of her. In and out, in slow strokes. Sweet, sweet, slow torment.

"Blade, what are you trying to do to me? Kill me?" she asks with humor written across her face.

"Yeah, Alessia, with pleasure, you read my mind, baby." I grind my dick a little harder on the one spot that drives her crazy.

"Fuck, Blade, please don't stop, take me the rest of the way with you." She pleads with me, locking her legs around me, telling me play time is over. "I want your dick in my pussy when I come all over you. God, do not stop!" Her chest is heaving from breathing so hard.

Grabbing one hip, I grind firmer and heavier down on her pussy until I feel her tightening around me. Trying to hold back from blowing my load too early, I breathe in and out through my nose to release some of the tension. I keep my hard, unrelenting pace until I feel her let go, arching herself up and moaning for me.

Watching her face and feeling her pussy coming hard, pulsing around me, there is no doubt in my mind that this woman was made for me in every way.

CHAPTER 22

Blade

Pulling up next to my brothers on the mountain ridge, we stand back and wait for that piece of shit, Skid, to meet up with his contact. Tank looks exhausted from following and babysitting this asshole around this past week. He's leaning against the back of the rock crawler truck with his eyes shut. We hear a familiar rumble of a bike and see dirt kicking up across the old desert dirt road. Spider crawls over to the ridge with his spotting scope that catches pictures, and he watches.

Down by the old, beat up building, one of the cargo trucks we've been watching is parked outside. About thirty miles out of town, in the dead center of nowhere, no one would even care why this truck would be making a stop. The rest of us crawl forward, with Spider anxious to see what they pull out of the truck ready to be unloaded.

Skid parks his bike and heads toward the old building when the door swings open and an older man walks out. Around his fifties, he shakes hands with

Skid. Spider's phone crackles next to us just as the speakers pick up Skid's voice. I turn to stare at the phone and Spider beams at me. "I stuck a bug in his cut under a patch before we came out here."

Skid asks the man, "Haul went okay while I was out of town?"

"Didn't have any problems with the Battle Born down south since most have been camped out up in Reno, like you said. We have this load and another one next week. Johnny wants you to get control of the club, Skid. It's hard enough hauling this through Vegas and then Reno. Reno is our drop. Johnny's not happy Blade is up here."

Skid's voice drops low and menacing. "Watch what the fuck you say, motherfucker, you know shit of the club life, how it runs." Skid steps closer to the guy. "You guys and the old Prez fucked up when you let them take the club over, that's all on you. Help me get this shit loaded into the building before the train gets here, and I want my cut for the intel. The rest will have to work out in time."

The man slaps a rolled-up wad of cash in Skid's hand, then, walking over to the back of the truck, he flips the back open and young homeless looking boys and girls come walking out down the ramp.

My stomach drops looking over the kids that are maybe anywhere from twelve to eighteen-years-old as they hold their hands over their eyes to protect themselves from the beating sun. I feel like I need to puke at the sight of these terrified kids all huddled together.

Skid jumps up, picking up an eight-year-old girl and handing her over roughly to the man, like she's a piece of trash. I close my eyes and look down, unable to imagine these dicks who want to buy these kids. I know the sex trade, especially with homeless kids and the drugged-up parents who sell them off.

This is bad, so bad. Stryker forbids any sell of anything underage to come across our territory. We knew the old Prez was selling sex and drugs, but this is much worse than we thought. Selling kids on the black market is beyond fucked up.

Tank growls behind me, "We ain't letting those kids get on that train." He backs up to stand by the truck and calls in the backup who's waiting on our signal. "Come in ASAP, everyone alive, Skid and one other man and about six kids. Everyone alive." Hanging up his phone, he crawls back over to us.

The high pitch noise of dirt bikes sounding from the distance gets louder. The man and Skid look nervous, horridly pushing the kids into the building, except for one. Skid grabs a young boy by the hair and jerks him back against him as a shield just as four riders rush in from different directions. Two brothers come from the west and two from the east. One of them is laying down the bike hard on the side, kicking up a huge dirt cloud in Skid's direction.

The dust settles enough to see that he rolled to the other side of the truck. Popping back up onto his feet and tossing his helmet off, he pulls a gun from his boot. My boys make me proud, even though, at this range, it's hard to tell who's who with their dirt bike gear on and not their cuts.

Skid panics, pointing his gun in all directions, trying to find a way out. Pissed off, he screams at the guy who brought the truck in, "Where's your fucking gun! Dumb asshole!"

The man at least looks embarrassed enough to say, "In the truck." Rubbing a hand over his face, he looks resigned to the fact that he's not going anywhere. Skid aims his gun and shoots him through the skull. "Motherfucker," I growl.

Skid is feral, stepping back till his back is against the old building. His crazy laughter crackles through the speakers. "I'm not letting you take that pussy to torture and question. Any of you step even a hair closer to me, I'll pop this boy in the head right before I grab one of those bitches inside."

Solo, Pawn and Cowboy are off their bikes which are parked on the opposite side of the building to where Skid is standing. Solo and Pawn lift Cowboy by grabbing one boot each and heaving him up.

He pulls himself on top of the building and crawls over the rooftop. Solo sneaks around one side of the building, as does the other prospect, Pawn. Skid's crazy eyes catch Solo moving in. Ripping his gun away from the kid's head, he takes a shot at Solo as he ducks back behind the building. Cowboy jumps down on top of Skid, tackling him and the boy to the ground. Solo and Pawn run forward and pull the boy away, taking him into the building and securing all the kids.

Cowboy and Wrench fight with Skid, finally taking his gun and pinning him to the ground.

Not wasting anymore time watching from up here, we jump in the truck. We need to get out before the train makes it here. I tell Tank to stay back with Spider and watch for trucks and to see what happens after the train pulls in. Axl jumps in with me, racing down to clean this up.

By the time we are down there, Skid's bike is in the back of the hauler. Not having time to be gentle, we move the kids back into the hauler and slam the door down.

"Axl, drive this piece of shit truck to the old warehouse." Axl nods in understanding, jumps in and drives off. Gunner and Wrench throw a hog tied, pissed off Skid in the back of my truck and the dead body on top of him.

"No time, get the fuck out of here, meet up at the mine," I yell out with the nerves I feel crawling up my spine. The brothers jump back onto their dirt bikes, kicking up dirt and making tracks to meet me at the mine.

I'm peeling out right behind them. Not wanting to make the ride too comfortable for Skid either, I hit every washed out whole or bump in the road.

Ten minutes later, Tank sends a text saying the train pulled through after a quick stop. Driver didn't get out, and, seeing no truck in sight, geared the train back up and left. He and Spider are heading to the warehouse to help Axl.

What an absolute cluster fuck this all turned into. Speeding as fast as I can to get to the mine, I just have an uneasy feeling and need to get this shit all over with.

This is just the beginning of a long fight. Breadcrumbs we keep coming across that just lead us to more questions, answering only a few along the way.

CHAPTER 23

Vegas

Blade has not called all day, so I pace and try to keep busy. I know he doesn't need me calling or distracting him. All afternoon I've been working in the bar getting caught up after being gone for too many days. My thoughts have me plagued with anxiety that's seeping into my thoughts no matter what I do.

As the night wears on and drink after drink is being sold, all I can picture is the storm that's brewing. Praying we all make it alive and in one piece.

"Vegas, you okay?" James squeezes my shoulder from behind me.

"Yeah, you got five? We need to talk." He follows me and shuts the door behind him, taking a seat across the desk from me. "Shit's brewing, I can feel it. The game has changed. Not only with the MC, but with me. What I'm thinking is that Johnny should be all up in my business right now. You told him I would be out of town for a few days shopping. He didn't text me once. He's been tipped off. We are missing a pawn here in this game, James. I can feel it, someone's in the shadows and we are missing it. We need to find them to score this round."

Letting out all my fears, I can see that James feels it too.

"I agree, Vegas, this situation either intertwined you and the club with purpose or fate, possibly both. I haven't heard from Johnny either. I do have eyes on him, but nothing has been reported as abnormal. We both know that doesn't mean anything."

"I'm going to talk with Papa tonight and give him a heads up. Maybe he can send an MC brother over that Blade trusts and have info flowing back and forth under the radar. Other than all this drama, I'm worried about Jenn too. She hasn't said what's eating her up and she won't anytime soon, maybe not ever. We may have to pry it out of her one day, so just watch her?" That's another concern I have but feel guilty that I can't focus on right now.

James' face falls a little, a telling that he already sees or knows of what's going on. He cares for her, you can clearly see the love in his eyes. "I'm trying, I'm really trying to break through that stubborn woman, a piece at a time. I don't know that what I'm fighting for is even worth the pain it brings me." James breathes in a gulp of air and settles back into the chair. I'm not the only person fighting this life. Fighting for happiness.

"James, I wish I could take the pain for you, have answers for you, but know that whatever you need, I have your back. In life, there are no guarantees except for some pain and some happiness along the way. Karma, that ugly twisted bitch, owes us, we paid our dues. Keep fighting. She'll pay up, eventually."

I hope that James can feel he has a friend who cares. Without saying anything more, he leaves, getting back to watching the bar.

Dialing Papa's number from my cell, he picks up after the first ring. "*Hola, mija,* what are you doing? Aren't you working tonight after your little vacation?" He's teasing me as if he really thinks I didn't deserve a few days off.

I shake my head and smile. "*Si*, Papa, I'm still at work. Thank you for giving us a few days at the house in Tahoe."

"*Mija*, you're welcome, but don't thank me. That's our family house, you can use it when you want. Just text me when you're up there. Now, I know you have something on your mind, best get to it, baby girl. *Que pasa*?"

I almost want to cry hearing that Papa knows me so well, and the stress I'm carrying, he can feel it too. The one man I need, Blade, is out doing only God knows what, and this game is deadly.

Sucking back the tears, I bring forward the fighter in my soul that always wants to win. I start telling Papa all that's happened since he left with Momma and Snake, right up to when I just talked to James. Letting it all out, even my fears.

Papa is quiet. I can tell he's digesting all my words and the story I just vomited his way. Then he finally speaks. "I hear two voices at war in you right now. Let me be your Papa first. *Mija*, you got to love and have faith in your man even when you are falling apart in fears and uncertainty. Blade needs to focus on protecting his club and you. Give him your faith first, always. He needs this from you to be strong. After, when it's done, tell him all that's in your heart and let him focus on you. Let him build you back up. Your *madre*, me and Snake will hold you up till then. This is our family, our bond, we will never break it, *si*?"

Feeling that crack in my heart toughen up stronger, I'm ready to hear the rest.

"Alessia." Oh shit, he only says that when it's the Prez I'm speaking with. "For once, you called when you needed to, *gracias*. I think you could be right. You know well enough that I can't tell you anything within the club. I will contact Blade and send a man after we have Church." The line goes dead. Fuego went to work.

Taking a few minutes to gather myself and the thoughts running through my head, I start plotting my next play with Johnny and who he could possibly be working with. A startling bang at the back door has my hand at my chest, and I struggle breathing through the blood pumping in my ears. "Son of a ...", another loud bang.

"Open up, *Princesa*, your Papa sent me."

"*Tio* Cuervo?" Feeling excited, I open the door to the very straight and serious face of Cuervo.

"You know your Papa trusts Blade. Doesn't mean that you're not his baby still. He's had eyes on you even when you didn't know. He asked me to come in and check on you. Don't worry about Johnny. I'm keeping his ass busy. He hasn't had time to contact you even if he wanted to. Doesn't mean I don't think he has a snitch on his side. Keep your eyes open and your gun loaded and on you at all times."

He kisses my forehead and shuts the door, going back outside into the darkness. That's where Cuervo has always felt most at home. Cryptic and shady as hell, but I love all their crazy, every last brother in this MC.

We never fight alone even when we are our own worst enemy.

CHAPTER 24

Blade

"Motherfucker!" Skid screams into the air. His head pops up and he's howling at the ceiling. He's chained in the middle of this dark, dingy, old building at the mine. His body makes an X, with his arms and legs spread out. The chains are the only way he is staying upright.

We think this building used to be where they would process the gold, but now it's our torture chamber. Hooks are everywhere, along with chemicals, which I will find out what they are for later. I make a mental note to have the prospects do an inventory later this week.

Back to this dirty fucker. "Skid, I can only cut you so many times before you bleed out, and I know you are counting on it. So, I'm going to do what I've been holding out on. Solo, hand me the torch."

Solo tosses the small torch to me. I grab my lighter from my pocket with my other hand. I open the valve and a small hiss of propane leaks out. When I strike my lighter, Skid looks over to me, then the fucker passes out. Nope, not good enough. "This limp dick fucker isn't going to black out," I growl to no one in particular.

Searching through my bag, I find the syringe and small bottle with epinephrine written on it. Taking an almost lethal dose, I plunge the needle into the vein of his neck, purging his body with a wake-up juice cocktail. The next time he goes to sleep, it will be for good. I toss the needle into a metal bin nearby and grab the white sports tape. I tape his eyelids open and count to thirty. Sure as shit, right on schedule, his head snaps back up and he tries to scream. Oh, I taped his mouth shut too. For fun. Skid's eyes bug out, his face turning bright red, the veins in his neck pumping erratically to his accelerated heartbeat from the heart that probably wants to quit.

Smirking over to the boys, I point to him. "That shit looks painful, doesn't it? I bet his mind is all kinds of fucked up. Wants to die, but, at the same time, the drugs keep it all ticking along." I sigh, feeling inpatient that this isn't more fun than I thought it would be tonight.

"Skid, this isn't going to be getting any easier for you. *You* know and I know, you're not going to die today. You aren't going to give me everything I need so easily. We'll keep you here as long as it takes."

Getting back to the torch and lighter, I start all over again. Lighting the torch and stepping closer to Skid, I say, "You may not tell me today, but you will."

Searing the big cut on his left arm, his agonizing moans and groans fill the darkness. I step back and Solo puts out the fire with an extinguisher.

I follow the same process with the right leg. The smell of torched flesh hits our nostrils, and Pawn gags, then steps to the back for some relief from the stench, returning couple of minutes later.

"Solo, Pawn, you two keep him alive, give him a penicillin shot. Chain his right arm to the corner." Following out the orders, they move Skid as I asked them to. "No food, no water, no heat." With that, I leave Skid to have one of the longest nights of his life, if he makes it. He won't get much sleep either with his eyelids taped open.

Solo goes with me outside and I light a smoke, taking a long drag. "Prez, why didn't we question him?"

"He's not giving us anything today. He knows what happens out here. We have to do what he doesn't expect. Catch him off guard, in pain and sleep deprived. We'll have a better chance."

Taking another pull, we continue to stand in silence. It's late and damn cold out here compared to the Las Vegas winter.

"Grab Pawn, we need to head over to the warehouse."

Walking into the warehouse, I have this thought that some of these kids may have heard or seen something. If I can only convince them to talk. The space isn't as shitty as you would think. We bought it off some hipsters that tried to turn it into a trendy little hacker spot.

"Axl, where are all the kids?"

"Set them up in the large corner office, thought the smaller space would be better for them. Called Kat over here, the nurse who used to date Tank, to come help us out." Axl runs his hand through his hair, clearly agitated. "There are some very young kids in here, that just does not sit well at all with me. The little ones had no clue what they were taken for."

He lets out a sigh. "I hope Kat can help us find some places for them to go. What are we going to do with them? We can't just throw them back out on the street, and we can't have them go running to the cops either."

"I know, bro. First, we need to talk with the oldest, bring her out here." Axl looks wearingly at me as if he really thinks I'm going to hurt her.

The petite young girl steps out from the office and walks closely behind Axl, stopping there, glued to his side.

Moving myself over to a table with chairs, I ask the young girl, "Can you sit down with me? I have a few questions for you. We have a friend on the way to look at everyone. I promise I won't hurt any of you."

Axl turns himself sideways, and I see that the she is wringing her hands together. Giving her a moment to decide, I encourage her by pushing the chair out with my boot. Another minute passes and my patience's wearing thin along with it. Finally, Axl coaxes her forward by lightly touching her shoulder, and she moves, then gingerly sits in the chair in front of me.

"Can you tell me your name and how old you are?" I try to speak a little softer and quieter than I care to.

She breathes in deeply and shakes her head back and forth. "I–I'm not anybody, haven't been for a long time, but my mom, before she died, called me Tami. I'm seventeen, and I'm a runaway."

"Tami, where did you live, and how did you end up on that truck?"

She starts shaking her head again, not wanting to speak, and starts crying, then pulls her little trembling hands to her face and starts sobbing into them. "Don't put me back into foster care, please! I won't tell the cops or anyone that you took us from those men, just please don't turn me into foster care!" She's crying harder, unable to look at me or control her sobs.

I'm not the man for this shit. I don't care where this girl came from and I won't send her back. My blood pressure is shot, and I have no patience left to sweet talk my way through this, but I try again.

"Tami, you got a raw deal in life it sounds like. Let me help you out, get you off the streets and in safer places, but, first, I'm going to need you to pull your shit together. Answer some questions. Can you do that? Then, I'll find the right person to help you out. We never have to talk again."

Tami sits a little straighter at my frustration, seeming to trust the real version of me and not the sugar coated one. "What do you need?" she asks quietly, dropping her hands, hiccupping and raising her brown eyes at me.

"How did you end up on the truck? Tell me every detail of how and what happened," I let out a heavy a sigh as I finish my request.

"I steal food or money. Since I've been living on the streets since I was fifteen, it's how I've survived in New Mexico. There are lots of communities where groups of kids live together, watch out for each other. One girl I knew, close to my age, said she heard of a deal going down. If we could get in before the pick-up, we could make enough to start over.

We snuck in and waited for the Hispanic guys to leave, but they never left. Just drank so much tequila till they passed out. We grabbed the leather bag they had and ran out. Eventually, one of your men caught us. His patch said Bear, he found us not long after we took the bag. Said that he scored two dumb bitches and was going to sell us."

Tears start pouring down her cheeks, her voice growing quieter. "He raped Amanda, then put us in the backseat of his diesel truck. He took the bag with him in the front. Outside of Las Vegas, there was a stop where he got into a fight with another guy from your club that pulled him over. He called him Buck. There was what sounded like a gunshot. He then dragged the dead man in the back of his truck. I don't know what happened to him. Eventually, Amanda and I were separated when we were sold."

She's shaking from reliving her story, and I should feel bad, but all I feel is intense rage at hearing the confirmation of who really killed Buck.

Axl hangs his head in total defeat. Bear knew what he was doing that day in the meeting. He knew it was a matter of time before we confirmed it was him. He died way too quickly instead of facing Stryker, like he deserved. The old man is going to be so pissed when he hears this.

"Tami, what was in the bag?" I ask her, unable to look at her from the anger I know is seeping from my gaze.

"We didn't want to steal, but you have to understand, th-that we..."

"I don't give a fuck why you stole it. Hear what I'm asking you. What. Was. In. The. Bag." Unable to keep looking away, my deathly gaze hits her. I'm forcing her to see death in the eyes of the man that she needs to answer to.

"Raw, uncut diamonds." From her pocket, she pulls out what looks like a small dirty crystal, and she places it on the table between us. "You can have it back." She looks down at her hands again.

Picking up the stone, I look at it in my fingers, gazing at what must be worth more than this girl will ever make in a lifetime, and a smile tugs at my lips at what she just gave me.

"Funny thing is that this little rock is worth so much money, but also has cost so many lives. You know what will happen to you if you keep it?" She shakes her head no. "You can't sell it to a bunch of thieves, they will take it and kill you, costing you your life. This tiny rock is your death. Never play with thieves again." She nods in understanding

Bam! The backdoor swings open, hitting the wall and forcing all of us to point our guns, waiting. Only, it's not a threat walking through but Tank, with a very pissed off Kat over his shoulder. What the hell is that woman wearing?

"Tank! You freaking big assed asshole! Put me down! I said I would help!" Tank reaches up, laying down a hard smack right on her leather covered ass. Kat's long black hair flies through the air as her back arches from the blow.

"Easy, Kitty Kat, you're scaring the kids, and the boys are about to shoot your loud, mouthy ass. It's a nice ass, though, and I don't want them to shoot it, K-love." He rubs the spot he smacked, making Kat squirm more. Pulling her down the front of his body, he places Nurse Kat down on her... knee-high black leather boots? What the hell?

She shoves him away from her with both hands planted on his chest. Or at least she tries moving the beast, when Tank kisses his fingers and touches her nose. "Calm down, Kitty Kat, we can play later."

Grabbing her temples, she rubs circles and takes in deep breaths before dropping her hands and storming forward to stand in front of the table. She is definitely the dark to Tank's light in every way. The woman has many tattoos on her body, including on her hands, and deep brown, dark eyes.

"Hey, I'm Kat, you must be the President of these merry little misfit fuckers?" She sticks her hand out at me and I stand and shake it back.

"Blade, and yes, I'm the President," I say while forcing to keep down a grin. "You a nurse?" Scanning her very un-nurse like attire, I ask, "Can you check over these kids? Help us find them some safe place to go?"

"Yes and yes. Tank, haul in my bag and stuff in, k, hot stuff?" Kat holds her hand out for the young girl, then takes her in another office to look her over.

"Tank, as soon as she got the kids looked over and situated, we have Church. Make it in two hours for an update. Solo and Pawn can stay here and help Kat if she's not finished by then."

"I'll be there with an update." He moves outside to grab Kat her supplies, while Solo and Pawn follow to help.

"Cowboy, roll with me. Text Stryker, Ice and Fuego, conference call for Church in two hours." As I'm giving him his instructions, I text Vegas.

Me: Gonna be a late night, meet me at the clubhouse, bring Dana. If she leaves to grab a bag, James or security goes with. James stays with Jenn all night or she comes too.

Pulling out from the warehouse, my mind is running over tasks that I need to do before Church. Number one is finding Spider and getting an update on the owner of the warehouse in California where we followed the first truck.

CHAPTER 25

Vegas

A vibrating noise and flashing lights catch my attention by the cash register where mine and Dana's phones are kept. I take a twenty from the young guy in front of me and put it in the register, peeking at my phone while doing that and seeing a text from Blade. Anxious to get back and read it, I hand the kid his change.

He grasps my hand along with his change and pulls me farther across the counter. He's looking to be cute and flirty, but the position also pushes my girls in a better view. Little dick.

I pull my hand back and stand upright as I stare at the obnoxious little punk until he meets my eyes. He smiles a little puppy smile and winks at me. "Damn, woman, you are fine."

Rolling my eyes at him, I throw back, "Whoever you are, you obviously don't know who you're messing with. Don't touch me again. Run along and play with the girls your own age, okay, cupcake?"

Dana chuckles a little farther down the bar, throws the kid a sympathy smile and hands him another shot.

"On the house," she says, then makes a motion with her head and eyes, signaling him to move along. The kid finally leaves, and she asks, "What's got you bent, Vegas?"

"Don't know yet, check your phone." We both reach for our phones. I read the text from Blade to meet up at the clubhouse. Which is fine, but shit is far from fine.

Dana groans, "Really? I have to camp out at the clubhouse at night now? We haven't been in lockdown since we lived in California. This is all your fault, you know, Ol' Lady." She pokes her finger into my chest.

"It was bound to happen, and you know it," I smack her hand away. "This does have to do with all the MC Chapters, better that we don't have to go all the way to Cali. At least here, we get to work and have a life, so quit the bitchin'. What's up anyway? Are you upset that Axl will be there?" I'm curious as to why *she's* so bent now.

"Ugh, Axl said I'm staying in his room, and not to worry because he already grabbed my sheets and pillows and 'girly shit', to come straight there after work. I don't want my shit in his room there! Now I need to buy all new stuff to take home, the moron! How the hell did he get into my house anyway?" She questions me with a pointed glare.

"Well, Blade took my keys to get a set of copies, so I'm guessing Axl got a copy from my copy? I don't think Axl is too worried about your boundaries. *You* are his boundary, you hear what I'm sayin'?" I'm trying hard not to laugh at her, but he's too damn cute not to like him for her.

"We haven't gone on one date, Vegas, we haven't done anything! How can he see me as his? Makes no damn sense to me, how can he even like me?"

"Same way you like him but won't admit it yet. You connect, you can spend all the time you like getting to know him and date. Over the last few years, have you found anyone who can piss you off like he can? Or make you daydream about him like he can?" I know she won't answer, so leaving it at that, I walk over to Jenn.

"Yo, bitch, you got a sleepover with James till this shit blows over with the club."

"Are you freaking kidding me? For fuck's sake, can't wait for you all to get these assholes dealt with."

"I hear you, girl, you and me both." Jenn flips a switch and a new song plays. Sitting in the chair behind the booth, I text Blade back.

Blade

Church is about to start when, finally, I get a text back.

Alessia: Okay, big guy, we are all set. Dana is coming with me and James will stay with Jenn. See you in a bit. Almost closing time.

Relaxing a little bit that everything is okay with Vegas, I pocket my phone. The speaker on the table dings with a call-in notification.

Spider connects the callers through. "Hey, we have the conference call up, who's with us?"

The speakers crackle a little.

"Ice and crew."

"Stryker and crew."

"Fuego and crew."

"Alright, we've got some updates you all need to hear. We followed Skid to the drop off. He had about six kids they were selling off. From what we've dug up, that's what the old crew were dealing with on the side here. Getting a cut from also transporting raw diamonds for Johnny. How far up the food chain that goes, I don't know yet. They were working together to transport the kids and the diamonds. All but two kids went into Group Housing Care back to California. Luckily, they were just snagged and thought they had been kidnapped. Their parents sold them off to Skid for non-payment on drugs they were supposed to sell or were using. Fuego, can you send a few men to take care of the parents?"

"*Sí*, it will be done by tomorrow." The venom is clear in his tone.

"Thanks. The other two older kids, we've been holding onto. They saw us kill the driver paid by Johnny. The girl is the one who knew about the diamonds. I'm not big on killing kids, wanted to speak with you all before we did anything. That's not all. The girl said Bear was the one who caught her and a friend running away with the diamonds. He took the girls, then, outside of Las Vegas, he was in a fight with Buck, shot him and put his body and bike in the back of the truck."

"Where the fuck is Bear?" my old man growls.

Taking a deep breath, I explain what happened just months ago, when Axl killed him. "But we have Skid waiting for you. If you want him, his life is yours. A little cut up, but one piece still."

"Fucking save that cunt for me! I'm riding up tomorrow, he will die by my bare hands." The phone sounds like it's cracking, but it's a wall and a fist, or a chair and a wall. Buck was one of the oldest members in the club. Left behind an Ol' Lady and his kids.

"He's yours, Stryker. Spider is going to give you all an update on the warehouse in Cali where we found the first hauler." Sitting back, I let Spider take the floor.

"We figured out with Vegas' help that Johnny can hide assets under a fake name. We hacked into the

Court data bases to figure out who owned property. The little dead lady who owns the warehouse of whore haulers is Tanya."

"What the fuck are you saying?" Stryker is lost by his anger and he wants every word verified.

"*The* Tanya from the Las Vegas chapter, she was feeding Johnny information and the club here in Reno. She was fucking for intel. When Blade came up here, she made a play for a spot in his bed again. When that didn't work, she ghosted, and we haven't found her since. Haven't spotted her with Johnny, but I can only confirm right now that they still are calling. I've got men out looking for the skanky bitch."

Ice, the Elko Prez, breaks his silence. "If she comes up, hold her. I have business to finish with that cunt. She came looking for a place when you all cut her loose. She paid for her stay by taking whatever any member wanted to give her. I had a few drops going missing. I want her to confess she ratted my men out."

The room is deadly silent. My heart is pounding in my chest because I know what Ice is asking for. It won't be a quick and easy confession. What do I care though? The bitch came out to play. She better be able to back up her choices.

"A few of my men and myself are on our way tomorrow until the bitch is found," Ice finishes, sounding as cold and emotionless as his road name.

"Aye, when she's found, she's yours, belongs to you and your crew," I slam the gavel down.

Church is out.

CHAPTER 26

Vegas

I see Jenn lost in her zone as I'm watching her bounce from foot to foot, enjoying the rhythm of the beat and the song. Feeling left out, I jump in on her solo dance. She's playing *Island in The Sun* by Weezer.

I feel myself getting swept away in the memories of our younger, more carefree days. Shoulder to shoulder, Jenn and I laugh and smile like the kids we used to be. James joins in, and we're making a little trio of fun. We try to signal Dana over to us, but she laughs and shakes her head no. That doesn't last long before Jenn and I tackle her out from behind the bar. James, the sweetie that he is, gets the other security guard, Nathan, behind the bar.

We continue our horrible dance moves that we believed we mastered through the nineties, and belt out lyrics we know by heart. The songs never change. And we haven't changed either, never will. We'll always be the young girls at heart that have grown into bruised women who are fighting for their happiness.

Even though we've been on the same road together, we've each had our highs and lows. Jenn can be fierce and guarded and can communicate best through songs. She's giving us this moment, a slice of time that won't be lost in this world of chaos and pain.

Hips bump, arms up in the air, the dance floor is opening up space for us. We are a force of strength and the bar patrons can feel our energy. Jenn, the girl can sing, pretends she has a mic and points at us while getting lost in her role as the lead singer. For a rare moment, we can see the real, unguarded Jenn. Her beautiful strength shines bright.

Just like old times, Dana and I become her backup dancers and singers, allowing her center stage. We hit our practiced sweet dance moves with a little kid and play, and finish with a bang of the old twerk, always a crowd pleaser. The bar erupts into a howl of appreciation and whistles. High-fives and hugs are passed around.

The best part of owning your own bar? You can do whatever you want, and with your sisters by your side.

All too soon, the bar closes, tables are wiped down, chairs are placed on tabletops, money tallied from the cash register. Handing James a beer, I give him a wink. "You and Jenn have a sleepover tonight?" I tease him. "You pack Trojans or a sleeping bag?"

James shoots me a glare. "Funny, Vegas. You knocked up yet, Ol' Lady, going to pop some babies out for that man, huh?" I shudder at his words.

"That's just mean, James! God, even though someday that will happen, that's the scariest thought in the world right now. I don't even want to know how that actually works or the aftermath." I shiver again, imagining the worst. "Asshole!" I look over at the girls. "Jenn, you and Dana ready?"

Standing up, I hear a, "Yep" from Dana and a, "Fuck, yeah," from Jenn which makes me look over my shoulder at James. He shakes his head, "Not like that and you know it."

"Maybe you should take a play from Blade and Axl and claim that woman?"

"She isn't ready yet. You know, since Blade, you've gotten rather nosy," James scolds.

"Maybe it's time we all lay the past to rest and move forward, and being around Blade made me realize that."

"I hear you, but, Vegas, some of us are still living in it." James looks over to Jenn who's throwing her purse over her shoulder, then strides our way with Dana.

Locking up the door to the office, Jenn walks out with James, both heading toward his truck. I give a silent prayer to the stars above to make love happen for them.

The bar area is packed at the clubhouse even though it's three in the morning. Smells of weed and cigarettes filter through the air. My eyes scan the crowd of brothers playing pool. On the opposite side of the bar, guys watch an orgy of whores touching, grinding and licking each other.

Seems like a few of the guys are missing. Must be that Blade and the top men from his crew are still in a meeting. I look away from the show and see that Pawn is behind the bar, tending.

"Yo, Pawn, throw me a vodka tonic?" I smile at him, then hand him my purse to put behind the bar for now. Dana sits at my right, handing him her purse, too. Looking to my left, I spot an exotic creature. The bitch is captivating. She's going to be my friend, just doesn't know it yet. Anyone this badass has to be.

I tilt my chin at her, then point to myself and Dana. "Vegas, this is Dana, you?"

"Kat," she hesitates, looking a little unsure of where I could go next with this exchange.

Pawn settles the score for her. "Vegas is Blade's Ol' Lady and Dana belongs to Axl."

"I don't belong to Axl." Dana's eyes are scrunched together, annoyed he claimed her to him.

"Sure you want to say that out loud where these club whores and their crew can hear you?" Kat asks, questioning her. "Way I see it, if you're not claimed, good for you, but you also invite those whores to make passes at Axl, or his brothers to do the same to you.

Just saying, either way, be sure." Kat pulls her drink to her red lips, her dark brown eyes assessing Dana's face.

I like her a lot, shoots it right at you, no bullshit. I shoot it back at her, "Who's claimed to claim you?"

Kat's lips pick up on one side, "Ah, wouldn't you like to know?" She puts her glass back onto the bar top.

Pawn puts us out of our misery again. "Tank's lady." Kat glares at the little shit for ruining her game.

Dana laughs, "That big pain in the ass is after you, huh? No wonder you could read my face. Misery loves company. Move over here, we need to join forces against those two."

Dana is usually more centered, but her nerves are shot, and I know it for sure when she orders lemon drop shots. Shit, misery does love company.

"Shit-faced for three coming up!" Pawn says, not as excited about this as we are. He makes a pitcher of them, sliding three shot glasses our way, along with the pitcher.

Dana holds her glass up to us, "Here's to the love we thought we had, to the love we want, and to the booze to drown out the empty space in between." The three of us clink glasses and down the shots. They are damn good. And deadly.

An hour or so passes and so does the pitcher. Vodka and lemon hum through our veins. Everything is a whole lot more interesting and fun.

Kat grabs from Pawn's hand the joint that he rolled for her. He states with pride, "Straight cut, primo green, not laced, you ladies enjoy." He smiles like a proud poppa.

Kat pulls it to her lips and, with a very nineteen fifties look, leans across the bar to Pawn. He lights it and winks at her while she pulls a deep breath in, then passes the joint to me. When in Oz, or was it Rome? Well, whatever the fuck it was, I do the same. Pulling in as much weed into my lungs as I can, I then pass it to Dana. She's never done this before, maybe I'm a bad friend, can't say I care in the moment, because, hello. Dana takes it from me, looks it over, and all our eyes are on her.

A long thick cloud of smoke released from my lungs hypnotizing me. Kat's already let hers out, and the bar is clouding over. I swear my buzz almost gets busted when Dana takes a small drag. Shocking me to my core. She passes it to Pawn, who drags, passes and blows.

On my turn, I drag and my seat spins around. Blade's face has the look of a predator in his eyes. Before I can blow out, he fuses his lips to mine and shotguns off my hit. My gaze is transfixed on his powerful eyes. He doesn't let it go.

Dana takes the joint from me. Pawn passes a new one that he just lit to Blade. Blade exhales the drag he took from me. Taking a new drag, he pulls my face to his. This time, *I* shotgun from his mouth, sucking in his hit into my lungs. He passes the joint to Tank who's protectively standing next to Kat.

Letting my drag go into Blades face, he grins. The universal sign of 'let's go fuck'. Leaning over me, he kisses my mouth, dragging his strong lips down my jaw, pulling my hair over my shoulder, kissing and sucking down my neck to my ear.

"My girl's been bad, smokin' and drinkin'. What was the lemon, Vegas, that I taste on your lips? I love it." His nose runs up my neck again, then grabs a lime wedge off the bar, and signals Pawn who hands him a tequila shot.

He runs the lime up my neck, placing the wedge between my lips. He shakes some salt on my neck, shoots his tequila, licks up my neck, causing me to shiver, and bites the lime from between my lips, then tosses it on the bar. Lime and tequila explode on my taste buds.

In my haze, Blade pulls me up from my chair and seals our lips together, tasting the lime and alcohol from each other. Fuck, that was hot, all of it. I thought between the shots and bud, I was waisted, but Blade intoxicates my soul with his.

His hands run down my ass, squeezing me hard and grinding his dick into me. "Missed you, baby, have a good day at work?" he asks me in a raspy voice. He sits down in my seat, picking me up and sitting me in his lap.

Dana starts clapping while talking to Kat. "Did you see that? That right there," she points between Blade and I, "That is how you greet your woman, right there." Surprised, Axl lets his drag out, choking and coughing at her words, confessing she wants passion without her realizing what she just did.

"Princess, I have all your needs right here, but it isn't happening tonight. The first time I take your lips, I will take your body. Just be warned, if you kiss me, you're mine. I would rather take you sober, but I'll take you anyway I can. You getting drunk to keep me from you and my bed won't work. You're sleeping with me." Dana stares at him and they stay locked in a silent war, although, I can see a little less fight in her eyes.

"Fuck, Blade, he just killed it with that one, that even made me feel a little shaken up." I hope Axl works out for her.

"You dickheads are really putting me in a tight spot here." Tank looks a little lost for once. Obviously, Kat is this man's kryptonite.

"Easy, lady killer, you don't have to confess your undying love for me. Keep it casual." Patting his chest, she turns back to face the bar.

I'm a whole lot out of my mind, but even *I* can see the desire in her eyes for a love like that. Damn, Tank, I'm going to dig right in the middle of this later.

Blade shakes his head like he can read my thoughts. Killjoy, I tell him back since we can communicate with facial expressions now.

The next morning, maybe noonish, Dana and I are in the kitchen cooking sausage, bacon, potatoes and eggs. I'm hung over as hell, but also hungry. That's odd, but considering what we did last night...

My eyes glaze over remembering...

Blade pulled me into the room, turning the music on his small speaker. Our bodies were so hot for each other's touch. I slowly took my clothes off for him. Stripping my body bare, I danced for him in this small space. I felt his possessive eyes tracing the lines all over my body. The body that he owned, every inch of me.

I crawled over to him and kneeled on the floor to remove his boots and socks. Blade lifted his ass up to pull his boxers and pants down to his knees. My hands removed them the rest of the way for him as he grabbed his shirt to lift it over his head. I saw his arm muscles jumping at the movement.

"Touch yourself, show me your hot cunt. Touch my clit, get it hot for me." Blade stroked his cock, until it was steel. The sight had my chest expanding, panting breaths of my desire for him. Getting lost into the song on the speakers, I threw my head back, letting my hair touch my ass. I started massaging my tits, pulling on my nipples and twisting them for him.

"Now, Alessia! Touch my pussy, I want to see your wet cunt coat your fingers, baby."

Doing as he asked, I spread my pussy lips apart, and two fingers dipped inside, then moved to my clit with slow, hard strokes, then back inside, then back to my clit a few more times.

"Stop."

My eyes found his just as he was reaching for my head, pulling me toward his dick. "Suck me, baby, suck me hard. Don't stop touching your pretty little pussy, make us come, baby." And I did it until we both came.

Blade then lifted me up to sit facing him in his lap and started playing with my wet cunt. I felt him getting harder for me again. Laying me on my back on his bed, he licked and sucked my pussy until I came again, then licked me clean. He slowly lifted himself up and over me, then slid inside in one smooth thrust.

We loved and caressed our sweaty bodies until the sun came up...

"Is this bitch still high?" I snap out of it when I hear a sarcastic Kat ask Dana about me as she's drinking her black coffee. She analyzes me like a puzzle that she needs to solve.

Dana answers, "Nope, I think she's hungover and still high on Blade though. I asked her how the rest of her night was, and she got this faraway look in her eyes. She was daydreaming, I didn't want to shake her out of it."

"Must've been one hell of a fuck then," Kat reasons with Dana.

Turning to them, I respond, "Oh, it was. I think Blade knows G-Easy turns me on. He played *Lady Killer*, song gets me so hot. It was like we were in our own porn. The world a faraway place. Clothes came off, touching ourselves, then each other. Fucking till the sun came up. Every orgasm he owns. Never felt anything so strong. His intensity wraps around my thoughts and heart, and I bow to whatever that man gives me."

I notice Dana making faces. "Dana, what is that face for?" Why can't she appreciate this story? Annoyed at her facial expressions, I stop talking.

"You kind of got lost in your lovers' monologue to realize who's standing behind you." The tart little bitch looks pleased that I was caught.

"Oh!" Turning around, I see that, behind me, at the door, Blade, Axl and Tank are all smiling ear to ear.

"Hey, you guys hungry?" I ask, hoping they'll all drop it. Reaching for a cup for Blade, I fill it with coffee, and hand it to him as he bends down and gives me a big kiss.

"Not as hungry as you are. Word of advice, though," Tank says chewing on a piece of bacon. "Keep that story to yourself, because, if I was a bitch, I would try to jump your man's bones the first chance I got."

"Whatever, Tank," I roll my eyes at him. "The girls are heading out to the gym, then work. Kat, are you coming to work out with us?"

"No," Kat states. "I have to look for a job, I need a new start. I'm not going back to nursing." She is sitting in a chair, sipping on her coffee and wearing Tank's shirt. Looking at Dana, I see that she's also wearing Axl's shirt, and he looks happy about it. I'm the only one dressed in clothes, well, my workout clothes.

"You can work at the bar, I have another project I'm starting. You can cover my shifts. If you find something else, good, if not the job is yours," I shrug like it's not a biggie. At least now I don't have to find another person to run the bar. Win-win.

"Okay, let's eat, then we'll go." Just like that, Kat joined our circle.

"I'm coming today," Axl informs us.

Dana turns, "To do what? Watch us working out?"

"No, I'm going to watch *you* working out. And make sure you all don't get blazed to and from anywhere else." He gives Dana a pointed look. I don't know if he's mad about it because she was high or that she did it to keep him at arm's length last night.

Dana roll her eyes. "Doesn't matter, you're not my man, you can't stop me!"

"Doesn't matter? The next time your friends hand you pot, just say *no*! Better yet, I'll kick Pawn's ass for giving it to you. Did you hear that, Pawn!" Axl yells back at her. He follows her back out the door, still arguing with her.

Kat whistles low, "When those two finally get it on, it will be hot."

"That's what I keep saying, a slow burn into an inferno." We hit knuckles in agreement.

Kat, Dana and I take the Tahoe to the gym. Well, we were driven by our guard who is in the front seat talking on his phone. Axl, just like Blade, wouldn't allow me to drive my own car. He stole the keys and locked just the front door against my protests. Idiot.

Stretching out my tight muscles, I catch Jenn walk through the door of the gym, with James chatting with Axl as she walks over to our group.

"What the hell did you bitches do last night without me! You smell like weed and a hangover still. Look me in the eyes, Dana. Did they pop your blaze cherry and I wasn't there? I'm so freaking pissed I wasn't there. Who the fuck is this?" She looks over to Kat who raises a brow.

"Vegas and I popped your girl's cherry. She was so sweet too," Kat mocks her. "Oh fuck, Axl looks a little mad right now." She points her black long nail to Axl and James who walked up closer.

Jenn starts laughing, "I'm Jenn, you are sticking around because I can use you now that these two are getting all domesticated. And Axl is giving you some hateful looks. I can't wait for you guys to spill what happened last night."

"That's my cherry pie! You girls won't be popping anymore of her cherries, the rest are mine!" Axl sounds possessive, a little hurt even.

I feel a little bad, but not really, so I goad him on. "Axl, I've popped so many of her cherries over the years, she's been mine way before yours. I've tasted her Cherry Chapstick..."

"The fuck you have!" Axl growls back at me.

Dana walks over to Axl, keeping the rouse going, touching his arm. "We were in high school, wearing our white nighties, watching a movie. I said, 'I wonder what it was like to kiss a girl.' We turned and stared at each other..."

Axl does outright growl, picking Dana up, and her legs wrap around his waist. Pinning her to the wall, her hands are in his hair as he claims her lips and body. Fuck, they just went legit.

"Hang on, girl," I cheer her on. Hmm, he's got good technique.

"Can I start my class, or should we wait for them to finish?" Matt, our workout instructor and new friend, asks.

"Matt, this is their first real kiss, be a peach, yeah, and let them ride this one out? Besides, this is good for business. These chicks are so worked up watching, they are going to go hard to work off that show." I turn my focus back to the said show.

Matt chuckles, "Just too bad I'm not that into it."

Axl still has no room between himself and Dana. Her feet are at least on the floor now. He pulls back a little to peck her lips and turns around with a monster woody in his shorts. Then he walks up to me and barks in my face, "Mine."

"Dude, we've never kissed and never will," my hands go up in defense. "She's my sister, you freak, you need to work on your bullshit game. It's been hella weak. Go take a cold shower before I puke!" I wave my hands for him to go away.

"Don't need a cold one." He grabs Dana's hand and drags her into the locker room. James is standing in front of the door. They got the bro code down pat.

CHAPTER 27

Vegas

Walking into the Battle Born Tattoo, I wave hello to their new receptionist and Tank on my way to Blade's room. Stepping in and setting his sandwich on his light table, I see he's got a customer in his chair and he's about to finish an eagle tattoo on the man's chest.

Bending over, I give him a kiss a on my way back out. "I'm heading over to the old shop, meeting with the contractor. Come find me when you're done here?"

Blade nods and kisses my lips one more time. "Sure thing, babe." He winks at me and gets back to work.

Walking outside, I whistle for Tugger to follow me to the back of the property where the old shop is right up against the mountain, and my favorite spot on this property. He jumps up and down, running around my feet, excited that he gets to come with me. A white construction truck with a company logo on it meets me out front.

"Hey, I'm Henry, we talked on the phone. I have the plans to convert this building to the brewery you wanted." The older man holds his hand out to shake.

Grabbing his hand, I say, "Alessia DeRosa, let's take a look at what you have." I spot James out of the corner of my eye heading this way. Always my backup.

For the next hour, we negotiate what I need him to do and what work I have set aside for the club brothers to build. We both agree that construction on the inside can start, and we both agree on the outside in the spring. The first heavy snow hit last night, Thanksgiving is a few weekends away. I would rather not get too busy before the holidays anyway.

"Thanks for coming out, Henry. I like your plans to start with one kettle to brew the beer, then add on as we grow." I shake hands with him one last time and we say our goodbyes.

"I'll be in touch, Alessia." He leaves us standing in front of the new Battle Born Brewery that's about to open this spring.

"Vegas, the girls are working in the bar. I'm going to head inside to check on them now. You wanna come with?" James asks. I know he would rather I headed in, but really?

"Nah, James, go help the girls out. Check in with Kat often too, okay? In case she needs help," I tell him, which I know he will do anyway.

Inside of the old shop, I turn off the office light when Tugger growls and points his face in the direction of the front door that's now slightly ajar. The wind is whipping the door open and closed. Snow is coming down hard, scattering all over the floor.

Tugg's low growl and snarl has my spine tingling in suspense and fear. Checking my waistband, I feel my handgun there. Crouching low, I whisper to Tugg, "Stay with me, Tugg. Stay quiet." I pat him on the head and stand up, keeping my back to the wall.

I watch the shadows while moving around the old tools and work benches. Tugg does his job and stays by my side as we creep around the shop as quietly as possible when a tall figure steps forward.

Johnny.

He lunges for me, pinning me with his body to the wall, his hand over my mouth. "Did I scare you sweet, Vegas? Come here, sweetie," he taunts at me. "Should have known you were using me all along. Didn't figure it out till you skipped town."

Tugger is growling and snarling louder at Johnny. "Good women are so hard to find, you know. I was planning all along to take you in as my own until I found out how sad you really were. Fucking Blade out from under the whores of the club to get your piece of the action."

Tanya, the bleached blonde bitch, steps out of the shadows. Should've known she was the piece I couldn't figure out.

Tugger lunges and bites into Johnny's leg, then pulls back and growls. Johnny pulls his gun out and points it at Tugger. I kick my foot up at his gun and the shot goes off through a wall somewhere, but not at Tugger. Throwing the heel of my hand at his nose as hard as I can, I feel blood spraying all over my shirt.

Tanya tries to hit my head with a wooden board, but I see it coming and raise my left arm to cover the blow. Pain radiates from my elbow to my shoulder; the fucking cunt just angers me more.

I'm distracted when Johnny hits Tugger over the head. Tugg flies through the air and hits the concrete floor, lying there limp. My heart squeezes in pain at seeing him not moving.

Johnny's hands go around my neck, choking me and slamming my head against the wall. The lights go out. I'm feeling dizzy and Johnny lets up just a bit. Taking both of my hands straight up as fast and as strong as I can between us and through his arms, I bring my elbows down on his arms managing to break his hold on my neck. I knee him in the balls and punch him again in the nose when he bends over in pain.

Using the seconds I gained to get away, I pull my gun out from the back of my pants. I stay down, then crawl to get behind Johnny. I will shoot this motherfucker in the head myself for hurting Tugger.

The light from the moon shines in through the window, and that's when I see a figure going by. I hope it's someone to back me up. If not, I'm totally screwed here.

The light switches back on and Blade's standing in the doorway, holding his handgun.

His right eye twitches from the anger he's holding back when he looks from my neck to Tugger who is lying on the floor. He steps closer into the middle of the room, and Tanya, the skanky ho, starts crying as if she wasn't a part of trying to kidnap or kill me. She runs toward him and attempts to throw her arms around him. "Blade! Johnny was kidnapping..."

"Shut the fuck up, bitch." Blade backhands her across the cheek with the butt of his gun, sending her flying to the floor. Lifting her hand, she feels the cut that the hit left behind.

Blade maneuvers cautiously to Johnny who raises his gun to Blade with hate, jealousy and vengeance in his stare.

"Wasn't it enough for you to take the territory, you had to take the girl, too, right? Take it all, Blade. You couldn't just keep fucking that whore on the floor who I'd sent and paid to suck club cock. Keeping all of you distracted with her used pussy. One look at Alessia, and you stole her from me!" he screams.

Blade shrugs, "Wasn't so hard, she didn't want you. She was always meant to be mine." Tanya gasps in surprise to hear the words fall from his lips so easily.

"And the driver you killed at the train stop? You had to kill my brother, too?" Johnny shakes with anger at his accusation to Blade.

"I didn't. Your little snitch, Skid, did that all on his own. We busted in on their drop. Skid popped the fucker because he knew he'd sing. Had I known he was your brother, I would have shot Skid and tortured the dirty, kid raping bastard myself," Blade sneers. "Don't worry, we have plans for you."

Tanya raises her hand to fire a shot off toward Blade. Johnny catches her movement, raising his gun as well. Hoping Blade and I are quick enough, my aim is steady on her hand when I pop off one shot at the same time that Blade shoots at Johnny's hand.

Timing is everything, they say, and our timing is perfect. Dropping their guns, they both hunch over and grab their hands in pain. Blood is flowing to the concrete, painting it red.

Tank, Axl, Cowboy, James and the other MC Presidents come in, storming into the shop. Papa's eyes land on mine and I see the fire burning in them. He races toward Johnny and punches him in the face, only to have Tank pull him off right before my brother, Snake, jumps on him.

I could care less, so I turn around just in time to see the Elko chapter Prez pulling Tanya to her feet by her nappy weave.

Panicking, I'm pushing people out of the way, trying to get to Tugger. Finally reaching him on the cold floor, I drop to my knees. He looks so still and barely breathing. I take my coat off and wrap him in it. My tears blur my vision as I'm trying to find my way out.

Blade's hands stop me from moving. "Alessia, what happened to Tugg?" he questions with worry in his voice.

"Johnny hit him over the head, I got to get him to the vet now." He helps to get me through the door. We are running as fast as we can with the snow coating the ground. I feel like vomiting, so dizzy that my feet slip from under me and the last thing I remember before it all goes black and very cold is Blade yelling my name.

Blade

Hearing a small grunt behind me, I look through the darkness, but can't see Alessia anywhere. Until I look down in the snow. She is laid out, face down and Tugger next to her. "Alessia!" A roar erupts from deep in my soul, shattering at the thought of her leaving me and our dreams. Leaving me all alone.

I run back to her and pull her over onto her back, checking her pulse to make sure she's still breathing. I don't want to leave Tugg, but I have to.

Hauling Alessia's cold, limp body to my lap, I cradle her to me and kiss her forehead. I see a tear hitting her nose and realize I'm crying. I try to remove what snow I can from her body to stop it from soaking into her clothes.

James comes running, panicking, but doing better than me, and manages to take control of the situation.

"Get her into the office! I'll get Kat, and I'll call the paramedics! Go!"

He picks Tugger up, then follows me into the office at the bar and sets Tugg's lifeless body on his bed. He sends Kat in, and, behind her, Jenn and Dana follow. Kat asks me what happened and calls 911, setting her phone on speaker next to her. She does as she is told, checking Alessia's pupils that are dilatated.

James is alerting everyone in the bar to leave. It feels like hours pass by instead of minutes. All I can do is hold her hand with my shaking one. Fuego and Snake come busting through the back door, cursing and yelling at seeing her lying there passed out. Alessia's eyes start to flutter. I'm wagering everything as I pray to any god out there that, if he is listening, to please save her.

James comes into the room and updates us on what's happening. "The EMT's are outside."

I pick Alessia up and race with her to the ambulance. They don't have the gurney out before I barge into the back of it, yelling for them to go.

I let her go enough for them to put an IV in, and her eyes flutter a little more until they're open. The paramedic asks me what happened. "She was attacked in her office, some guy had her in a choke hold and hit her head against the wall." That's all I can say, anything more and I may cry. Once in this lifetime is enough for me.

We finally make it to the hospital and Alessia is unloaded and taken into the ER, thank whoever that she's awake now. The nurse tells me to wait in the damn waiting room until her physical and head CT is finished.

It feels like hours later before Fuego, Snake, Dana, Axle, Kat, Jenn, along with the rest of the Cali and Reno family members come in to give us support. That thought pisses me off. Family. Alessia is mine and I should own her fully. Thought I had all the time in the world. As soon as she's better, we are making it happen.

Axl grips my shoulder and sits next to me while we wait. He hands me his cell to look at some pictures. "Thought these might cheer you up?"

Scrolling through, I find picture after picture of Johnny being raped with tools, missing body parts, same with Tanya. Ice really did a number on her. I could only recognize her hair by the end, the most brutal rape murder I have ever seen. I would bet she squealed all her secrets before the torture even began, trying to save herself.

Handing the phone back to Axl, I do feel a little better knowing those two paid for what they did.

A tall, fair lady wearing a lab coat steps through the doors two hours later and looks around the waiting room. "Family for Alessia DeRosa?" Fuego, Snake and I step forward and the lady raises her eyebrows at us in disgust. "She has a concussion and will be staying the night, the rest she can tell you. You can go see her two at a time, room 220."

Ignoring the uppity cunt, Fuego and I race towards the room she gave us. We barge inside, and there she is. Her face is a little pale and she has bags under her eyes. We stop by her bed. Fuego stands on one side and me on the other.

"Baby girl, *mi niña*, how's your head?" Fuego's heart is plainly shown on his face as he speaks softly to her.

"No worries, Papa, I'll be home tomorrow. I got some good hits in too." Alessia tries to grin at him. "Didn't take them all myself, you know?" She tries to joke around with her old man, but I can see through the poker face she has in place.

"Baby girl, your momma is going to have my ass when I tell her," Fuego smiles at her and continues, "Snake and I are going to crash at your *casa*. See you tomorrow, get some sleep, *sí*?" He kisses her forehead and then walks out.

Alessia reaches for my shirt and pulls me to her to hug me. "Tell me everything is okay with Tugg, Blade," she pleads as a tear falls.

"James took him to the vet. He'll give us a call when he has more information, okay?" I push her hair back with my fingers, and she shakes her head, not believing me. "Is he alive, Blade?"

"Baby, I haven't heard, but not hearing anything means he's still being worked on, so that's good, right?"

What I don't have the heart to tell her is that it's touch and go. Johnny cracked his skull, and the vet is trying to get the swelling to come down. I'll tell her tomorrow.

The next hour is a whirlwind and I'm thankful for it because it keeps her distracted. Kat has a lot of pull with the nurses here, which helps a lot since visiting hours ended a long time ago. At some point, the nurse gives Alessia something in her IV that knocks her out cold. I'm lying next to her, spooning her tight, not willing to let her have the bed to herself. I need to feel her next to me as much as I need my next breath, my chest hurts so bad.

The shadow of a man blocks the light coming from the hallway. Hawk looms in the doorway. "I wanted to come and check in on her, after everything." He is talking to me, but his eyes move over her face.

Getting up to my feet, I signal for him to follow me out to the waiting room which is, thankfully, empty. "Hawk, I'm not sure I really appreciate you coming by to see her. She's mine, she wears my patch. Why are you here?"

"Regret, pain, fuck, I don't know. If I could go back, I would do it all differently. I would have loved her more. Been the man I had promised her I'd be."

"Does it really matter now? You had her for years, but you never really claimed her."

"We were damn kids, man, when we ran off and got married," he replies a little agitated.

"Still, where was your patch claiming her for all others to see? You never really claimed her because you knew she wasn't yours," I throw back, not willing to give him an inch.

"You haven't married her, and if you ever let her go, I'm coming back for her. I can't fight you for her, Blade, you're one of the Club's Presidents," his voice is full of regret and pain.

"That's where you're wrong." I need to make sure the fucker understands Alessia will never be his again. Thumping my fist against my chest, then pointing to his face, I say, "If she was yours, you would kill me for her. You wouldn't wait for her. You come back again looking at her like you have been, and I will kill you. It's your last warning, *brother*. For my woman, I'll kill anyone, don't care who the fuck that is, brother or not, Prez or not. Alessia is *mine*."

CHAPTER 28

Blade

I feel a light touch across my forehead, waking me up. Just as I'm trying to pull myself back to sleep, I feel it again.

"Blade, Tank brought the Tahoe, we're going home in about twenty. Wake up," Alessia tries coaxing me from my deep sleep. Opening my eyes, I kiss a bare spot above her gown, right on her chest, and then her lips. I get up and stretch my sore back, ready to get my woman and me the hell out of here.

"Well, if it isn't my favorite little soldier. You get some sleep with that fat ass taking up most of your bed, honey?" Tank's voice booms into the room out of nowhere.

Vegas laughs happily, moving to give Tank a big hug. "You're such a dork, but a lovable dork."

Tank's big arms wrap around her and lift her feet up and off the floor. "Right back at you, honey. Go grab your clothes so we can get your scrawny, ninja ass home." Tank makes motions of Vegas fighting with fists, then kneeing the air, bowing to her fighting honor.

Mischief laces her eyes as she shakes her head, laughing at Tank. "Thank you, honey. I needed that, dork."

Tank tosses me the keys and walks back out. "Thanks, fucker!" I call out to his retreating back as I hear him whistling all the way down the hallway until he reaches the elevator.

Shutting the door, Alessia hangs up her coat. Finally, we are home after a long night. I sit on the couch, hoping like hell that I can close my eyes for a few hours. Alessia sits in my lap which I want, but it worries me that she feels she needs a safe place.

"What's wrong, Alessia, what's in your head?" I ask while rubbing her back.

"My baby died, Blade, my baby is gone." She says it so quietly that I worry I heard her wrong. A big, fat tear rolls down her cheek and hits my cut, and she wipes it away with trembling fingers.

My heart starts racing in my chest. "What are you telling me, Alessia?" Last I spoke with James, Tugger was still fighting his way back home.

"I was pregnant, and, with what happened yesterday, I started bleeding, so they did a pregnancy test last night when I said I wasn't raped. Then, they removed my IUD, said I would need to replace it." She takes in a shuddering breath and continues as I sit there in utter shock. "Since I was pregnant, and that shouldn't have happened, they had to take it out."

She stops for a second to gather her thoughts, and her next words gut me. "But, somewhere inside of me, I feel like I killed our baby. I shouldn't have been in that building alone. I should have left with James. It feels like it's my fault."

She starts crying over the grief of losing a baby she didn't even know we were having. I rock her and try reassuring her until she finally falls asleep. I can't let go, so I hold her for the next thirty minutes.

Feeling confused and tired, I decide to call my mom. After I lay Alessia down in our room, I make the call. "Hey, Ma, did the old man make it home to you yet?" Stryker took Skid back to Las Vegas with him. Said he was going to make his torture last for months. I was all too happy to get rid of the traitor.

"Hi, honey! Yes and no. He's in Las Vegas, has a few things to wrap up before he heads home. What can I do for you? Not that I don't want to talk about me, but what is going on that's got you worried?"

"Can't tell you all of it, but Alessia, Ma... She lost a baby last night. She didn't even know she was pregnant." I feel my heart breaking all over again as I pour my heart out to my mom. "I don't know what to do to help her. I called because I was hoping you could tell me. The whole thing really confuses me. I'm sad, but, honestly, I was just so relieved that she was okay."

I swallow and take a breath because the next words out of my mouth are selfish. "I can stand to lose a whole lot, but I'll never be able to stand losing her."

My mom is quiet for a long moment that seems to stretch forever. When she starts talking, I can hear the sadness in her voice. "Makes sense, Blade, she would feel the same way if she were you. To her, she lost a part of you in that baby, a baby she wasn't even aware of so that she could protect it. She loved that baby instantly when she knew it was there because that baby was yours too."

I hear her softly sniffling while trying to find words that would bring me comfort. "Now her hormones are reacting to what her body was geared up to take on. Be patient and loving, and, when the time is right, push her out of the sadness and back to living for the future. Just give her some time to grieve what she lost and remind her that you both still have a future."

"Thanks, Ma." I feel lighter somehow after hearing her take on this, and I can only hope that I can be the man that Alessia needs me to be while recovering from this trauma.

"Love you, and, Blade, bring your ass home more often, and bring Alessia with you." We hang up just as there's a knock at the door.

James, Jenn and Dana walk in with a drowsy looking Tugger. Our badass dog fought for Alessia, and I can't help but grab him from James and hug him to my chest. Walking with him into the bedroom, I lay him right next to Alessia's head. He scoots up and licks her face, then again and again until she moans out, "Tugg, use the doggy door, why do you always... TUGG!"

She startles him with her scream, and happily barks back at her, thinking it's play time. Pulling him to her, she peppers his face with kisses and tears.

CHAPTER 29

Alessia

The weeks following that have been hard. I've kept Tugg at my side all the time. Some days, I felt pretty functional, others, I would feel so sad that Kat, Dana and Jenn would do something so funny to each other, or tease the guys, that it would pull me out of my funk. A couple of days Blade and I would stay in and he would hold me, watch movies with me. My favorite was when we would go shooting. Or play pranks on Tank. Kat had some great ideas.

Last night, Tank said enough was enough when we gave him an O'Doul's in a mug all night long at the bar. He drank the 24-pack telling us all how invincible he was until we showed him what he was really drinking. He said we were just being mean, and that the next prank meant war, and he didn't care what Blade said, he didn't give a shit if it made me happy anymore.

"What's got you smiling, baby?" Blade asks with some concern in his voice, and I wonder if he thinks that our next prank will be on him.

"Just laughing about Tank last night, that was a lot of fun. I also just realized that I can't use what happened as my crutch anymore. Tank will declare war, and, honestly, if he does anything to my boots or my hair, I would have to kill your Road Captain," I state very matter of factly.

"Can't kill the boys, Vegas, and, yeah, it's probably time to let up on your coping mechanism. Which is really funny, but we can't keep the torture going. Tell you what, go right ahead and prank the prospects. If they can't out mastermind you and your evil crew of chicks, they can't get patched in." Blade is joking, but I'm already group texting the girls with what he said.

"What are we doing in downtown Tahoe? Thought we were meeting my parents at the cabin?" I look at Blade confused because this feels off and my senses are telling me he's up to something.

Parking the truck, he walks around the other side and opens my door. The cold air hits my legs and I freeze instantly. Burr, a shiver races through my body. It's cold up here.

Blade takes my hand and leads me to the bench we sat on a month or so back. We sit down in the same spots we sat in before, and it sort of feels like we've come full circle. It's so beautiful with the Christmas lights already out and the big snowflakes piling up on our beanies.

Blade turns to me, grabbing my hand. "Alessia, that day we came up here to go shopping... I knew that day that I wanted you to be by my side for the rest of my life. I bought a ring that day, and I wish like hell that I would have given it to you and eloped to a chapel then. Your dad would've had my nuts if your mom missed your wedding, but I would've done it, and it would've been so worth it."

We both start laughing, our mixed warm breaths clouding around us. I can barely see anything through my tears. I can't believe this is happening and I almost miss what he says next.

"Here I am asking you today to wear my ring and stay by my side and have my babies. Every day, we gamble with time, betting on the outcome. Will you place your bet on me and go all in? Will you marry me, Alessia?"

A warm tear streaks down my freezing cheek. The thought of having a baby, the thought of marrying Blade, they both make me so happy. A laugh escapes my mouth as I answer, "Hell yeah, I will!"

I throw myself at him and start peppering kisses all over his face while looking back into his eyes and thinking how far we've come. It feels like a lifetime when it's been where it's been for just months.

"Okay," Blade starts rubbing his chin. "What do you say, highest card wins?" He pulls out a deck of cards from his coat pocket. "You pull, and I pull from the deck. If I get the highest card, we march into the casino wedding chapel and we get married right here, right now."

"You're on, shuffle the deck," I screech out.

Blade shuffles the deck three times and looks at me. "Ladies first." He fans out the deck in front of me and I pull a card, showing it to him. Queen of diamonds. Damn, please be higher.

Blade pulls a card and looks at it. He doesn't say anything for a moment, and I'm about to cry thinking I won, but really lost, when I notice him fighting back a grin as he turns his card over. Ace. That's a low card. Or so I thought? "Wait, what is the Ace in this game?"

"Baby, that's an Ace. That's the highest card you can pull in this game." He pulls me to my feet to smack my lips with a greedy kiss.

Not taking a minute more, we run into the casino. I stop abruptly, surprised to see all the brothers from the Reno, Vegas and Cali chapters, then my parents and his parents are waiting inside for us. My head is spinning when the girls rush over, eager to see me.

"Go with the girls, Alessia, they have your stuff upstairs in our room."

I am speechless for a change.

An hour later, after the girls have curled my hair and redone my makeup, I feel ready. Looking in the mirror, I laugh, because there is not one thing in my outfit that screams white wedding. Black silk blouse tucked into a black leather skirt, with black knee-high boots. Yeah, definitely biker bitch status, no white wedding for me. Best part is, my girls look just like me.

Jenn hums low in appreciation, "This is definitely Vegas. Blade does you good, girl."

Dana checks the text on her phone. "Let's get moving, Axl already texted me five times in the last twenty minutes. Blade wants you in the chapel. Now," she says and tosses her phone back into her bag.

Stepping off the elevator, I see Papa and Snake waiting for us. "Baby girl, you look beautiful, time to get you to your man." Taking Papa's arm, he leads us across the casino floor. The farther along we get, the more I notice the MC brothers have gathered around, walking to the sides and behind us.

Getting to the entrance of the chapel doors, I see Blade standing at the end of the aisle, and looking up, he finds me staring. He looks so handsome in his black jeans and boots. His head is freshly shaved on the sides and a tiny Mohawk is up the middle.

Since it's not a real traditional wedding, Papa just keeps walking down the aisle until we reach the end and he places my hand in Blade's.

The girls go to stand off to the side and the officiator starts talking, keeping all the lines straight forward, with not a lot of extras. Honestly, I don't care for weddings or the mushy sentiment in front of other people, so I am okay with the 'get it done' ceremony.

Finally, we get to the end. "Will you take William Johnson to be your lawfully wedded husband in all things, until death do you part?"

"I do," I speak up, barely able to contain my giddiness. Blade takes my hand and slides on my finger a classic vintage, small carat, in white gold ring. It's beautiful.

"Will you take Alessia DeRosa to be your lawfully wedded wife in all things, until death do you part?" the officiator asks Blade.

"I do, for this life and the next," Blade calmly states but his hands squeeze mine.

"You may now kiss the bride."

And it's done. We are husband and wife.

Stepping into each other, our lips touch, and I feel Blade's hand running behind my neck. I open my mouth to deepen the kiss, and whistles ring out. Pulling back, I ask Blade, "Take me to bed? I've missed you." I need to reconnect with him on the most basic level.

With no other words, Blade turns and leads me away to the elevator. The whole ride up, my back is to the wall as he kisses me, soaking in every part of my body. Rushing into our room, clothes start flying off, boots hit the wall. All that's left is my garter and thigh high stockings.

"I want to kiss and lick every part of your body, but I need to be inside of you more," Blade says against my neck. "Can I have you, Alessia Johnson, put my baby inside of you tonight?"

"Yes."

I choke back the tears and fear, and bet again on this man and our future as Blade makes sweet, slow love to me.

EPILOGUE 1

Blade

Two weeks have passed since we got back from Tahoe, and I have a surprise for Alessia. I'm patiently waiting for her to come in and see what I did. The bell rings above from the shop door, then I hear her voice. "Hey, guys, is Blade in his room?"

"Yeah, he's been working on something, head on back," Tank says.

"Hey, lovey, what did you need?" she says as she's walking into my work area. "Holy shit, Jazzy, is that you?!" She runs forward and gives her cousin from California a hug. This is the cousin who did all her rose tattoos before.

"Damn, girl, I may have to move. You did not tell me there were so many fine brothers up here", Jazzy tells her while she smacks Alessia on the arm. "Or at least I'm coming to visit more often."

"No," Tank yells from his room. "We've met our quota for crazy bitches in their crew."

Alessia whispers really low, "He's having girl problems, don't worry about him."

"I can hear you!" Tank's on a mission now.

"No, you can't," she yells back. "What are you two up to in here?" Her gaze finds mine, looking me over, then her eyes land on my chest. "Wow," she steps over to me looking over the blue and gray rose I had Jazz tattoo.

"For the one we lost," I tell her. Alessia's eyes gloss over and she closes them as I pull her to me, kissing her lips. "And I had her tattoo my wedding ring."

Her eyes pop open and she grabs my hand to see a calligraphy A on my ring finger for her. She laughs out loud, "I can't believe you did that! Is that for the Ace or for Alessia?"

"Believe it. You're next, and it was for both." Sitting her in the chair I was just in, I pull off her wedding ring, then trace out the band tattoo, a thin filigree band. Turning on my gun, I permanently put the band on her finger, branding my heart to her.

EPILOGUE 2

Alessia

"Blade! Get your ass up, it's time to go. FU....CK!"
Standing next to the bed, I place my hands on the edge.
A cold sweat breaks out, covering my skin. I put my
head down and grab onto the side of the sheets,
waiting for the strong, painful contraction to subside.
"Motherfucker."

Blade jumps up, ready for action as soon as he
realizes that I'm in labor pain and not from any
outside threat. He climbs over the bed to get to me.
"Alessia, what's going on, we need to go to the
hospital?" He lovingly runs his hands over my arms
and face.

"I would think so being I'm dying from these damn
contractions, Blade! I would say yes, we need to go to
a goddamn hospital, shithead," I scream as I feel
another one coming.

He pulls his hands back from my verbal slapping,
and I can't say that I feel too bad about it since my
insides feel like they are ripping me apart. Kissing my

forehead, he doesn't say another word, handing me a sundress. He gets me into the Tahoe after one more contraction paralyzes my body.

It's the middle of summer, I'm miserable and extra cranky in this goddamn 100 plus degree heat. I'm so hot. Rolling my window down helps me to cool and calm down a bit. His eyes betray his calm exterior, as they go from me to the road. He reaches for my hand and holds on to it all the way to the hospital, trying to take the pain away from me until we get there.

Once we are at the hospital, Blade's stuck at the front desk giving them the insurance information, while a nurse wheels me into a room. She hands me a gown, asking me if I can change into it by myself. I take it into the bathroom and I mechanically exchange the sundress for the hospital gown when another contraction hits me. Kneeling on the floor, I try breathing through it. The cold tiles from the floor call to me.

Lying down, not giving one fuck as to why but just because of need, I try absorbing as much of the cold as I can. Blade finds me there, and he bends to pick me up, looking scared to death. "Alessia, are you okay, baby?"

Not waiting for me to answer, he rushes to place me on the bed, then turns to face the nurse who left me alone. "You let her change all by herself? While in labor? In a bathroom? She was on the floor. I do *not* want to see you in here again! Get another nurse in here!" The poor woman, looking terrified, turns to leave the room just as Papa walks in, laughing.

"*Mija*, your Momma is here to take care of you. Looks like you'll need it since Blade will scare all the nurses away." He kisses my forehead just as another contraction hits me. "Hang in there, baby girl." My mom walks in the room and he turns to kiss her, then leaves, knowing it's about to get real ugly up in here.

This one contraction lasts longer, feels stronger, and scares me with the intense pressure of need to push. This can't be good.

Mom walks over with a washcloth and ice chips, handing Blade the cup and placing the cloth on my forehead. "You can do this, Alessia, I'm right here with you. I'm not leaving until I get to hold my grandbabies."

"Momma, I need to push, it feels like I need to push. It hurts so bad," I cry out to her, pleading with her to help me. Blade is at my other side, hovering by my head, unsure of what to say. He looks at my mom for guidance. "Oh shit, my water just broke!" A warm flood of water coats my legs.

Mom grabs a handful of towels and starts wiping my legs dry, placing a few more under me. "We got this, Alessia, rest in between contractions, okay?"

Blade takes my hand as the young female doctor walks into the room. "Hello, I'm Dr. Hill, I'll be checking to see how far along you are. Can you place your feet up on the bed?"

Dr. Hill checks to see how far I'm dilated, a worried look passing her features. "Alessia, you're going to be delivering these babies rather quickly. I'm going to set up, do not push until I tell you, okay?"

Nodding back at her, I agree, "Okay." Exhausted, I roll my head to touch Blade's arm, then reach up to hold on to him. After a few more contractions and cries of agony, Dr. Hill is down by the foot of my bed.

She places my feet in the stirrups, scoots in closer and looks up at me. "Okay, momma, on this next contraction, I want you to push with everything you have, every time. Dad and Grandma, can you two grab her legs and push them up to her chest when she's ready?

Blade

Alessia screams, sweat running down her forehead and neck. I'm so proud of her. She's in so much pain. It's killing me to watch her go through this. Holding her leg back, the trembles of her muscles weaken me to my core. I rub my hands over her legs when the contraction passes.

Tears streak down her face. She was too far dilated to have an epidural, but she's hanging in there. "Blade, I'm so tired, I feel so tired."

Wiping her tears away, I try to bring her comfort. "You can do this, baby, you are going to bring these babies out into the world. Then you get to sleep, and drink coffee again." She gives me a weak smile, then closes her eyes.

Her body tenses and she sits up to push again while Cindy and I encourage her to keep going. Then my son's head appears, followed by the rest of his body, and my world stops for a second. I snap out of it and tell Alessia, unable to stop my own happiness, "You did it, baby! Cortez is here! He's here, baby. You can do this one more time, one more time, little momma!"

Dr. Hill hands me the scissors to cut the cord, resting the baby on Alessia's chest. Cindy and my mom, who I didn't even see coming in, are helping to clean a wailing Cortez. Both grandmas are wiping tears from their eyes. I lean down and kiss my beautiful wife and momma to my babies. Eventually, the nurse takes him to look him over and clean him up better.

Alessia's body gears back up as a new contraction hits. Cindy comes rushing back over to take her leg. With some more encouragement from us to keep going, by 3:43am, Easton Johnson is born. Alessia starts bawling, "We did it, Blade, our baby boys are here!"

I smile back at her and hand her the pair of scissors. "Yeah, Alessia, Cortez and Easton are here. Now cut the cord."

She grabs them and starts cutting Easton's cord, laughing and crying at the bawling baby in her arms, cuddling him to her chest. Cindy walks over, carrying a sleeping Cortez and handing him to me. Moisture hits my eyes at the sight of my boys.

BONUS

Alessia Johnson

two and a half years later

"Cortez, stop messing with Easton!"

Running past a laughing Blade, I pick Easton up and off the floor to save him from Tez. All the twins want to do nowadays is fight, and, at almost three, it can get a little vicious. Tez is always the first to throw a truck or some other toy at Easton, always ready for a fight.

Blade is no help, as always. He wants them to work it out themselves. "You know that as soon as you let them fight it out a few times, Tez will learn to back off when Easton holds his ground."

Kissing Easton on the cheek, I pass him to Blade to take to the kitchen table for breakfast. Then, I pick Tez up and follow them in there where I strap him to his highchair.

Tugger looks around the corner, and, when the coast is clear, he lazily lays on his bed with a grunt, relieved the twins are out of the way.

Blade comes over and hugs me from behind, rubbing my six month pregnant belly. "How are my girls doing?"

I look at my boys and sigh with happiness. I believe, from deep inside my soul, that, no matter what, I didn't lose my baby when I miscarried all those years ago.

They just came a little later, in a set, together.

THE END

SNEAK PEAK OF NOTHING LASTS FOREVER, AXL'S STORY...

PROLOGUE

Axl

The bass hits the speakers and the stage lights dim, except for a spotlight in the corner of the stage. The fans scream, "GNR! GNR! GNR!"

Axl Rose and the rest of the band strut out with a guitar raised high. Drumsticks flip up high in the lights and then they're caught behind the drummer's back. Stage lights of all colors beam around in all directions. The band takes position as *Sweet Child O' Mine* starts rocking the crowd.

It is 2006, at a Guns N' Roses concert at the MGM Grand Casino. Me and the boys pass a joint around the group. Smiling, I eagerly take my first drag for the night as deep as a I can. The smoke hits my lungs hard. I hack and choke it back up. Blade laughs and grabs the joint from me to take his own drag.

"Easy on the grass, dickhead, we have the whole night." He shakes his head at me and hands me a cold beer. The foam hits my hot, dry throat, it is so good.

Song after song plays through the speakers as we laugh, smoke and drink. My mind is so fuzzy that faces and bodies blend in the crowd. Living it up to my youth, I am experiencing everything that I can.

Since we are pledging in as brothers in the Battle Born MC tomorrow, there are no guarantees in this life after that, only for right now. That's exactly what I do, I live for right here and right now, nothing lasts forever.

Some stupid drunk asshole behind me plows into my back, spilling my beer on my GNR shirt and pissing me the fuck off. Handing it off to Tank, I turn to shove that motherfucker back. Stumbling a few steps forward, he turns back around to face me. "Sorry." He says it, but not really giving one fuck that he slammed into me as he smiles like the dickhead that he is. Dickhead turns back around to his date, throwing an arm around the hot blonde bitch that he's with.

"Take this little punk ass bitch down, and then take his bitch." Tank is shoving at my shoulder to get to it, then crosses his arms, waiting for me to deliver.

Spider, Blade and Tank surround me. The anger and vengeance pump like a shot of adrenaline through me. Grabbing the smiling asshole's shirt, I whip him around to face me, then throw my fist high and wide into his nose. Blood splatters with a crunch from the force of it. His right hand comes flying from down low up for my face.

Ducking to the right, I dodge the uppercut, and swing my weight forward, hitting him in the stomach with a jab. The force of it arches him toward me, and my left fist smashes his cheekbone. That's followed by a right and another left. The punk is left lying on the ground.

The security guards come running toward us to haul both of our asses out. Blade catches one of the them, palming him some cash. The passed-out dickhead is taken out of the pit.

I walk over to the scared blonde that's nervously looking around for an escape. Grinning her way, I show her my party boy face as I take her hand in mine to apologize.

"Sorry, princess," I say while stroking my thumb over her knuckles. "That prick you came here with was an asshole. Come party with us, and I promise I'll be good."

I spot that she has a disposable camera in her hand. I pull her close to me. "Come on, beautiful, take a pic with me? That way you'll always remember this night and then you can trust me, because you'll have my picture on your camera."

Encouraging her further, I snatch it from her hand and pull her body close to mine. She giggles nervously with our backs to that stage. I slide behind her and place my hand on her stomach while my other hand holds out the camera. I rest my chin on her shoulder and we both smile when I push the button to snap the picture.

She turns around, so I grab her by her shirt to pull her to me and lay a smacking big kiss on her juicy pink lips while snapping another picture of us. Her hands go straight to my chest for balance, and then she relaxes herself into the kiss.

I start walking backward, and Blondie follows me over to the guys. I pocket her camera as I introduce her and take my beer back from Tank. I wash down that hot kiss with a cold drink.

Blondie eyes me over the white plastic cup that someone must've given her, then grabs the bottle from my hand. She shoots the rest down and pulls me toward her for another kiss.

The smell of grass pulls me away from her lips. Tank hands out the joint to us, and Blondie grabs it, then takes a short drag from it, coughing it back up almost immediately. I laugh at how cute she is. Between the two of us, we manage to finish it off. Her beautiful hair catches the light, drawing me to her body.

More chicks from the crowd join our little party up front by the stage. Blade and Tank each have a handful of bitches entertaining them. The songs play on through the late-night hours. Hot bodies continue to grind and touch. Sweat, weed and alcohol permeate the air.

More grass goes around, and the boys and I are lit. We are so high off weed and hormones. Blonde Girl and I rub all over each other when she grabs my dick and pushes her tits against my chest. She yells over the noise into my ear, "Let's go to the bathroom!"

She pulls on my hand and starts walking forward. My feet and dick anxiously follow her. I watch her ass that's covered in a denim skirt and her long, lean, tan legs in a haze.

Excitement laces itself around my intoxicated mind. The primitive need to touch her tits and pussy takes over. We make it to the bathroom where I shut the stall door and spin Blondie around. She trades me places and ends up with her back against the door.

My hands find the bottom of her GNR tank and pull it up over her tits, palming them and loving how soft they are. Sucking one nipple, then the other, my hands find her toned thighs, and I push her skirt up.

I pull my mouth from her breast, releasing the nipple with a pop to gaze over her almost naked body. I run my fingers over the pink thong she's wearing, then move it to the side. I start pumping my fingers in and out of her tight pussy.

Blondie moves forward and starts kissing and nipping at my ear. I grab the condom from my back pocket while she keeps kissing my neck up to my lips. My fingers rub her clit and fuck her pussy.

She undoes my pants, pushing them, along with my boxers, down far enough to get my stiff dick out, before rolling the condom on.

Lifting one of her legs over my hip, and then the other, I push her against the door with my body, and sink my dick into her very tight pussy. She howls out in pain, only to be drowned out by *November Rain* as it blares around us.

Not taking the time to think too much of it, I use her body to pound out my release. As soon as I come into the condom, her feet hit the floor and she is straightening herself up. She pecks my lips and is gone before the song is over.

Best fuckin' concert ever.

CHAPTER 1

This story goes back to the night the girls get stoned...

Axl

Coming out of Church, I think over what Blade and I relayed to the other chapters, the information that our club gathered on Skid and that other asshole, Johnny.

Having answers to deliver gives us pride, but also leaves us feeling tense and angry over unresolved issues.

That is until I turn the corner and find the bar full of smoke. Not terribly uncommon, except for the fact that Dana is sitting with the girls with a lit joint between her fingers, and big smiles stretched across all their faces.

Blade reaches the bar before Tank and I even have a chance to get there. Watching Dana take a hit off the joint is hot as fuck, but it also pisses me off that she did this at the club without me here. Any of these assholes could approach her.

I take the joint from her hand and give her a stern look. I don't know how to handle this shit right now. So, I take a couple of long drags of my own while chatter goes on around me. I breathe the stress out with a long cloud of smoke.

I snap out of it when Dana starts clapping while talking to Kat. "Did you see that? That right there," she points between Blade and Vegas, "That is how you greet your woman right there."

I start choking and coughing out my next drag at her words. Did she just confess she wants passion without her realizing what she just did? Her outspoken thoughts throw me off guard but excite me at the same time.

Pushing my chest against her back, I tell her all too happily, "Princess, I have all your needs right here."

I step back to look down at my dick and catch her eyes staring at it too when I look back to her flushed face.

"But, it isn't happening tonight. The first time I take your lips," I run my thumb across her bottom one and bring her eyes back to mine, "I will take your body. Just be warned, Dana, when you do kiss me, you will be mine. I would rather take you sober, but don't mistake, I'll take you any way I can. You. Are. Mine. You getting yourself drunk and high to keep me from you and my bed won't work. You're still sleeping with me. And in my bed."

Gently, I keep her chin still with my fingers while holding her gaze with my lustful one.

Dana's tantalized eyes are locked with mine in a silent war of control over herself. And not moving an inch out of my hold.

"Fuck, Blade, he just killed it with that one. That even made me feel a little shaken up." I hear Vegas, but I don't lose sight of Dana's light blue eyes. So rarely will she look at me in the eyes.

I run the tips of my fingers across her forehead and down around her ear, tucking her golden blonde hair back.

"You dickheads are really putting me in a tight spot here." Tank pouts like a little bitch, causing Dana's face to move in his direction. My hand loses the touch and connection I desperately crave with her.

"Easy, lady killer, you don't have to confess your undying love for me. Keep it casual, big guy," Kat lets the fucker off the hook.

Feeling frustrated, exhausted and in need of sleep, I grip Dana's shoulder. "Let's get to bed, princess, I'm beat." I nod my head in the direction of the rooms.

Dana's body hesitates, but her eyes tell me she knows where she's sleeping. I, for one, am excited to see those long, lean legs wrapped around me. I mean, wrapped in my sheets. No, I definitely mean both me *and* the sheets.

Finally giving into the inevitable, she stands at my side and tells the group good night. I fist bump my brothers, and Tank gives me a nod of approval and a wink like the kid he is sometimes. Dumbass.

I lead Dana with my hand touching her lower back, and she leans into me just slightly the further down the hall toward my room we get. I open the door for her and she walks past me.

She steps over to where I placed the bag I gathered from her house earlier. Sitting down next to the bed in a chair, I smile as I watch her looking for her pajamas. I'm very happy with myself that I didn't pack any. Can't say that I'm sorry about it.

Her head whips in my direction and she eyeballs me with her icy blue eyes. "I know that you went through ALL my clothes, Axl. Where the hell are my pajamas, you asshole!"

I stand and close the distance between us, pulling her taut body against mine. One of my hands lands on her hip and the other behind her head. I speak softly into her ear, "Princess, you will wear my shirts to bed from now on or nothing at all. I give you choices, Dana."

Letting her go, I reach into my small dresser and hand her an original concert t-shirt from back in Las Vegas, one of the many, but also one of my favorite memories from when I went to a Guns N' Roses concert.

She looks at the shirt a little shocked, or confused, but grabs it and takes it, along with her bag, to the bathroom.

Stripping out of my clothes down to my boxer briefs, I listen to her move all her shit around on the counters. The sound of it is gifting me with a sense of peace.

Blade did give me the option of staying at her house with her. I said no knowing that she would be forced to sleep in the same bed as me if we stayed here. I'm a dick like that.

A few minutes later, she steps out from the bathroom wearing only my t-shirt. The light cascades around her, making her long blonde hair and toned legs shine.

Fuck, I want, no, *need* to see the rest of her gorgeous body, but I hold myself back. Barely.

"Where did you get this t-shirt from?" she asks as her fingers nervously toy with the hem. I watch her thigh muscles move as she steps closer to the bed. Her questioning gaze finds mine as she slides her body next to mine under the covers.

Rolling over onto my right side, I prop my head up on my hand. "I got that shirt at a concert we all went to a while back in '98, in Vegas. It was a hell of a crazy night that night. I remember only a few things. We smoked a hell of a lot of bud. We drank our weight in beer." I run my hand over hers under the covers.

"I've been to a few of their concerts too. We could go together, if they ever put on a show in Las Vegas again." She lets a long sigh out. Rolling to her left side, facing me, she smiles when she asks, "Tell me about that concert, was it your first?" Running my fingers from her calf up to her knee, I pull her body closer to mine, resting her leg on my hip.

Laughing a little, I say back, "Well, let's see, I was sixteen then, and my dad took me, Blade and Tank for my birthday. That was the first time we blazed with our dads. Half of the club was there that night. He bought me a shirt, I can't wear it anymore, fucking thing is so small. I wanted to be Axl Rose, the lead singer, so bad, I wore a red bandana on my head, too. I was a skinny ass, little punk kid. My dad started calling me Axl, the brothers caught on, and that's how I got my road name."

Dana's eyes sparkle back at me in amusement. "You're very close with your dad, aren't you?" She tries to stifle a yawn back as she brings her hand up to cover her mouth

"Yes, my dad is pretty badass. We can talk more tomorrow. My princess needs her beauty sleep." I kiss the corner of her mouth and rest my left hand on her waist.

Dana snuggles into me and relaxes her hands on my chest. Within minutes, she is lightly snoring. My body shakes a little when I try to quiet my laughter at my little snoring, stoned, drunk princess.

ABOUT THE AUTHOR

Scarlett Black is the author of the Battle Born MC Series. Not really knowing where a story will take her is what she loves most about writing. She strives to write about strong women and the men who love them. She believes in love and the miracles that come from it. She enjoys giving her fans a happily ever after worth melting their hearts. These may be books, but they are written with her heart and soul. She is Battle Born. Are you?

www.authorscarlettblack.com

Made in the USA
Monee, IL
30 October 2020